THE WOMAN IN THE WOODS

J. A. BAKER

B
Boldwood

First published in Great Britain in 2023 by Boldwood Books Ltd.

Cover Design by Head Design

Cover Photography: Shutterstock and Alamy

A CIP catalogue record for this book is available from the British Library.

Paperback ISBN 978-1-80415-388-8

Large Print ISBN 978-1-80415-387-1

Hardback ISBN 978-1-80415-386-4

Ebook ISBN 978-1-80415-390-1

Kindle ISBN 978-1-80415-389-5

Audio CD ISBN 978-1-80415-381-9

MP3 CD ISBN 978-1-80415-382-6

Digital audio download ISBN 978-1-80415-385-7

Boldwood Books Ltd
23 Bowerdean Street
London SW6 3TN
www.boldwoodbooks.com

Dedicated to all writers everywhere.
May those words keep flowing.

There is always one moment in childhood when the door opens and lets the future in.

— *GRAHAM GREENE*

A memory is a beautiful thing. It's almost a desire you miss.

— *GUSTAVE FLAUBERT*

1

_____

I was twelve years old when I died. Twelve years, six months and three days to be precise. Six years later I was reborn, released from prison, given a new identity, a new life. A fresh start, different outlook. I was a changed person, quite literally. New name, another version of me. Like a snake shedding its skin, I slithered away from my old life and started again, viewing the world through a different lens, allowing for a more balanced perspective. That was what they told me while I was inside, all those psychologists and behavioural therapists, the stream of doctors who probed and delved into my head, that I had to have a more balanced view of the world, focus on the future, not let the past dictate who I am, who I could be; that I had to embrace the positive aspects of my life and ignore those dark shadows that without invitation, elbowed their way into my brain, trampling over my recent achievements, leaving me feeling deflated and alone. I use the word achievements very loosely. Small steps would be a more appropriate phrase. Better suited to who I was. I hadn't achieved anything worth speaking of. I had existed within those four walls, stayed out of trouble, kept my head down and not drawn any negative attention to myself. That was enough. While others around me ranted and seethed, thrashing about in their beds, biting and spitting, banging their heads against brick walls and screaming for hours on end, I had remained silent, letting it all unfold around me. I didn't have the energy to be badly behaved. Instead, I would lie there on my wafer-thin mattress night after night, eyes closed, counting down the days to freedom, blotting out the anger and the frustration, the terror and the feelings of utter hopelessness that crowded my mind. I did my best to ignore the darkness that crept in and dreamt instead, of blue skies and sunny days, of green meadows carpeted with daisies and buttercups while horses cantered around nearby fields, their long silken manes blowing gracefully in the soft warm summer breeze. They helped me cope, those thoughts and imaginings. The carefully created animated existence I dreamed about night after night. Those picture-perfect visualisations helped me to stay connected to the outside world, to remember that there was a life beyond those brick walls. A life that at some point, I would be able to join. And then one day it happened, I was told that I could leave, that I had met the requirements for settling back into the outside world. I was rehabilitated. A new person. An alternative me. A cleaner and happier version of the child I once was. I was ready to face civilisation and move on from the past. Recalibrated and no longer out of kilter with those around me. A new me. A better me.

Heather Elizabeth Oswald disappeared and Mary Campbell was let out of a young offenders' institute having served her time for a heinous crime that sickened and appalled the nation and the world at large. I was free. I left Heather behind and emerged as Mary, the girl I was about to become. Except there were no cantering horses ready to greet me upon my release, no rolling meadows and fields of buttercups. I was placed in a small flat above a greasy chip shop that stank of stale fat, the all-pervading smell permeating through the fabric of my clothes and clinging to the carpet and curtains. Tin cans rolled and clattered around damp alleyways in the wee small hours, dogs barked continually, drunks shouted and fought outside my bedroom window. It was hell and heaven all rolled up into one big fat sodden mess of a life; everywhere filthy, noisy and confusing, but at least I was out. I had a new life. I could start again. Be whoever I wanted to be. Be the person I had always hoped I could be.

That was over forty years ago and now, here I am, still here. Still breathing. Still the same old me, the person I always was, who I will continue to be until the day I die, because for all the trite acceptable words that professionals use to describe rehabilitated prisoners – people are what they are. Deep down, none of us ever really change.

Do we?

2

THE WRITER

A pulse takes hold in my throat. I swallow and run my fingers through my hair, trying to appear confident and unperturbed. She's there again, sitting at the back, features sculpted, complexion chalk white. Striking – that's how I would describe her if asked. A striking individual with poise and grace, and an uncanny ability to unnerve me with her pale skin, piercing azure eyes and direct gaze. I blink, rub at my eyes, trying to make sure I'm not seeing things. She turns away then faces me again.

I shift in my seat and stare down at my roughly written notes, the words blurring and merging as my eyes mist over, a small amount of fear beginning to grip me. It's always the same; anxiety coupled with excitement before I begin, which almost always dissipates once I start to speak. I do my best to ignore her presence and focus instead on the task in hand. As usual there are empty seats that will fill once the time for my speech grows near. I prefer a larger audience. It comforts me, massages my ego. It tells me that people still like my stories, that they are prepared to take time out of their day to listen to my ramblings. I suppose I need their adulation. It props me up, keeps me going. Keeps me writing. As pedestrian and inane as it sounds, it's true that without readers, writers are nothing. I like to picture the people who read my novels, sitting curled up with one of my books, devouring every word. Even as I'm writing the grisly details of a fictional murder, I want them to feel relaxed and captivated by my prose. Bewitched by my words. Does that make me sound sad and rather shallow? Maybe that's because it's true. I live alone in a small cottage near the river; a house surrounded by trees and a tangle of overgrown shrubbery, and I crave the applause and praise of other people. I need them to fill the void in my life. The gaping hole that may never be filled. I'm a half person. Incomplete. A partially written story is what I am. Perhaps that's why I enjoy my career so much; telling my own stories full of mystery and intrigue to try and plug the abyss that is there in my own existence; the parts of me that my brain won't allow me to remember. The memories that are either dormant, refusing to reveal themselves, or gone forever, never to return, exploding out of my brain after a speeding car knocked me to the ground, taking away my past and almost my life.

The rumble of voices has me staring up at the crowd, my prepared script a blur of swirling grey in my peripheral vision, the words swimming and distorting on the page. It's now a full house. One hundred and twenty or so seats and each one taken. A sudden surge of people all eager to soak up my words of wisdom and read my books. Relief blossoms within me, unfurling like the petals of a newly formed flower as it embraces the early morning dew and half light of the new dawn. I want to throw off the mantle of worry that is perched on my shoulders and lose myself in the milieu of the moment. And yet there is an undefinable ambience about this place today, something that is putting me on edge. As if an incident is about to happen. An unforgettable occurrence. Something that will ruin the day and dent my fragile veneer of confidence.

I shrug off that feeling and gaze out once again at the spread of people, my waiting audience. My readers. She's still there with her pale skin and unbending posture, her body rigid and straight as an arrow. Her expression is harder to see, now lost amid the sea of faces that await my speech. I feel easier, more able to focus on my script knowing her penetrating stare isn't so visible, knowing her face is lost amongst the crowd. I'll be able to think clearly, push away the anxiety that is beginning to have me in its grip. Perhaps it's her presence that's doing it, making me nervous and discombobulated. Maybe she is the reason I'm expecting some sort of unwelcome event to happen. Seeing her once in a crowd is forgettable, twice, noticeable, three times, deeply unsettling. This is the fourth time and I'm feeling distinctly out of sorts. Nervous and agitated. I unclench my jaw, rotate my shoulders to loosen my joints. Just a face, that's all she is. An avid reader. A fan. I squirm at the use of that word. Fanatic – it conjures up images of somebody so consumed with an idea or a person that they will go to any lengths to get what they want. An extremist. A maniac. I don't want her to be a fan. I don't even want her to be a reader of my books. I just want her to stop attending my talks and to leave me alone. I have many readers who come to see me, to chat and get their books signed. She isn't like them. She is indifferent. Unsmiling and unresponsive. A face in the crowd. A possible threat.

The room suddenly takes on an air of expectancy, as if something monumental is about to occur – the walls, the bookshelves, the people: their faces, their minds, swollen with anticipation and perhaps even a touch of fear. Outside, the town hall clock chimes 5 p.m., each peal of the bell in perfect synchronicity with the thud of my heart, each ring reverberating through my chest like stampeding cattle, crushing me. Trampling my body underfoot. Sucking every last bit of oxygen out of my lungs.

I take a long shaky breath just because I can, to convince myself that I'm not dying, that I can breathe and function like a normal person, and I scan the crowd, searching for a sympathetic face, somebody who will help me recalibrate myself. A pair of caring eyes, a half smile, a tilt of the head to convey their compassion and show interest in what I'm about to say. They all help to soothe my nerves, rebalancing my mind, suppressing the root fear I have that something will go horribly wrong, that I'll stumble over my words, lose my train of thought, that somebody will ask me a difficult question, one that I cannot answer, and then everyone will laugh at my ineptitude before gathering up their coats and bags and leaving in disgust. Nobody will ever buy any of my books again. I'll be a laughing stock. A failure. That has never happened. Ever. But there is always a first time. And I don't want it to be now, while she is sitting watching me, scrutinising my every move.

A gentle-faced, friendly-looking lady sits at the front, her pale blue eyes brimming with kindness and expectation. I keep her in my sights, smile at her and grip my papers with clammy fingers. She wants me to succeed. They all do. That's what I tell myself as I clear my throat and stand up, ready to do my talk. I inhale deeply – in through my nose and out through my mouth, my lips curled into a small O shape – and I begin.

* * *

It's over before it's begun. That's how it feels. I glance at the clock on the wall of the now almost empty library – 6 p.m. I've been speaking and answering questions for almost an hour. Only a few people remain, everyone else having left looking happy, a copy of my latest signed paperback tucked under their arm. She is still here, however – Chalk White Woman – that is my new name for her. She is sitting watching me, only looking away to briefly stare outside at the impending storm clouds that hang in the sky, their grey bellies engorged with rain. Despite her frequent attendance at my talks, not once has she ever spoken to me or asked me to sign a book. She has asked no questions, never engaging with either me or anybody around her. She simply sits there, staring ahead, eyes full of ice, her expression austere and unyielding.

I stand up, determined to ignore her, watching as the final few attendees leave. I refuse to acknowledge her presence or her apparent dislike of me; her body language screaming at me that her malice for me runs so deep it is practically subterranean. No words have ever passed between us; no interactions, verbal or otherwise. There is no reason that I can think of for her to act this way and yet here she is again, watching me from under her lashes, her body unmoving. That is, until she stands up and begins to walk towards me. My scalp tightens, ice prickling each hair follicle. I turn away and pretend to rearrange my already perfectly stacked pile of books, my fingers fluttering over the dust jackets, tracing a line over my name printed there on the cover – I. L. Lawrence. The sight of it still has the power to make me misty-eyed and awestruck. I'm lucky in so many ways. I would do well to remember that, to stop dwelling on my fears and insecurities and focus on my successes. Having a hole in my memory has damaged me in more ways than anyone will ever know. Every now and again I think that perhaps they are coming back, the images of my past, fleeting thoughts and visions jarring with me, only for them to disappear as quickly as they arrived, leaving me feeling confused and out of kilter. A stranger in my own life.

I hear the shuffle of her feet along the wooden flooring, can almost feel the heat of her body and smell the buttery aroma of her breath wafting close to my face. Except when she does eventually arrive, there is nothing, as if she isn't actually there at all. When I do pluck up the courage to look up, she is standing next to me, the corners of her mouth turned up into something closely resembling a smile.

'Hello,' I say, barbed wire cutting at the soft flesh of my throat, my voice clipped and laced with foreboding. I swallow and soften my tone. 'I hope you enjoyed the chat and the readings.' My voice is hoarse – no more than a whisper – fear rendering me almost silent.

She nods but says nothing in return. Part of me wants to keep speaking, to keep her here and find out what her motives are, work out what it is she wants from me. Another part of me would like to push her away, to tell her to stay the hell away from me and never attend any more of my talks, that she unnerves and scares me with her staring eyes and unfathomable cold mannerisms. But I can't. So instead, I point to the small pile of books on the desk and give her a wide smile.

'Would you like to purchase a signed copy of my latest novel? They're available at a reduced price. Cheaper than the local book-shop.' My voice, a friendly whisper, belies my true feelings. I've learnt to put on an act, to mask my innermost fears and sentiments. After the accident I had to learn how to be me again. Whoever that person actually was. I'm still learning. Every day is a lesson.

Alicia, the librarian, gazes at me from where she is standing on the other side of the room, her eyes full of curiosity, her expression one of bemusement before she turns away again and continues with her work.

I rub at my neck, suddenly feeling clammy and feverish. A line of perspiration coats my brow and sits on my upper lip.

'I might,' Chalk White Woman says, her face still pallid, her mouth now unsmiling. She has returned to her usual frosty demeanour and stands motionless, watching me.

My eyes stray to the clock on the wall. Soon the library will be closing. I need to leave here, to make my excuses and get as far away from this woman as possible.

'Well, if you don't fancy buying one, you can always loan one from this library. They have copies in stock.'

I should be encouraging her to buy one from me but need her to leave. I need her to leave more than I need the money, even though at the present time in my life, every penny counts. She doesn't reply, those deep blue eyes never leaving my face, studying me, watching for a fissure in my veneer. Waiting for me to crack. In my peripheral vision, I see her hand moving, her long slim fingers pushing a slip of paper underneath the cover of the book that sits atop the small pile of novels on the desk. My skin suddenly feels icy, my face flashing hot and cold. The thick pink scar that runs the length of my face and zigzags across my hairline, flares and tingles, small sparks of anxiety sizzling at my flesh.

Without saying another word, she moves away and walks towards the door. Alicia doesn't appear to notice as she passes, her head lowered while she tidies her desk. Chalk White Woman leaves without uttering another word or showing any gratitude, the door slamming behind her with a dull thunk. Still, Alicia keeps her head down, immersed in her work. Suddenly we're alone, just the two of us in the building, a hush taking hold, a silence enveloping us.

I watch Chalk White Woman's retreating figure through the glass panels of the door. Her slim body slowly disappears amongst the thinning crowds outside, distant and ghostlike. Only then do I open the book and retrieve the piece of paper she placed inside, my heart a heavy thud in my chest, my fingers clumsy with dread and anticipation.

The walls close in, the floor falls away beneath me when I read the words written there, the print swimming and looping on the paper. I blink and try again, each word, each letter like a knife being pushed deep into my abdomen.

I know who you really are.

Six small words that have the capacity to render me incapable of moving or thinking rationally. I swallow and push a strand of hair out of my face. My body feels heavy and numb, my limbs wooden when I try to move. Beneath the words is a grainy monochrome picture of a young girl, her features blurred, the image too distant, too indistinct to see her face properly.

'Everything okay there? I thought I heard you say something. I was just about to lock up.'

I clear my throat and look up at Alicia into her dark quizzical eyes. She is probably thinking of a dozen different ways to politely ask me to leave the premises. It's getting dark outside. Everybody else has left. She wants to go home. I'm willing to bet she has a loving partner, a nice clean house and a pet that sits by the door waiting on her return. Her partner will have cooked dinner. The table will be laid, complete with serviettes and maybe even a lit candle between them, everything set out on a crisp white tablecloth. I think of returning to my cottage; heading down the crooked lane that leads to my driveway, manoeuvring my way through the towering trees that surround my property. I shiver at the sheer anonymity of it all. The darkness. The indescribable loneliness. Then I think of Whisky, my wonderful canine companion and feel my heart swell with love. It's not all bad. I have somebody at home waiting for me at least. My trusty old dog. My best friend. My only friend.

'Yes. Sorry, of course. I'm ready to leave now. Just need to collect my things.'

The piece of paper slips from between my fingers and flutters to the floor, its glaring whiteness incongruous against the dark wooden flooring.

'Oh here, let me.' We bend down at the same time, our heads colliding when we lean forwards to scoop it up.

'Sorry,' I say, my exasperation and anxiety spilling out. My desperation for her to not see those words a palpable force between us, but it's too late. She picks it up and hands it over, the sight of it in her palm sending a sickly sensation spearing across my gut, making me light-headed and nauseated. The room takes on different dimensions. Pieces of broken glass collide and shatter in my head. I stare down at it, at the slightly crumpled piece of paper and blink repeatedly to clear my vision. I've got it wrong, become confused somehow. In Alicia's hand is a receipt. Not a note. No picture. No words. Just a small nondescript receipt for a snack from the local café.

My eyes burn with unshed tears. I swallow and try to act normally. I must have been mistaken and picked up the wrong piece of paper. Next to me, Alicia makes a slight moaning sound and rubs at the side of her head. I'm abruptly riddled with humiliation and doubt. It was definitely there, that note. The picture. Those words. I saw them. I'm not going mad. Am I?

Without waiting to see if she is injured or upset or completely bewildered by my strange behaviour, I grab at my belongings, snatch up the receipt from her hand and make my way to the door, my feet barely touching the ground, the words I felt sure I saw written on the paper etched into my mind, forever embedded into my brain as if carved onto tablets of stone:

I know who you really are.

The heavy door swings closed behind me, the noise reverberating into the near stillness outside. I step over the threshold and head out into the growing chill of the night.

3

SUMMER OF 1976

It wasn't the heat that was getting to her, even though her shirt was sticking to her skin like cling film, it was the boredom. The days stretched on and on, everything still, the landscape, the world in general in a lull; crops, lawns, flowering borders deprived of water for almost a month. Adults draped themselves over fences, chatting to neighbours, bemoaning the water bans, their bodies listless and floppy in the unrelenting heat as they wiped at their brows and stared up at the azure sky, searching for clouds, praying for any amount of rain to break the dry spell that they had endured for what felt like an age.

The pavement was hot beneath Heather's backside as she sat, watching the world go by, the concrete absorbing every drop of warmth, retaining it and firing it back out onto her already hot and sticky body. She didn't mind so much. Not like the adults who droned on and on, their voices echoing into the hot cloudless sky.

Too bloody hot to think straight

When will it ever end?

I see Kevin at number 36 has been washing his car again. No water shortages for him then, eh?

Heather suppressed an eyeroll at the sound of the chatter, rested her chin on her knees and allowed her mind to wander. They were all idiots anyway. She'd heard her mam and dad say that over and over again. Her family wasn't like the others in their street, all the gossipmongers and do-gooders. Nobody could tell her family what to do, especially her dad. He paid for his water and would use as much as he bloody well liked. That was what he would mutter when the neighbours' talk drifted his way. Fuck the government and fuck this drought. She heard that line a lot as well, mainly when he was drunk, stumbling home from the pub late at night when she was supposed to be tucked up in bed asleep, his voice a loud rumble in the kitchen below her bedroom as he paced the floor, opening cupboard doors, searching for more drink and if he got lucky, some scraps of stale food. Heather would lie there, the thin sheet that was draped over her body, pitted with holes big enough to fit her fingers through, her limbs languid, her stomach growling and grumbling. Hunger. It was always there, an over-active gremlin that inhabited her belly for days on end. Images of roast dinners and apple pie and long, large glasses of lemonade filled her thoughts. And then she would fall into a fitful sleep where dreams of the brightest colours flooded her brain only for her to wake the next morning to a wash of grey, the flimsy thread-bare curtains doing little to block out the early morning light that flooded her room, accentuating the peeling wallpaper, the mouldy ceiling and bare floorboards; the heat of the early morning sun heightening the smell of urine that rose from her bedsheets in unrelenting waves.

She sighed and drummed her fingers on the ground. Who cared about it being too hot anyway? Soon autumn and winter would roll in, angry and fierce, the brisk wind howling in their faces, the cold biting at their skin; shards of ice stabbing their fingers and toes like tiny sharp swords. Then they would all complain about that too. Heather decided that sometimes, grown-ups just enjoyed moaning. If it wasn't the cost of living it was the drought. If it wasn't the drought, it was the heavy snow. And if it wasn't the heavy snow, it was the rain and badly behaved kids trampling on their front lawn, crushing their geraniums and dragging mud into the house. There was always something.

A shadow passed overhead, a rush of birds clouding Heather's view. Bastard pigeons. That's what her mam and dad called them.

'Fucking shitehawks.' She shouted it into the air, clapping her hands before standing up and stamping her feet, the tarmac feeling like liquid under her summer sandals that slapped loosely against her heels, the straps frayed, the soles as thin as worn cotton.

'Heather Oswald, wash your mouth out with soap, you filthy child.'

The soft summer air felt warm and delicious on her tongue as she spun around and stuck it out at Renee Milward. She couldn't help but stare at Renee's huge pendulous breasts and broad hips. A swathe of pale green material clung to her bulges, accentuating her ample girth.

'You got a baby in there, then?'

Renee shook her head, ignoring Heather's acerbic remark and turned away, strands of damp hair breaking free from her hairband. Dark wiry springs were laid flat against her forehead, shiny and wet, plastered down with tiny droplets of perspiration that sat in an arc around her hairline and ran down the side of her face.

Always said no good would come of that kid. Like mother like daughter. Renee's voice rang out in the open air, her words directed at nobody in particular.

Heather felt her stomach plummet, a sharp pain sliding from left to right across her abdomen. She ignored Renee's comment, pretending that it didn't bother her. Words. That's all they were. Empty meaningless words. Heather had learned to disregard them over the years, the malicious rounds of gossip that had been spread about the neighbourhood because of her family and how they were.

How they were.

Three words that had the power to cut her in two. They didn't. She had long since stopped taking notice of what anybody said about her and her family. She knew how to shake them off, those nasty words, and watch them glide away into the ether like liquid mercury. She also knew that Renee didn't have a baby in her belly. She was just fat. Even her arms were round and dimply, her fingers like stumpy little sausages. In truth, she really liked Renee and didn't know why she had just said that about her having a baby in her belly. Sometimes when Renee was in a good mood, she would give Heather a bag of sweets or if she was feeling really upbeat, she would throw in a bag of crisps and a can of fizzy pop.

'Here,' she used to say as she shoved the goodies into Heather's hot little hands, 'get these down you. And don't tell yer mam or dad that I gave you them. It's just between us, yeah?'

Guilt stabbed at Heather's chest and tummy for being mean. Sometimes insults just fell from her lips. She visualised her mouth like a dumper truck tipping out tonnes of gravel and spreading it out on the ground. All those rough stones and chippings making people fall and hurt themselves. That was her words, the stuff she said. Designed to maim. Used for maximum effect. She wanted to not say anything, to not spew out those insults but just didn't know how. Maybe it was to stop their words. A way of getting in the first insult as a way of defending herself and her family.

She looked up, an apology on her lips, twirling on her tongue like sticky candyfloss but Renee was nowhere to be seen. She had already bustled off somewhere, disappearing out of view. Lesley Harcourt was there though, standing on the other side of the road with her slick clean hair and lilac ribbons, wearing long embroidered jeans and a tight-fitting T-shirt. She wore a bra as well. Eleven years old and the first girl in class to wear one. Heather thought of her own flat chest, her narrow hips and unwashed clothes. Shame burned at her, a flamethrower under her skin scoring at her bones. Lesley's dad had a job in town. He wore a posh suit, drove a car and they went on holiday every year to somewhere that wasn't local. Not Scarborough or Filey or any of the other seaside towns along the north east coast. They went to places that Heather could neither remember nor pronounce. Places she had never heard of that screamed exoticism and excitement. Sometimes they would go on an aeroplane, flying up amongst the pearl white clouds like famous people with loads of money, while other families from around here were lucky if they managed a week in a caravan at Crimdon Dene. Heather had never been away anywhere. Not even Scarborough or Filey. Their family didn't go on holiday. Ever. She didn't know why. It's just how it was. Actually, that was a lie. She did know why. It was because her mam and dad drank away any money that they had but she was too wise to ever question it, to ask them to stop and use some of it to put aside for a week in a caravan somewhere where there was a beach and a stretch of azure water that lapped around her ankles while she frolicked and played in it, eating ice-cream and having the time of her life.

A thrum pulsed at Heather's neck as she watched Lesley head over towards her, a swagger in her gait. And wearing lip gloss. Lesley Harcourt was wearing lip gloss, her mouth shining like buffed glass, her lips parted slightly in a half smile.

'What you up to?'

'Nothing.' Heather poked the drain cover with a stick before dropping the broken length of twig, aware of how immature she looked, aware of how immature her behaviour was. Suddenly, poise and grace felt important. Poking sticks into things was stupid and childish. Mouthing off to neighbours was uncouth and uncalled for. She needed to watch and learn, to outgrow her embarrassing ways. Be more like Lesley. Less like herself and only speak when she had something interesting to say. When she got home, she would sneak into her mam's make-up bag, maybe steal some old mascara, a lipstick if she got lucky. Once her mam got off her face on gin then nothing else mattered. She'd never notice. She would wake up the next day, hair matted to the side of her head, her face a funny pale grey colour, those small snake-like red veins spread over her cheeks. Her eyes would be glassy and unfocused for most of the morning until she'd had her cigarette and cup of tea and had brought herself round. It didn't bother Heather. It's just how it was in their house. She was used to it. Expected it. Anything different would scare her, make her think that something was wrong. Her family fraying at the seams was normal in her little world. She preferred the familiarity of it all, the predictability of her mam and dad's behaviour, how they let her do whatever she wanted while they were busy supping their bottles of gin and white rum, and cans of beer. She could put up with the permanent hunger pangs and the cold in the winter when there wasn't enough money for coal for the fire. She didn't even mind the darkness when the electric got cut off 'cos they didn't have any coins for the meter. But now she was in the presence of Lesley, clothes and looking nice felt important. Essential. If the likes of Lesley Harcourt was going to be her friend, then she needed to improve how she looked, not be the scruffy, smelly kid from Tunstall Street. It was time to shed that particular look, be somebody different. Somebody better. Prettier. If only she knew how or had the means to achieve it.

'D'you fancy a wander to the park?'

Heather's face heated up. Her fingers and toes tingled with anticipation. The park. She was about to spend the day at the park.

With Lesley Harcourt. Forget the intense unrelenting heat. Forget the greedy gremlins in her belly that leapt about and knocked against her ribcage. She had a new friend. A pretty, glamorous new pal. Things were looking up.

'Yeah, course. Why not?' She glanced away, her gaze fixed on the horizon, on the low shimmering sun and slope of the nearby hills, hoping her laconic reply and cool distant demeanour hid her true feelings. Being too eager was not the way to go. Lesley would see straight through it if she became too animated. Think her an idiot, not worthy of any attention. And she desperately wanted it – that attention, was hungry for it, devouring every word, every look that Lesley threw her way. Her need to be needed was almost a physical thing, something that bulged beneath her bony frame and snaked through her veins.

'Great. Then afterwards we can go down to the stream, see if anyone's about.'

It felt as if somebody had lifted Heather up and was pulling her towards the sky. She was as light as air. Giddy at the prospect of spending the day with Lesley. Her latest new friend. Lesley's name floated around her head, rolled about her mouth, sliding over her tongue in a silent swift movement, the feel of it a delicious flavoursome thing, like raspberry ice cream and chocolate sauce all rolled up into one big gorgeous glutinous mess.

'Come on then, slowcoach. What you waiting for?'

And without turning to see if Heather was following, Lesley Harcourt ran over the road and disappeared down an alleyway, the sound of her footfall and the tinkling of her laughter drowned out by the roar of passing traffic.

4

I like the darkness. I like how it encroaches in barely discernible notches, shifting ever closer until it arrives suddenly, obliterating everything, shutting out the defects and flaws of the day. I love the anonymity of it. It allows us time and space to grieve over our mistakes and misfortunes. We can be alone with our thoughts and free up our emotions, not be forced to paste on a smile and go through the motions of polite conversation when everything around us is falling apart.

The drive home is therapeutic, my mind raking over what just happened. How I reacted. What I saw and what I thought I saw. How rude I was to poor Alicia, turning and fleeing without giving her an explanation or an apology, without asking if she was okay and whether she was injured. My flesh puckers with shame. I make a mental note to call her later in the week, tell her how sorry I am, that I suddenly felt unwell and had to leave in a rush. I will tell her anything but the truth. That's because the truth is a slippery evasive thing. It falls through my fingers like water, never staying long enough to fully implant itself in my brain. I'm not sure I would fully recognise the truth if it jumped up and hit me in the face. The fear I felt when I saw that note and read those words was very real, like being catapulted back in time, but then like a thief in the night, it was snatched away and shredded before being thrown to the four winds. Much like the slip of paper that contained that blurry image, that too vanished. I should be used to it by now, my unreliable memory, the way things from the past dip in and out of my brain. Recent events stick; every word in my books, every plot, every character and their motives strongly rooted in my thoughts, but happenings and episodes from my past are harder to locate, hiding somewhere in the recesses of my mind. Dark and secretive. Unreachable. I can't understand it, how that picture and those words disappeared, replaced with something drab and mundane. An everyday item. A receipt. A silly slip of a crumpled receipt from a local café. I did see it, didn't I – those words? That pixelated face. They were there. And then they weren't. Here one minute, gone the next.

I turn on the radio, the music lulling me into a near hypnotic state, and try to not dwell on it, the fact that I'm fractured and faulty, my brain always letting me down, leaving me frightened and discombobulated.

I sigh, place my hands tightly around the steering wheel and focus on the road ahead. I need to stop this – going round in circles, torturing myself. Trying to recall the past, convincing myself that I'm close to finding out who I was, only to suddenly discover that none of it is real, that I am using the lives and memories of others to fill the gaps in my own mind, inserting their thoughts and actions and tweaking them to fit the narrative I've constructed for my own life. Aside from my scars and memory loss, I'm a healthy individual with a well-ordered, albeit lonely life and a successful career. I'm single, have no children and no living relatives. I have a dog called Whisky. I own some expensive pieces of artwork and antiques, a hobby I took up once my books started to sell, yet I have no or few recollections of my early life or anything that came before the accident. Not an accident actually. A hit and run. I was left for dead by the side of a country lane, my life hanging in the balance. Nobody was ever caught and held to account. With so few clues left at the scene, it's doubtful that the perpetrator will ever be found. That is my life; it's who I am now. Not who I was. With no living relatives and neighbours or friends who know or ever knew anything about me, I am a mystery. A stranger in my own life. An enigma. And now here I am, doubting my own mind, what I saw. What I *thought* I saw. I'm tired. That's the only explanation for thinking that receipt was something other than what it really was. It was some type of hallucination. A dream. I've heard of it happening before – people who don't get enough sleep, begin dreaming while they are awake. My sleeping pattern whilst getting my most recent book written, edited and published has been scant and sporadic, snatching at naps here and there, getting up in the middle of the night to complete chapters and plug plot holes. I'm not thinking straight, imagining things that don't exist. The human brain is a complex structure and can often make us think we have seen things. Optical illusions, mirages, they are all tricks of the mind. That's what that slip of paper was – a trick of the mind. An illusion. A cruel deception. I would very much like to know who I really am, have thought about it a lot. I have scoured the internet and found nothing of note aside from my birth which was registered on an ancestry site. I've written about it in my most recent book, created a character who has lost their memory. I thought it would help, be cathartic and liberating, a way of dragging myself out of this pit of despair. I was wrong. It has had the opposite effect. It has made me unbalanced and exhausted. It has caused me to see things that aren't really there.

The cottage is in darkness when I pull up outside. I turn off the radio, the crunch of tyres on gravel such a familiar sound to me, I barely hear it any more and yet tonight, it feels heightened. A reminder that I'm alone in this place. With only my German Shepherd, Whisky, for companionship, tonight's solitude feels sharper than usual. A jagged blade in waiting.

I know who you really are.

Anger rises in my chest. I want to slap it all away, shut the image of that piece of paper out of my mind. Shut the image of *her* out of my mind. Pretend it never happened, that she didn't saunter up to me and make contact after watching me for so long now. I close my eyes and rest my head back on the headrest. It didn't happen. It can't have. There was no note, no words. No picture. I imagined it. All of it. I must have. And yet it felt so real. The goosebumps that rose on my arms as I stared down at it, they were a tangible thing, something physical that occurred. The note was not. It can't have been. But her? She was there. I'm sure of that part. Or at least I think I am. With the passing of time, it all feels skewed in my head, everything jumbled and blurry. A notion implants itself in my brain, a tiny pinprick of a thing that balloons until I can no longer ignore or dismiss it. What if there was a note but it somehow fluttered under a desk and the piece of paper that was handed to me belonged to somebody else? It's a plausible theory. More than plausible. It's a distinct possibility. Distinct enough to stop me thinking I'm losing my mind. I want to believe it, that somewhere under a desk in the library is an old image of a young girl with that phrase written beneath it. I want to believe that it existed because if it does exist then I'll know that I'm not losing my grip on reality and that thought scares me more than she ever could.

I open my eyes and sit up, then turn off the engine, squinting at my reflection in the rear-view mirror. An old lady stares back at me, my scar a scarlet streak of lightning that slices across my features. Even the most carefully applied make-up fails to disguise it. If anything, it heightens it, makes it appear more pronounced, my flesh puckered and vivid.

I know who you really are.

Tomorrow morning, that piece of paper will get swept away by the cleaning team, discarded, and thrown in the bin. It will no longer exist. If indeed, there ever was a piece of paper.

I sigh out loud, a breath rattling in my chest. God, this is torture. I lean forward, resting my head on the steering wheel. If that woman does claim to know who I really am, then she is lying. It's impossible. Or highly improbable. How can she possibly know who I really am when even *I* don't know the answer to that? Or maybe I do. Maybe the thoughts I occasionally have are real. How would I know for sure?

I climb out of the car and head into the cottage, drop my bags on the kitchen floor, switch on the lights and fill the kettle. I open the back door and watch Whisky head outside into the darkness for his final pee of the night, his ageing stagger a sign that sometime in the near future, he won't be around. Then I will know true loneliness. I shut out that thought, put it in a locked box in the farthest reaches of my brain. It's a dilemma for another time. I have enough to focus on at the minute. Enough to keep me awake at night, that woman's face occupying my dreams.

Outside, an owl hoots, its call ringing into the still of the evening. It's only 7 p.m. and yet it feels like midnight. Not for the first time, I question why I live where I do, why I bought such a remote property, tucked away in the woods, separate from the rest of civilisation. I must have had a reason. According to the documents I have in the house, I bought it twenty years ago. It took me ten years to pay off the mortgage. It was fairly cheap when I bought it. At some point, I redecorated and made the place look presentable. Made it home. And then somebody ploughed into me with their vehicle and removed all that I knew from that time, out of my head. When I came to in the hospital bed, my agent was sitting at my bedside. The police found her number in my purse and called her. No family. No close friends. An agent.

'Who am I?' Those were my first words to her. 'And who are you?'

She explained that I had written a book and she had secured me a deal. The book was due to be published the following month.

'We could use your accident and memory loss to your advantage,' she had said a few days later during one of her strained visits, her head tilted to one side in faux sympathy as she eyed up the many tubes that were inserted into my body. 'It can be a hook to draw people in. Readers love to hear about the lives of authors. Any trauma can be used to help sell books. It's a story, a way of garnering sympathy and boosting sales. What do you think?'

Something inside me folded, my insides recoiling in resistance. Fear screeched through my veins. It felt like a bad idea. Gruesome and unbecoming. I had no idea what it was, some deep-rooted visceral reaction to her words. I didn't want to be viewed in that way, my newly scarred face, my life on show to the public, so I refused. I didn't want to be viewed in any way. I just wanted to curl up and disappear. We parted company some months afterwards, our differences too great to ever be repaired. As much as I wanted to sell books and become successful, having my own personal suffering exposed to the waiting world and using it as a marketing tool felt like a step too far. I was already feeling fragile and vulnerable, my life stripped of its core; the very essence of me a deep hollow. With no memory, it felt like my insides had been scooped out and thrown away. I had to start again, relearn how to live my life and with nobody around to guide me, it took a lot of time and effort. I knew then that I was alone. I also knew that the other me had possibly lived her life in complete anonymity for a reason. I just didn't know what that reason was. I had nothing to go on, nobody to ask. In all the time I have lived in this cottage since the accident last year, I haven't had a single visitor. No friends calling around for coffee, no family members popping in for lunch. Not a single soul. Which makes me think that there is something in my past that is unpleasant. Something I am hiding from.

I make myself a cup of coffee and sit at the table, ruminating over the woman at the library and how her appearance has stirred up so many unwanted questions and thoughts. I should have followed her, asked what she wanted from me and yet something stopped me, some subconscious fear that had me rooted me to the spot. What if a part of me does remember and I'm blocking it out? What if the note does exist and those words were some sort of threat? But then again, what if it doesn't and I'm losing my mind, slipping into the darkest of corners with nobody around to help me?

My gaze roams around the room as if searching for answers. The bottle on the windowsill catches my eye. Even while I am sitting here, my hands firmly clasped around a mug of hot coffee, I can feel the shape of the glass against my palm, the smoothness and solidity of it. I can recall clearly how jarring it felt when I discovered it; a fleeting memory pinballing into my brain, making me feel breathless and frightened, and then leaving just as rapidly as if it had no right to be there.

It had been a long day. I had been sitting at my computer, working for hour after hour without a break and needed to get out of the house, to feel the sun on my face, drink in the clear cerulean sky, and so I stepped outside and headed down to the river with the intention of simply resting on the riverbank and taking in the scenery. I pulled on my boots and took a short stroll down to the water's edge. That's when I spotted it – a bottle floating downstream. Quite the cliché. Without thinking, I waded into the slow flowing current and picked it up. It had been a natural reaction, as if I was being driven by an invisible force. A hand from the past, pushing me on, trying to dredge up those memories. And for a few transitory seconds it worked. I was the other me again, knee deep in water, the movement of the river stirring up those latent thoughts, bringing them to the surface. The heat of the sun, the azure sky, the gentle trickling of water. And darkness. An over-whelming sense of complete darkness and terror. Not external darkness but an emotion from within. Something inside of me. Something chilling without end. A deep well of wickedness. Clutching the bottle, I had waded out of the river and ran home, hoping its presence in the house would unearth more memories.

Whisky pads back into the kitchen and lies down beside me with a thump, his thick bristly fur warm against my legs.

'Come on, old man. Let's get that door closed and settle in for the night, shall we?' He stares up and licks his lips, his sad eyes rheumy with age. 'Here's hoping you've got a good few years left in you, eh?'

He watches me as if to tell me that he's not going anywhere anytime soon. I hope he's right. Whisky is the only real close friend that I have. His demise would rupture my life beyond recognition. He's my anchor. My rudder in an unsteady and often frightening world.

I stand up and rub at his coarse fur, my fingers disappearing into the depth of his black and golden coat. 'Come on, old man. Let's get that fire going. See what's on the TV. Just you and me, old fella. The pair of us together. Partners in crime.'

5

SUMMER OF 1976

The park was empty.

'Nothing happening,' Lesley said, her voice a thin drawl. 'What do you wanna do now, then?'

Heather sat on a swing, placed her feet on the floor and pushed back, her legs straight out in front of her as she sailed high in the air. The swish of the slight breeze glided over her bare arms, fingers of cool air massaging her thin bruised limbs. A tingle rose in her belly as she went higher and higher. She was an angel on its way to heaven. A god-like creature with wings. Nothing could reach her when she was soaring up in the sky like this. Nothing. Not her mam with her loose fists or her dad with his stupid drunken ways and cutting insults. She was out of everyone's grasp. Alone and untouchable.

'Swings are for babies.'

They sliced through her, those words, stopping her in her tracks. Heather placed her feet on the ground then stood up, the world still swimming around her. Her eyes felt dry. Her mouth, her throat was full of sand, every word an effort. That felt like a stupid thing to do, to try and push herself higher and higher on that swing, pretending she was up in heaven with God. She had made herself look like an idiot. Now she would have to work twice as hard to get back in Lesley's good books, to appear cool and be the sort of girl that people like Lesley Harcourt wanted to hang around with. Which Heather wasn't. She knew that, but she was willing to try. To learn. She was eager to be liked. Desperate even. She would do anything to be part of Lesley's gang. Anything.

'Thought you wanted to go down to the stream?' Heather's cheeks and neck felt hot and dry, her brain full of fireworks that were exploding simultaneously.

'S'pose so. Thought you might like to stay here and play on the slides and the climbing frame like all the little kids do.'

She shook her head so hard it vibrated, the bones in her neck crunching and twitching, blood pounding in her ears. 'Nah. Like you said, swings and parks are for babies. I'd hoped there might have been some lads here that we could talk to, but looks like they've all gone off somewhere else.' The words left her mouth, alien and untethered. She had no idea why she had just said that. She didn't even like boys. They were boring and stupid and had spotty faces and backs. One of the boys in her class had teeth so big they filled half of his face. She didn't like any of them and they definitely didn't like her. Not that she cared. Not any more. Now she was friends with Lesley, nobody and nothing else mattered. She'd seen the other girls in school wander around in pairs, arm in arm, best friends together, and had been consumed with envy. Now it was her turn. Her turn to shine, to prove just how interesting and grown up she could be. She was going to have to work at it, to think long and hard before she acted, rid herself of her impulsive childish ways, but it wasn't impossible. Somewhere inside her was a young woman. A fledgling teenager who was itching to emerge from her cocoon and be free.

'Lads round this way are *so* immature. Not worth our time.

Come on,' Lesley said, pushing her hair behind her ears with such style and charm that it left Heather breathless. She was captivated, her eyes glued to her new friend. The pout of her mouth, the curve of her hips, even the swell of her breasts; it was everything Heather wanted for herself. Everything she dreamed of being. 'Come on then. Let's go down by the stream,' Lesley continued. 'We can hop over the fence on Church Lane and cut through the woods. I've got something to show you.'

* * *

'Over there, next to that wall. That's where she lives.' Lesley pointed, her long pink nails shimmering in the dappled light that filtered through the branches of the large oak tree that stood tall and proud next to the stream. Candy pink. That's what that partic-ular shade of nail polish was called. Heather had seen it in the Avon catalogue. Not that she or her mam ever bought anything from it, but Shirley Dennis dropped it off all the same, week after week, hoping for a sale. Heather would sit, fingers tracing a line over the alluring pearl-like colours displayed in the small glossy book, fantasising about what it would feel like to place an order. How exciting it would be to take receipt of the delivery, opening that white paper bag as it was handed over, plucking out those eye-wateringly expensive items she had ordered and holding them aloft like they were small nuggets of solid gold, studying them, turning them this way and that, her eyes drinking in the array of bright lustrous colours. Nail varnish, lipstick, bubble bath, perfume. She longed for them all.

Heather screwed up her eyes and stared at the brick edifice that could barely pass as a house at all. Her own home was scruffy and stank of stale cigarettes and booze, and if they had any money for food, fried eggs and sausages, but this was something else completely.

'Somebody lives there?'

'I told you. She's my nana but we don't talk to her or see her any more 'cos she's mean and moody. A right old cow my mam says. I think that... ' She stopped speaking and turned away, her voice trailing off into the distance, her eyes lowered to the ground.

'But there's a hole in the roof? And some of the windows are broken.' Heather's voice rose an octave. 'What happens when it rains?'

'Then she gets wet, doesn't she?' Lesley shrugged her shoulders and jutted out her bottom lip. 'According to my mam and dad, she's just getting what she deserves.'

Confusion tugged at the edges of Heather's thoughts. She had no idea why somebody deserved to get wet and live in such a horrible rundown house. Maybe she was a witch. She kept that thought to herself, still unsure of the parameters of this new relationship. Still unsure of whether such thoughts would result in her being ridiculed. Witches didn't really exist. She did know that, but sometimes thoughts sprang into her mind and came out of her mouth before she had time to stop them. Maybe all that would change now she was friends with Lesley. She would watch and learn, become the fledgling adult she had always wanted to be.

'And anyway,' Lesley said, 'it hasn't rained for weeks and weeks and it's not gonna rain for another month or so, so it won't bother her, will it?' She looked up to the sky and held out her hands, shrugging dramatically. 'Not exactly wet around here lately, is it? Everything's as dry as sand.'

She gathered up a palmful of soil and let it fall through her fingers, its powdery texture falling at her feet. 'See?'

Heather nodded. That made sense. It was still a weird-looking place. And what about when the weather turned and the dry spell finally broke? What then? She brushed away those thoughts. It wasn't her problem. 'Why does it look empty though? As if nobody lives there?'

'Told you already.' Lesley pulled her T-shirt tighter around her body, staring down at her chest and flat stomach, looking from left to right until she was happy with what she saw. Heather felt her face flush and looked away, jealousy and adoration a heady combination that fired up her senses and pushed adrenaline through her veins. 'It's because she's mean and moody.' She turned around and began to walk away, a sign that the conversation was over.

It made no sense to Heather that mean and moody people lived in houses that looked scruffy and empty but she also knew that pushing it any further with more questions about holes in roofs and broken panes of glass could sever the friendship before it had had time to really begin. Their recently formed relationship could end up as fractured as the old lady's windows. Heather didn't know lots of things but she recognised fragility when she saw it, and their current connection was as brittle as strings of caramelised sugar. She needed to keep Lesley happy, do her bidding in order to be her equal. It didn't matter that Lesley constantly did the calling while Heather followed. She had a friend. And that was all that mattered.

'Maybe we should go and see her? While we're here, that is.' Heather tugged at a piece of her hair, the urge to pull it out completely so strong it was like a physical ache anchored deep in her bones. She thought back to the immediate whoosh of pleasure she got when she initially yanked out her first small fistful, the strands tucked firmly between her fingers, then the panic of having to cover up the small bald patch, combing over longer strands and plastering them down with cold water. That was last year. She had tried to keep it under control since then, especially after her mam found the bag of hair she had stashed at the bottom of her wardrobe and had screamed at her that she was 'a filthy stinking waste of bloody space,' but sometimes the urge was so strong it overwhelmed her, like picking at a scab or tearing and biting at a loose ragged nail. Sometimes things are there to be damaged and torn apart. It's just how it was.

'You reckon?' Lesley's voice was soft. Laced with concern. 'You really think we should go and see her?'

Heather nodded then shook her head, her cheeks flushing pink with shame. Once the words had left her mouth, she had wished them back. Lesley hated her nana. She had told her so only a few minutes ago. And yet her reply had been restrained. Compassionate even. Heather rarely saw her own grandparents. They lived in a big house in York and had unowned their daughter, Heather's mother. Or was it disowned? She could never remember the correct word for it, but they didn't speak any more 'cos of their daughter drinking too much and marrying Heather's dad. They called him 'that man.' Said he was responsible for dragging their daughter down into the gutter. Heather never really understood what that meant. They weren't homeless. She'd heard of tramps who lived in the gutter and although their house was messy and sometimes stinky and her curtains weren't thick enough to keep the light out, they certainly weren't and never had been, homeless. She had a bedroom and they had a living room and a kitchen. They hardly ever used the cooker 'cos there was never enough money for the electric or the gas but they had pots and pans in the cupboards. Not much food, but at least they had plates and cups and saucers to eat from when they did have some grub in. Sometimes they would get fish and chips from the chip shop but not very often as they cost a friggin' fortune. That's what her dad would say.

'Daylight bloody robbery,' he would yell as they unwrapped the paper, the smell of the salted chips and battered fish making her weak-kneed with hunger. She would always share her chips with her mam as it was too expensive to have her own bag.

'I never see my nana or grandad. They live in York and they're millionaires.'

Lesley's eyebrows shot up to her hairline. Her mouth was agape. 'Millionaires? Did they win the pools?'

More white-hot flames licked beneath the surface of Heather's face. 'Well, maybe not proper millionaires, but my dad says they've got too much money while we've got none and that they should share it about a bit, not be so tight-fisted and mean. Miserable old shites. That's what he calls them. A couple of stuck up miserable old shites.'

Heather felt the heft of Lesley's arm as her new friend linked it though her own and stood close to her, the warmth of her body making her clammy, the skin of their forearms suctioned together in the dry heat.

Listening to Lesley's voice when she replied was like being coated in warm honey. 'You see,' she said softly, 'I knew that about you, that we've got loads in common, you and me. I just knew it when I saw you there on your own. I knew then that we'd end up as best friends.'

Just like earlier when she was on the swings, she felt as if she was flying, rising through the air like a bird, wings outstretched, the cool breeze caressing her bare flesh, lifting her upwards towards the endless cobalt sky. This was it – the moment she had been waiting for, for all of her life. She was now a somebody instead of being a nobody. No longer weak and grubby, no longer that dishevelled kid at school who always had nits and stood alone in the playground, she had grown taller, fleshed out and become a proper person. Nobody could stop her now. Nobody could hold her back or look down on her or call her names. She was made of granite. With Lesley by her side, they could do anything they wanted. She could do or be absolutely anything at all.

6

I made no attempt to keep in touch with either of my parents once I was back in the outside world. I was living in a grotty seaside town on the opposite side of the country. It didn't matter anyway. Dad died eleven months after I was released and my mother followed him to her grave just two years later. Life without them was the same as when they were both alive – grim and desperate tinged always with a sprinkling of hope that things would improve.

My job as a cleaner was both mind-numbing and therapeutic. I was pretty much left alone to get on with it. Every so often my supervisor, Rita, would bark at me to get a move on or to pick up my pace. The other girls feared her but she didn't bother me so much. I'd endured worse when I was in prison. I had endured worse before I went in. Not that they knew that. I had a story about my past. My name was Mary and I grew up in the north east in the shadow of the hills, Captain Cook's monument a constant feature that sat atop them, but moved to the west coast to live with my auntie. I got a job and found a flat above a chip shop. That was pretty much it. Not that anybody asked. We did our work and went home. Some of the others used to go out to the local pub for drinks once we'd finished swilling out the public toilets along Main Street but I *always went straight back to my flat. Keeping my head down, being as unobtrusive as possible was my real skill. It was how I lived my life. It kept me out of trouble. Kept me breathing. I worked hard and played little, living my life in a straight line with no deviations. No cracks or crevices to allow the trouble in.*

'You're doing really well,' Angela, my probation officer used to say whenever I met up with her for my regular briefings. 'Many find it diffi-cult to cope with life on the outside but you've adapted brilliantly. Just keep on doing what you're doing and you'll be fine.'

So I did. I worked hard, even managing to save up some money. I had never had anything as a child, let alone savings, and every time I checked my balance, it gave me a warm glow inside. It wasn't much, just a couple of hundred pounds, but it was something and something is always better than nothing. The flat I lived in was a hovel. I could have spent some money on new decor but it was rented and would never be mine so I couldn't see the point. To outsiders, I was still a poor young girl living in a squalid flat, but with a small amount of spare cash, I felt like a million-aire. I realised at that point what money did – it gave people hope. Folks with proper hard cash behind them oozed confidence, made them feel like they could take on the world. That was me, I wanted to take on the world. I was desperate to fight back and yet knew I would have to live a low-key life, be as inconspicuous and unremarkable as possible for fear of getting recognised and a group of vigilantes turning up in the dead of night and burning down my flat. I also had to think of my probation period and how I was being closely monitored. Being well behaved was one of the conditions of me not being sent back inside. And I couldn't go back in there. Another stint would have been the undoing of me.

So instead, I continued working hard, keeping my head down, keeping myself to myself and having my regular meetings with Angela to let her know how my life was going. The fear was always there, however. That crushing terror of being recognised even though I had changed a lot over the intervening years. With newly shaped eyebrows, a shorter haircut that was a different colour and the fact that I had started wearing glasses, I looked like a changed person. I had also put on weight, my features no longer gaunt, my skin now fresher with a healthy glow. I wasn't that sallow-skinned, rake-thin child. The hunger I suffered as a youngster was something I vowed I wouldn't ever go through again. Near starvation and living in grinding poverty skews your thinking, makes people desperate. Makes them do desperate things. Terrible things. But that was the old me. Or at least that's what I thought. It's what I told myself time and time again, that my actions didn't define me. Until my thinking took a crooked turn, my bitterness and bile finding a way out and making me question who I was and who I really am now. Whether my badness is something that can ever be put to bed.

7

I wake with a start, the darkness a heavy shroud around me, and sit up in the chair, my head fuzzy with sleep. Orange embers are glowing in the grate of the fireplace. A small flame suddenly bursts into life, dancing and flickering up and down and side to side before disappearing as rapidly as it appeared. There is a strong smell of ash in the room. I'd been dreaming. No, not dreaming as such. It was a nightmare. Fear continues to cling to me, weighting me to the ground. My heartbeat pulses in my ears. Images. That's all I have. Vague visual remnants of the rogue thoughts that filled my head while I slept, too complex and unclear to fathom or put into words. Faces of children. Water. Screaming. I shiver and shake myself out of my stupor. Dreams and nightmares, my nemesis for as long as I can remember, which isn't that long at all.

My fingers reach down to touch Whisky's fur. I'm met with nothing, just a surge of cold air. The pulse in my ears quickens. He always sleeps beside me when I'm napping in the chair. Always.

I sit up, my thoughts already in overdrive, visions of Whisky lying somewhere in the house, in pain, waiting for me to come to him looming large in my mind. He could be ill or incapacitated. Or worse. I listen out for the soft pad-padding of his feet on the rug or the snuffle of his snores that tells me he's asleep somewhere in the house, and hear nothing, just a numbing protracted silence. Even the owls have remained quiet, the night air outside my cottage suddenly devoid of all the usual noises. No cawing, cooing or hooting. Nothing at all.

'Whisky? Where are you, boy?' My legs are heavy, my head fogged up, the residue of the dream still present.

He doesn't respond. There's nothing. No snuffling. No sound. Not a damn thing.

But then a swirl of cold catches me unawares, lapping around my ankles. I can smell it – the trail of outside air that has somehow crept inside, into my house.

'Whisky!' I'm shouting now. He should come lolloping through any minute, alarmed by my cries. Except he doesn't.

My fingers clutch at my throat. A whimper escapes unbidden. I run to the wall, my palm slapping at the light switch. The room is flooded with a spread of white. No Whisky. The house suddenly feels huge without him, my small living room a large expanse of nothingness.

The thud of my own feet booms in my ears as I run into the hallway and stare upstairs to the landing. Empty. His bed is empty.

'Whisky! Come on, boy. Where are you?'

I tear into the kitchen, a bout of dizziness causing me to stagger. I lean out and grasp at the worktop to remain upright, my fingers curled around the edge of the granite surface. The back door is open. Not ajar. Wide open. The heat of the house is seeping out, the cold air sneaking in. And still no sign of Whisky. I can hardly breathe. The old boy never leaves the house without me. Ever.

'Come on, lad! Where are you?' My voice echoes into the stillness of the night.

Not a sound.

My throat tightens. A gavel bangs at my temple.

I grab at a shawl that's hanging on the back of a kitchen chair, tug it around my shoulders, step into a pair of old boots and head outside, my voice reedy with fear. 'Whisky! Stop this. It isn't funny any more.'

My words are met with yet more silence. How the hell did he manage to get out? I cast my mind back, the memory of locking the door clear in my head. Or maybe not. I was tired. The note from the library was playing on my mind. It wouldn't be the first time I had inadvertently left it open, but it is definitely the first time Whisky has wandered out there on his own. In the dark. Late at night.

I grab at the torch that is hanging by the back door and shine it ahead, a beam of yellow highlighting the remoteness of the cottage and the sheer density of the nearby woods. It slices through the darkness revealing a tangle of branches and not much else. That's because there isn't anything else to see. I'm on my own in this place. Completely and utterly alone. Just me and the woods and the river.

Oh God. The river.

'Please, Whisky! Come on out from wherever you're hiding!'

Whisky hates water. He wouldn't go down there on his own. He just wouldn't, would he? My breathing is laboured, pins and needles biting at my fingers and toes. I don't have any neighbours, nobody to turn to for help. This is a whole new experience and I have no idea what to do next. The shawl is a hindrance rather than a help, constantly falling down my shoulders while I hold onto the torch. I shrug it off and watch it slip to the floor in a crumpled heap. I kick it to one side and step farther into the thick shrubbery and undergrowth, my clothing snagging against the branches and thorns that hamper me, blocking the route ahead.

'Whisky!'

I suck in my breath, holding a pocket of air in my lungs, and listen. The distant hoot of an owl after what feels like a never-ending silence fills the woods, echoing somewhere above me. Then the rustling of leaves as the wind picks up. A sharp snapping of branches underfoot. And then I hear it – a whimpering sound. Low, barely audible, but it's there all the same. Ice spears at my flesh, shards of it stabbing at me, ricocheting up and down my spine.

'Whisky? Hold on, boy. I'm coming!'

My legs are liquid as I half stumble, half run into the web of leaves and branches that trail over my face and snag at my hair. Something small falls into my mouth. I feel it squirm on my tongue and spit it out, coughing and gagging. Thin globules of saliva coat the lower half of my face, hanging like tiny silver threads from my chin. I wipe at my mouth and face, a small sob erupting from my throat. No time for self-pity. I need to find Whisky. He must be close by. He never leaves the house and wanders alone. He will be scared, upset. Wondering where he is. Wondering where I am, why I've left him out here on his own.

Another whine coming from the left. I stop, listen out and then head towards it, farther into the woods, farther into the darkness until I'm completely surrounded by trees and undergrowth. My chest burns. I suppress the wheezing sound that's coming from my throat, holding my breath, trying to listen out, waiting to hear the cries of my boy.

Mud squelches under my feet. Twigs break, the snapping noise ringing into the night. I pad around, my ears attuned to every little sound, my hands lowered to my sides, feeling out for Whisky's soft furry body, for the wetness of his nose, the soft silkiness of his large ears.

I hear it again. A low desperate whine. The sound of an animal in distress. My animal. My lovely old boy. Upset and suffering in the darkness.

I act on impulse, running without thinking, my instincts driving me on, heading towards the noise. Heading towards that lonely distressed cry. I need to find him, to be with him. Whisky will be lost without me and I'm nothing without him. He keeps me on an even keel. Gives me a reason to get up every morning and face the day. My dog and my readers, they're all I have.

Exhaustion pulls at me, my level of fitness excruciatingly poor. I swing the torch around, still listening out, my nerves jangling. And then I hear it again. Another plaintive cry that tears at my guts. It's close by, the noise. Sweat coats my palms. I slowly move the light over the ground, my eyes wide, searching, sweeping across the crushed branches and mulch of foliage and leaves, attempting to find the source of that awful howl.

And then I see it. The eerie glare of the fox's eyes as it's caught in the beam of the torch. And the bloody animal dropped at its feet on its back, its body twitching, its limbs urgently pawing at the air. A cat. Or perhaps a squirrel. It's too dark to see, my eyes blurry with terror and confusion.

More breaking of twigs underneath its paws as the fox darts away, disappearing into a nearby thicket. I'm at a loss as to what I should do. I can't even see what sort of animal it is. It's small, a mammal. It's not Whisky. He's still out there somewhere. I swallow and fight back tears. My Whisky, out there all alone in the cold and the darkness.

Before I can do anything, the small creature lets out a squawk and turns onto its stomach, its tiny paws scrambling about in the mud, suddenly righting itself and scurrying off up a tree, its tail bobbing about behind it. A squirrel, slightly injured but possibly saved by my approach but I still haven't found my poor dog.

It's difficult to control the tears, the lump that is wedged in my throat a huge jagged rock. I swallow and rub at my face with cold fingers. Where is he? Where is my boy? I feel it keenly then – the isolation, the lack of family and friends. I have no-one. Not a single soul I can turn to for help. Why is that? What have I done that is so bad that I am isolated, living out here in the woods on my own? Was it by choice or did something happen that drove me to live here? I try to ignore the small still voice in my head that is telling me that something is wrong, that Whisky's disappearance is out of character and a sign that things are about to change for the worse. Whether or not I closed the door is irrelevant. Whisky wouldn't leave without me. Somebody took him. I just don't know why.

It takes me another hour of frantic searching to realise that I need to call somebody. I'm not even sure whether I should ring the police or the local dog pound who won't be open at this hour anyway. Ringing 999 to report a missing dog isn't really an emergency. It's my crisis for sure but compared to violent attacks and murder and all manner of dreadful crimes, it doesn't come close to any of those wrongdoings. I'm aware that people often use social media to trace missing pets but since the only account I have is in my author name, I can't even do that.

All out of ideas, I track back to the house, fighting my way through the high knot of branches and shrubbery, stopping dead when I reach the back door. It's wide open again, not slightly ajar, not even closed which is definitely how I left it. This time I know that I'm not imagining it or doubting myself and my movements. Stirred by panic, I run into the kitchen and almost skid across the floor when I step onto the small piece of paper laid there, on the tiles.

You ruined my life so I've taken your dog. I know that he's all you've got.

I don't attempt to suppress the shriek that spills out. It fills the kitchen, escaping into the growing darkness outside and filtering through the treetops. I'm not imagining this note. This is real. Just to be sure, I reach out and snatch it up, laying it flat on my palm, and stare at it. It's real. This time, it's real. My body is heavy with exhaustion after tramping through the woods. Dread is pulsing through my veins. And still, I have no Whisky because somebody has taken him. Somebody whose life I ruined. I slump into a chair and stare at the ceiling, doing all I can to remember.

8

SUMMER OF 1976

She felt uplifted, waking every morning with visions of Lesley tattooed into her thoughts – what they would do together, where they would go – ideas speeding around her brain at breakneck speed. Life was suddenly amazing, each day painted with pastel shades: peach, pink, eye-catching yellow. No more drab grey days. No more hours spent wandering the streets alone, bored, and unwanted. Thoughts of the time they spent down by the stream with the dilapidated cottage and talk of Lesley's nana were far from her mind as they sauntered into town a few days later.

'Look,' Lesley said, her hand outstretched, palm turned upwards as they wove through the crowds of shoppers.

The sight of the crisp ten-pound note made Heather's insides leap. She had never seen that amount of money before and certainly not up close. The only cash she ever saw were the small wads of notes her dad brought home after working on a building site, and even they didn't last long, each one washed down at the local pub until they were gone and all that was left was the reek of the booze as her parents staggered home in the early hours, their voices slurred, their faces pale and waxy, at which point Heather

would take herself off to bed, stomach tight with hunger after she
had tried and failed to find something to eat, scouring the
cupboards for a few measly crumbs to fill her aching belly.

'Waddya fancy buying?' Lesley's voice was cool, as if she carried
ten pounds around with her all the time. She didn't. She couldn't.
Heather's awe of her did not run so deep that she was blind to such
things.

'Where did you get it?' The question was out of her mouth
before she could stop it, curiosity and a small amount of fear
driving her, forcing her to ask the unaskable.

'Does it matter?'

'I don't suppose so.' But it did matter. Heather was certain she
had taken it from somewhere. Even kids like Lesley didn't carry ten
pounds around with them as if it was nothing. It was everything. It
was probably a week's wages. Perhaps not a week's wages for
Lesley's family but for Heather's family, it was a fortune. She visu-
alised Lesley's house with the car on the driveway, her mam with
those gorgeous pencil-fit dresses. No apron. No snags in her tights.
No broken nails or bleary eyes; the remnants of last night's gin still
swilling through her veins. Lesley's mam would wear perfume and
have her hair permed and styled. Their house would be lovely too.
Not huge, nothing palatial but it would be clean and always
smelling of flowers and freshly baked cakes. No threadbare carpets.
No bedsheets stinking of stale urine. It would be nothing like
Heather's, that much she did know.

She thought that maybe they should take it back, check that
Lesley's mam knew about it. And yet, it was so tempting. The
things they could buy for that amount of cash. Her head spun.
Already she was imagining new shoes, maybe even a new dress.
She would love to have a pair of those flared embroidered jeans
that everyone was wearing. She'd never had a pair of jeans before,
let alone ones that had brightly stitched patterns woven up the

side. And if Lesley's parents had that kind of money lying around then maybe they deserved to lose it? Lesley's dad had a job. A proper job that he went to everyday, in an office somewhere in town. Probably in one of those big office blocks. She had seen him leave the house in his pale blue suit and get into his shiny car. He probably got paid loads. It's not as if they would miss it if he had a really good position as an accountant or something along those lines. She'd heard that he once worked at a bank somewhere in town.

Maybe she deserved to have this money. And besides, other people had nice things so why not her? The initial thrashing of her heart when she saw the money had slowed down and been replaced by excitement, a flush of happiness. She decided that it was actually quite exciting, knowing it might be stolen. It gave her a buzz, causing her skin to tingle and making her body feel as light as air.

'Come on. Let's get something to eat and then we'll have a look in the shops, see what we can get.' Even with that kind of cash, Lesley managed to sound calm and self-possessed, as if having ten pounds was nothing, when Heather knew it was everything.

Adrenaline surged through Heather's body, flooding her veins. She fell into step beside her new friend and sauntered towards the café up the side street off the main drag through town, the smells emanating from it making her mouth water.

'Two sausage rolls please, and two plates of chips.'

The lady serving behind the counter looked them up and down, her lip curling at the corner, a deep groove lodged between her eyebrows. Heather felt the thump of her heart as it bounced around her chest. She waited for the caustic remarks, the refusal. Their swift exit back out onto the street. Maybe spending money that was possibly stolen wasn't so easy after all.

'You got enough cash? We had two young 'uns in yesterday just like you two, and they wouldn't cough up when we asked them to pay.'

'We'll pay,' Lesley said, her smile saccharine sweet. 'Won't we, Heather?'

She nodded, her tongue glued to the roof of her mouth, her shoulders locked in position, the heady combination of exhilaration and fear pulsing beneath her flesh, making her hot and cold at the same time. She decided that she liked this new feeling. It made her feel alive, as if fireworks were exploding beneath her flesh.

'Well, you'd better or we'll have the police onto you. Not about to put up with any more of you bloody miscreants. It's about time you were all back in school, not roamin' the streets and bothering everyone.'

Lesley held out the ten-pound note, her fingers clutched around it, the money an incompatible sight in her small hand. 'Here. You see, I told you we had the money, didn't I? So that'll be two sausage rolls and two plates of chips, please.'

The woman eyed the money, suspicion and disdain still etched into her expression. Heather felt the floor sway under her feet. Static fizzed and popped in her ears, a thick line of white noise that echoed in her head. This was it – the moment when they would get thrown out, told off for thieving and chucked out onto the street.

'I'll get your change. Where you sitting?'

'Over there.' She pointed to a small table in the far side of the café by the window.

'Right, well here you go.' The woman huffed as she slapped the notes and coins into Lesley's palm. 'Not sure where young 'uns like you get the cash from. That's part of today's problem. Too much, too bloody young, if you ask me.'

'Well,' Lesley replied breezily, 'it's a good job nobody's asking you then, isn't it, 'cos this is my money. I earned it doing jobs around the house while I've been off school. Been cleaning cars and helping my dad in the garden, planting flowers and stuff. I even washed the windows yesterday so any money I've got, I earned through hard work.'

Her walk was an exaggerated sway as she made her way over to a table in the farthest corner of the café. Heather followed, stomach howling, her knees weak with hunger and shock. She wanted to look behind her, see the reaction to Lesley's words, but didn't have the nerve. It was one thing to mouth off to neighbours but another thing entirely to be rude to café owners who might call the police or a security guard because she and Lesley were considered a nuisance. Her mam and dad would kill her. For all their slovenly drunken ways, even the Oswalds didn't want the shame of being associated with a child who'd been involved in a skirmish with a café owner and hauled off to the local police station. She could practically feel the grip of her mam's bony fingers on her upper arm. The sting of her palm as it met with her face. She already had enough bruises to be getting on with. She didn't want any more. Besides, she was starving and didn't want to risk losing that food, to come so far and end up with nothing. She could hear the woman mumbling something about the cheek of kids nowadays and thought that a misconstrued look could result in them being thrown out and she was really hungry, having had no breakfast, so didn't want to miss out on those chips and that sausage roll.

'Did you?' Heather said, her voice a whisper. They were sitting by the window, passers-by glancing their way before shuffling off into the searing heat, their bodies weary-looking under the glare of the hot unrelenting sun.

'Did I what?'

'Earn the money like you said?'

Lesley shrugged, her bottom lip jutting out in defiance, an act of indifference that was so breathtakingly self-assured Heather felt as if she could hardly breathe. 'Might have. Why do you wanna know?'

'I just wondered. I mean,' Heather tugged at her bottom lip, chewing at a loose ragged piece of skin until a sharp pain sliced through her mouth, forcing her to stop, 'it's a lot of money, isn't it? You must've worked really hard to get all that, did you?'

'Maybe I did. Maybe I didn't.' A small eruption of laughter. Lesley's eyes bore into hers, a hint of mischievousness there.

'Did you *steal* it?'

More giggling, low and deliberate. 'Like I just told you, maybe I did. Maybe I didn't.'

Fear and intoxication at Lesley's casual manner shrivelled Heather's guts. She wouldn't get the truth out of her. Asking again was pointless. It would just make her new friend tense and jittery, possibly even angry. She might even get up and storm out, leaving Heather on her own and that's the last thing she wanted to happen. So what if she did steal it? If she did, then it wouldn't be right to just sit there and eat the food knowing the money she used to pay for it was stolen. She *was* hungry though. Really, really hungry. No supper last night and no breakfast this morning either. Loads of kids from school stole things – sweets from the corner shop, small bottles of cola or lemonade. It was just a game. The shop owners had loads of cash. They didn't miss it. Sometimes, the way they placed stuff near open doorways with nobody there to watch over it, it was as if they were asking for people to take their goods. It served them right.

The food arrived mid-thought and Heather watched her friend tuck in without missing a beat. No guilt, no hesitation.

Lesley looked up at her, eyes glinting with suspicion. 'Not hungry?'

Heather smiled, her mouth hitched up at the corners, the aroma of the hot chips and the buttery scent of the pastry on the sausage roll making her mouth water and loosening her resistance. 'Course I am. I'm starving.'

'Well get tucked in then. After we've eaten these, we'll go and get an ice cream from that pink and yellow shop over the street.' She pointed to the ice cream parlour opposite where a queue of people stood waiting, their bodies snaked along the pavement, faces wet and flushed from the burning sun that beat down on them.

The thought of an ice cream in the blistering heat was enough to make Heather swoon. What did it matter if the money was stolen? So far, nobody had missed it or reported it as having been taken. And anyway, what if Lesley was telling the truth and it was really hers? Being bold and sassy and letting her mouth run loose with adults was one thing but pinching large sums of cash and spending it on sausage rolls and ice creams would definitely result in Heather getting a good hiding if her mam or dad ever found out. Heather sighed, the thought of her parents darkening her day. The waste would rile them as much as the shame heaped upon their family, the thought of how they could have spent the money on themselves eating away at them. How they could have spent it on yet more drink. She often wondered what it was that attracted them to the booze. It made them stagger and fall about. It made her mam fall asleep in the armchair, her head tilted to one side. Sometimes her mouth would hang open and she would snore. Once, Heather had laughed and her mam had opened her eyes, caught her giggling and had practically flown out of the chair in a rage, whacking Heather around the side of the head for being, *'a cheeky little shit'*. It hurt, her ears ringing from the hit, but even then, she had refused to cry. Crying would have only brought on another slap. Crying was pointless, a waste of time and energy and only brought her more pain one way or another

A pain lodged in her stomach as she shovelled in the food. She stared down at the empty plate, realising she had eaten it almost in one go, forcing fistfuls of chips and greasy pastry into her mouth as fast as she could. She wasn't sure she had any room left for ice-cream.

'Tasty, eh?' Lesley's eyes were narrowed as she stared at her new friend, a tiny crumb lodged at the corner of her lips. Heather wanted to lean forwards and brush it away but feared the reaction. Their relationship was very new. Too new for brushing away stray crumbs and making Lesley look silly, like a baby who couldn't feed herself properly.

She nodded, wondering if she also had any flakes of pastry dotted around her own mouth or any stodgy pieces of potato lodged between her teeth. She didn't like the thought of that – sitting there looking ridiculous in front of her friend. It was bad enough having to wear raggedy clothes and to have fingernails with crescents of dirt under them. She didn't want to look like somebody who hadn't eaten in ages and who had gulped the food down in an undignified rush. It made her face go all hot and tingly, the thought of people staring at her, thinking she was dirty and greedy. Even though it was the truth. She'd been told it loads of times at home whenever she asked for something to eat.

'Not got nowt in. Always thinking of your stomach, you are, lass,' her mam would shout. 'Just a bloody eating machine is what you are. Can't afford to keep ya.'

'Come on, cheer up,' Lesley said, as if she were reading her thoughts. As if she was able to see right inside Heather's head. That was something else that made her shiver, made her feel dirty and ashamed, the fact that she was always thinking about her new friend, wishing she could be more like her. Wishing she could *be* her instead of the smelly, scruffy kid that she actually was. Lesley filled her mind day after day – her voice, her face, the way she walked. She was there when Heather woke and her face was the last thing she saw before she fell asleep at night and the more she tried to think of other things, the more her friend crept inside her head and lived there.

'Let's go and get that ice cream now.' Lesley's chair scraped across the floor. 'Race you there. Let's see if we can jump the queue, elbow all those weirdos out of the way.'

She led the way out of the café with Heather following behind, trailing in her shadow.

9

For the longest while, nobody knew who I was. Who I really am. I led a low-key life, stayed out of trouble, kept my private life, private. And that was exactly how I liked it. Until Ralph came along, that is. Ralph, with his smile and easy manner and effortless charm. He was like nobody I had ever encountered before. On a different level to me, to my family. To the person I had once been.

I continually questioned what he saw in me, convinced he could see inside my head, was able to penetrate the suit of armour I had wrapped around myself, around my emotions and thoughts. Convinced he would peel back the layers to reveal the real me, not the new better version of me but the dirty, blemished person lurking just beneath the surface. She was, and is always there, waiting in the wings, that awful naughty child, ready to make an uninvited appearance. I keep her at bay, keep her hidden and out of sight but because she is an intrinsic part of me, every now and again she appears unbidden. A sudden flash of temper. Bitterness and resentment if things don't go my way, that's when she rears her head, reminding me that she is still nestled deep inside me.

'No need to be so cagey and suspicious all the time, Mary,' he once

said when I asked him what he saw in me and why he had asked me to move in with him. 'I thought you loved me the way I love you?'

The look of hurt on his face was so real, his tone so damaged by my repeated efforts to keep him away from who I really was, the person I used to be, that I knew I couldn't ever tell him about my past, no matter how close we got, no matter how strong our relationship became. He wasn't made of stone; he was a gentle soul. Sensitive and caring. Our bond was strong but it wasn't unbreakable. It was a fragile thing, frail under pressure. And nothing lasts forever. Except death. The past had taught me that much. Death just goes on and on and on. The faces of the deceased haunting me night after night. I call them the deceased to protect myself, to protect my own mental health. Victims is what they are. Victims of a horrible unforgettable crime. A crime I was a part of. A crime that should never have happened. And yet it did.

And so, out of a fear of losing possibly the only man who would ever want to be with me, I let him into my life.

I moved into his flat and we rubbed along together very nicely, my story about losing my parents and being brought up in a series of foster homes before going to live with my aunt, holding water. The lack of photographs or anything to document my earlier life was testament to that fact. I lied and he believed me.

I left my job as a cleaner and worked at an office in town, again, leading a subdued existence. They were an amiable lot but fortunately for me, not particularly sociable. Most had young children and were keen to get home every evening. That suited me just fine. No impromptu visits to the pub. No Christmas parties. The fewer people I had in my life, the better. Safer. The chances of being recognised were almost non-existent, my new look so very different to the child I once was, but it wasn't a chance I was willing to take. Putting on weight altered my features, made me a healthy, shinier version of myself. I was no longer grubby Heather from Tunstall Street. No longer the scruffiest kid in town.

I had met Ralph unintentionally, our meeting a fortuitous affair. It

*happened one afternoon when I was heading home from my cleaning job,
his request to go for a drink a complete surprise to me. We had passed one
another a few times before on my way to and from work, often enough to
warrant a half smile or a nod of the head as we went on our respective
ways. On that particular day, I had accidentally bumped into him while
checking my watch and it went from there. He told me afterwards that it
had taken him weeks and weeks to build up enough courage to speak to
me. I didn't blame him for that. I wouldn't want to speak to me either
with my permanent anxious expression and hurried brusque manner.*

*There are days when I wished it hadn't happened. I loved him. Oh
God, I loved him like I had never loved anyone before, which in fact, I
hadn't. Attachments were difficult for me. Ralph was my first and only
relationship. And for the most part, we were happy. The sort of happy I
never thought I would ever know or deserve to feel. But in the end, things
turned sour and I was left alone. Had I never met him, grown close to
him, then I would never have had to suffer the gut-wrenching trauma
that followed. The gut-wrenching trauma of loss.*

*Correction, they didn't turn sour naturally. We hadn't reached the
end of our relationship. It certainly hadn't run its course. It was a
horrible painful split. Just as we were warming up, looking good together,
being a proper couple, that's when it happened. The revelation. My reve-
lation. His discovery of who I really was. And then the inevitable end
of us.*

10

I'm in the car revving the engine when I realise that I haven't locked the door to the cottage. Not that it matters. Even if somebody does get inside, without my Whisky there is nothing in there worth taking. They can have my precious artwork and antiques. They can access my bank account and take every penny I have because without my beautiful dog, all of it is worthless.

The car spins on the gravel when I turn and head out onto the lane that leads away from my house and back out onto the main road, the full beam highlighting the woods and the route ahead. I wind down the window, listening out for any sounds. For the sounds of my boy, out there all alone, waiting for me to pick him up and take him home. I try to not think about the note and what it could mean. It was different to the note at the library, which was printed, not handwritten.

The note I cannot find.

The note that might not even exist.

Fear and confusion combust in my head.

I wish I knew what happened back there in the library, whether it really happened. She was there. I know she was.

I'm not losing my grip. I am not losing my grip.

Whoever this lady is, this woman with the chalk-white complexion, she knows all about me. She knows where I live, she knows about my past. She also knows what the most precious thing is in my tiny little world and she has targeted it. Taken it from me and left me feeling terrified and bereft. Maybe she followed me home. Or perhaps she already knew my address although I have no idea how that could be. I've gone to great lengths to live privately, to keep my home life separate from my professional life. My initial guess that she followed me is probably correct. All she would need to do is drive a good distance behind me and watch as I turn off the main road down to the woods. The rest is easy. In my bid to live privately, I've inadvertently highlighted my existence here in the cottage in the woods. Now isn't the time to even think about that though. I just need to find Whisky, make sure he isn't hurt. Make sure she hasn't done something abhorrent to him. Carried out an unspeakable act of cruelty. What sort of person would abduct a helpless friendly old dog who is clearly no threat to anybody? I don't give that question any headspace, pushing it out of my mind as quickly as it appears.

Calling the police now seems like a good idea. I'll need to find the number of the local station or even drive there myself, tell them what's happened. Show them the note. But first, I'll drive around the lanes, stop and search the undergrowth, shout and scream his name until my throat is hoarse. What sort of a monster would do something like this? Taking the one thing that means the world to me. The only living thing I have that I care about.

Once this is over, I'm going to work out who she is and what it is she wants from me, this strange delusional woman. And how I can remove her from my life, go back to how things used to be – calm and on an even keel. Predictable. My recovery after the hit and run was difficult enough and now I have this to deal with. Anger ripples through me. Anger and confusion. What did I do to her? She claims I ruined her life. If I was such a bad person, surely I would know about it? There would be clues. What did I do that was so terrible? A hundred scenarios run through my head but none of them fit. Did I have an affair with her partner? Is that what this is all about? Is Chalk White Woman a woman scorned? If so, then she has overstepped the mark. Her revenge has got my attention. If it's a battle she is after, then as quiet and reserved as I am, I'm up for the challenge.

The wind picks up speed, whistling through the trees, the eerie rustling of the leaves and the creaking and groaning of large branches jangling my nerves, all these extraneous noises stopping me from hearing any important sounds that could lead me to my dog. I push all thoughts of Chalk White Woman out of my head. I will deal with her later. Right now, I need to find Whisky, make sure he is okay.

It's almost impossible to see through the woods to work out if he's in there and my search on foot proved fruitless, so I keep on driving. I swing the car out onto the main road, which is almost deserted, and hit the brakes, the car's tyres growling with resistance. In the distance, on the roadside I can see a shadow. A shape silhouetted against the backdrop of the last vestiges of an amber sky, the sun dipping and disappearing behind the hills, leaving the landscape swathed in an impenetrable velvety blackness.

A pulse taps at my temple. As carefully and quietly as I can, I clamber out of my seat and walk towards the shadow. I don't call out for fear of scaring him, but already I can see that it's my boy, the distant shape morphing into the instantly recognisable outline of a German Shepherd, his wide body and long loping back end a sight so familiar to me I almost cry out with relief.

I'm ten or fifteen steps away before he sees me, his body frozen with fear. Whisky is an old boy. A house dog who only ever ventures around the garden and into the woods with me, but never alone. I pray he is able to recognise me in the darkness and, after what he's been through, doesn't think of me as a stranger who means him harm. The last thing I want is for him to bolt. In his usual languid sluggish style, he stands up and begins to lope towards me. I talk to him, keeping my voice low and soft, whispering words of encouragement. Non-threatening. When he is a couple of feet away, I allow myself to cry out and he comes lolloping over, his head nuzzling into my legs. I drop down onto my haunches and bury my face into his, his tongue wet on my cheeks as he licks away my tears.

'How did you get out here, old boy? Who did this to you, eh?'

He stops and stares off over my shoulder as if trying to reply to my question. My hand is on his back. I feel it then – the rustle of paper that is attached to his collar. My stomach clenches. Another note. What is it with this woman and her love of writing fucking stupid notes? I'll read it later when we're back home. Right now, she isn't worth the effort. All I want to do is get my boy into the car and back home to the warmth and security of our cottage. I guess in a way, I really am fortunate living alone away from other people. For all I may have inadvertently made myself a target by being so isolated, at least I can disappear into my cottage and not have to speak to anybody. My faith in the outside world is already corroded and damaged beyond repair after the accident, and all events like this do is deepen my distrust even further.

'Come on, lovely lad. Let's get you into the back seat, get you warmed up and when we get home, we'll have some supper. How does a bowl of mince and gravy sound?'

He lets out a short sharp bark of agreement and we walk together across the muddy track. It takes three attempts to get him into the back of the car, his legs weak with age, his old body resistant to such heights. He's no longer able to leap the way he used to.

I try to block out thoughts of how roughly he was handled and how he was just dumped by the roadside and left to rot. Later. That's when I'll go over it all in my head, torturing myself with thoughts of him being shouted at or worse still, hit or kicked. But for now, I'm just relieved to have him back. Back with me, exactly where he belongs. I'd like to see her at this moment in time, this woman who means to do me harm. I have a few questions for her, like the hell does she think she is, doing this? She may find that she picked on the wrong person. Never mistake quiet for soft or stupid. She does that at her peril.

* * *

My wine goblet is almost empty. I head into the kitchen and refill it, the need for another glass of red so strong the feeling is almost overwhelming. One more and I'll summon up the courage to read that note. More bloody notes. Stupid, stupid woman.

Whisky is snoring beside me as I flop into the armchair. His head is lolling out of the basket and resting on the furry rug that is laid in front of the fire. He's exhausted, the shock to his system rendering him fatigued and incapable of doing anything other than napping. That plus a full stomach, the effects of which will have brought on a soporific sensation so strong, means he will probably sleep right through until morning.

I lean down and ruffle his ears, the silkiness of them never failing to make me smile. He is always there for me, his gaze, his body language so trusting it stirs up a visceral emotion in me.

The note sits on the arm of the chair, its presence a reminder that somebody could be out there right at this minute, watching us, planning their next move. No, not somebody. *Her.* The woman from the library. Chalk White Woman. I have no idea what game she is playing, but her face with those sculpted features is enough to strike fear and loathing into me, her unsmiling expression making my flesh crawl with trepidation.

I glance down at the slip of paper. I'm putting off opening it. The fact she managed to worm her way into my life, into my home and is currently under my skin, irritates me to the point of wanting to scream and throw her latest message into the fire. But I don't. I stare at it, wishing it would disappear. At some point in the past, I clearly caused her harm, said or did something to hurt her, either deliberately or otherwise, but Whisky is innocent in all of this. I need to protect him, keep him safe in his twilight years. He deserves that much and more. She is getting back at me through him. Why doesn't she just confront me? Is she a coward? Or worse still, is she unhinged? That thought stops me in my tracks. What exactly is she capable of and how far will she go to get even? Even for a deed I cannot remember committing. I'm almost certain I have led a normal life. No stints in prison, no crimes committed. As far as I'm aware I've never even had a parking fine or a speeding ticket. So what exactly am I supposed to have done? The idea that I slept with her partner is also hard to believe but not so outlandish that I rule it out; however, there is nothing in the cottage to suggest a torrid love affair; no love notes or photographs. No birthday, Valentine's or Christmas cards. Not a damn thing. Besides, wouldn't I have had a visit at some point after the accident? A text or a phone call?

The red wine coats my tongue, leaving a floral aftertaste that clings to the roof of my mouth. I take another swig and then pick up the missive. No more prevaricating. I need to get it over with. Whisky continues to snuffle and snore by the side of my legs, his body curled into a tight ball, paws snuggled up to his face. I open the note, determined not to be shocked or upset by whatever is written there. Or angry, although that is proving harder to do.

My face flushes hot and cold, my scalp turns to ice as I digest what she has written.

> Were you frightened for a moment there? Did you feel real terror at the thought of losing something you love? Welcome to my world, the world you created. Be prepared because this is only the beginning...

A threat.

My hands are trembling. Who the hell does she think she is? This time I do throw both notes into the fire in a fit of pique. I thought everything in my life was sorted. And now this. Since the accident, I have kept my life simple and structured. Just me and Whisky and my books, a successful symbiosis. I know what each day will bring and that's exactly how I like it. No bumps in the road. No unwanted deviations, or unexpected trials or tribulations. Being knocked down and left for dead was traumatic enough. I now like to live an uncomplicated existence. My life isn't completely trouble-free. Whose is? Life is tricky and complex and littered with difficulties and I do have my moments for sure, but nothing on this scale. She has appeared unbidden and uninvited and I want it to stop. I want her to go away and leave me alone.

When I finally came home from the hospital confused and frightened, my memory utterly fractured, I scoured the cottage, searching for clues about myself and how I lived my life, and found very little. Apart from a few childhood photographs, I found nothing of any substance. Nothing that would help me to remember who I was. It was as if I'd deliberately lived a sanitised existence, as if I had tried to smudge out who I used to be. Visits to the hospital to see a specialist did nothing. I was advised to take up exercise to improve brain function and cognition. They also gave me as much background on my previous life as they could but what they told me was what I already knew – that I had always been a writer, submitting articles to magazines and supplements under a pseudonym. I found no links to who I really was, just an old birth certificate and the death certificates for my parents. I did some research into my mother and father and my real name but nothing of any substance came up. Unless something major occurs in some-body's life like receiving an award or appearing in court, it's almost impossible to trace them. Even Google has its limitations. I was left with just names and addresses and not much else. That was all I had to go on. So one day, I made the forty-mile journey and visited the place where I grew up – a nice enough house in a small close. Nothing significant or outstanding about it. Just an ordinary three-bedroomed house in an ordinary town on the edge of Teesside. I sat on a bench and watched the neighbours come and go, wondering if any of them would recognise me, willing one of them to give me a wave and call my name. It didn't happen. I recognised nobody and they clearly didn't recognise me. I felt let down and slightly bereft.

Other patients who suffer memory loss go home to friends and family who help to put the pieces of their life back into place. I came home to nobody. I had already distanced myself from my agent at that point and our split came soon afterwards. Which left me with nothing. The fact that nobody visited me in hospital or cared that I was injured told me everything I needed to know – that I was alone and had lived like that for all or possibly most of my adult life. If there was anybody out there who knew me, they did not step forward at the time, to make themselves known. And they still haven't. With my recently scarred face, it's unlikely anybody will recognise or remember me. It doesn't bother me so much. I'm fairly happy like this even if it does feel a little lonely from time to time, and until the appearance of that woman and these letters, I had stopped looking into my past and had begun to concentrate on the future, but now I'm infused with a desire to know, if only to work out what it is she wants from me. What she thinks I've done that is so terrible she feels the need to follow me, sending me threatening letters and kidnapping my dog.

A sudden wall of exhaustion slams into me, a huge crest of foaming white water that forces me back into the chair. I rest my head against a large cushion, weariness weighing heavily on me. I'm too tired for this. I expend every ounce of energy I have on writing and existing. This feeling of anxiety and anger is a hefty cloak to wear. I don't want it and I don't have the time or the energy for it.

My eyelids are made of lead but I fight sleep, worried that something will happen if I nod off. The fire is dying down, the grate a dull glow of amber and ash that crackles and pops. I stand up and check all the windows, rattling at the handles to make sure they are all fully locked, then do the same with the doors, sliding bolts across that I rarely use, jamming them in place with a loud metallic clatter. Whisky can sleep in my room tonight, not on the landing which is his usual position. I'm not taking any chances. I'll push the chest of drawers up against the bedroom door and we will spend the night with each other, safe in the knowledge that if anybody tries to get in, we have one another for protection and comfort. This ridiculous woman with her pale face and pathetic notes can fuck off.

'Come on, boy.' I whistle and wait while he gets up and pads alongside me. 'Let's go and get tucked up in bed.' I get down on my haunches and hold his face in my hands, his wonderfully soft and furry face that has brought me so much joy and comfort over this past year. 'Who took you, eh? If only you could speak, let me know what she did to you. Who she is. Why she's doing this to me.' I stop and briefly shut my eyes then shake my head. 'To us. But don't worry, I won't let it happen again. I'll protect you, make sure you're safe.'

It's no surprise he went with her. He's friendly, led by his stomach and easily enticed with cuddles and treats. She took advantage of a gentle dog, his easy affable nature allowing him to be led away from his home. Whatever it is she thinks I've done, he doesn't deserve to be hurt or upset.

My next talk is in three days' time at a local bookshop in town. My stomach folds in on itself at the thought of it. I only started doing these talks out of necessity. A necessity that I sell more books, get my name known and keep my income steady while I consider my recent diagnosis; something else that will occupy my mind and stop me from sleeping, the thought of the tumour that is growing inside me, occupying my mind. When I'm not writing, I'm giving talks and when I'm not giving talks I'm writing, but always, *always* when I'm doing both of those things, I'm also pondering over my health and what the future may hold for me.

I will keep my eyes peeled for her when I'm speaking at the event. I'll be on the lookout for her alabaster skin and piercing gaze. And then I'll speak to her, find out who she is and what she wants. Tell her to leave me and Whisky the fuck alone. And if that doesn't work. Well, if that doesn't do anything, then it's probably time to get the police involved. Whether I want to or not.

11

SUMMER OF 1976

'Use your sleeve. Hurry up, she's coming.'

Heather wiped her mouth with the back of her hand, a smear of baby pink ice-cream streaked across her skin. Her flesh felt sticky, her mouth cold and sugary. Irena Wallis, the coolest, cleverest girl in school was heading their way. Heather looked down at her own bare legs and dirty ankle socks, thinking about her baby-like clothes and unwashed hair, and wished she was anywhere but here. Why was Irena coming over to see them anyway? The thought of it infuriated her, under her arms and round the back of her neck pricking with indignation. She and Lesley were a team now. Best friends. They didn't need anybody else. It was just the two of them against the world. Irena, as popular as she was, would be an intrusion into their recently formed little friendship. She would spoil everything, ruining their routine and marring their plans.

Lesley stepped forward and pushed back her shoulders, her hair falling into long chestnut waves down her back. 'Now then. Not seen you around in a while. Where you off to?'

Irena shrugged, her lower lip jutting out slightly, accentuating her perfectly shaped mouth with its Cupid's bow and shimmering lip gloss. 'Dunno. Nowhere really. Just hanging around the town for a bit.'

'Well, we're doing the same. Maybe we could all hang around together?' Lesley's voice was a chirrup, her enthusiasm for Irena's friendship as evident and obvious as the padded bra she wore that added at least two inches to her bust.

Heather's stomach tightened. She tried to mask her disappointment with a forced smile. Everything was fine as it was. She didn't want another girl joining them. She just wanted Lesley. Three was an odd number. Somebody always got left out when there was an odd number. And she knew it would be her. With their slim figures and fashionable clothes, Lesley and Irena were a good fit together. Heather was an add-on. A leg iron.

She tugged at a loose piece of thread on her sleeve, wrapping small lengths of cotton around her fingers and yanking at them. She felt Irena's eyes on her, that scrutinous gaze, the way she spent too long assessing her clothes, her hair and unmade-up face. She felt it as keenly as a slap on her bare flesh, the discomfit of it making her skin red with shame and hurt. This was it; the moment when she knew she would be edged out. Marginalised. Pushed aside and forgotten about while Irena and Lesley sauntered away arm in arm, their commonalities greater and more closely aligned than hers and Lesley's ever would be. She knew it had been too good to be true. People like her didn't have popular friends. They didn't have any friends at all. Suddenly the summer looked bleak, her days long and lonely. Stupid really. What did she expect? To suddenly be hanging out with the in-crowd? It had been short-lived, her friendship with Lesley. Something to be savoured, but the memory of it a fleeting thing, like catching a dandelion in one whole piece then watching as it rapidly falls apart in your hands, the breeze catching its fluff and dispersing it far and wide until it's no longer there.

'Yeah, why not?' Irena's voice was posh, her accent different to Heather's and Lesley's. She had moved up north from a village near Leicester last year. Her dad was also different to Heather's, different even to Lesley's who had a job and a car and everything. He was a managing director somewhere. Heather didn't even know what one of those was but it clearly paid really well because their home was the big one up on the hill, standing on its own with no other houses attached to it. It had a huge garden with apple trees in it. Rumour had it that they even had people who cleaned their house and mowed their lawn for them and didn't have to do any of their own housework. Seriously rich is what they were.

'You okay with that, Heather?'

Heather nodded, her nerves on fire, her limbs watery with discontent. It was all she could do to not turn and run away, leave the pair of them behind while she hid somewhere remote, away from the rest of the world. Up in the hills. She could go there, take the bridle path and spend the day walking, nestling herself amongst the trees and shrubbery. Take some time to lick her wounds and work out what to do next.

Irena's voice intruded on her thoughts. 'I love the colour of your hair, Heather. It's got some shades of copper in it. You should add one of those temporary dyes. It'll bring out the red highlights.'

The vice that was tightly clamped around Heather's skull began to loosen. She wasn't certain, but Irena's voice sounded genuine. No sarcasm. No words dripping with acid. No hidden meanings that she would have to unpick before answering. That had happened in the past when she had replied to somebody, convinced they were being friendly when they really were being sarcastic, accentuating Heather's lack of finesse, firing subtle scornful remarks at her that were designed to wound.

'Yeah, her hair is gorgeous, isn't it? And you're right. We should maybe buy one of those dyes today.' Lesley's voice also sounded real. No underlying tones of mockery or malice. Heather was accustomed to that type of talk, could spot it a mile off. But this – this seemed genuine, as if they really cared. Maybe they did. It was difficult to tell, their friendship still new and unblemished. No history to go on. No way of unpicking rogue comments and working out the subtle hidden meanings.

'I've got some money,' Lesley said, holding out her palm, a crisp five-pound note lying there, held in place by a handful of loose change.

'We won't need money,' Irena replied, a smirk teasing at the corners of her mouth.

'How come?' Heather's voice was muffled and echoey as if she was underwater.

Irena tapped the side of her nose and smiled. 'You'll see, Heather. Come with me and you'll soon see.'

* * *

She knew what was going to happen. They all did, but it was like the first rumblings of an avalanche – too big, too heavy, just too damn fast to stop. They knew that they all had to go along with it, not appear unfazed or scared. No chinks in their armour. Nothing that would allow the light out. Or the darkness in.

It began with hair dye and quickly escalated to small items of jewellery including a silver watch and a pair of earrings. By the end of the day, they had accumulated a hefty stash of stolen goods, their pockets heavy with trinkets and items of make-up.

The pain behind Heather's eyes when she took her first item soon dissipated, dissolving and transforming into something bigger. Something better. A buzz that filled her body like small bolts of electricity. She felt alive. Important. For the first time in her life, she owned things, had her own belongings – possessions that could define her, help her step back into the light instead of constantly lurking in the shadows, humiliated by her outward appearance and lack of social graces. These items that were hers would help her take that heady dizzying leap into adulthood. People would see her as a somebody, admire her even. She'd waited a long time for that moment and now with Lesley and Irena as friends, people who would have her back should anything terrible take place, she could be anybody. Anybody at all.

12

Nothing lasts forever. That is what I've heard people say. Except they're wrong, the folk who say such things. It's nonsense. Pain and heartache and periods of harrowing misery; they last forever. They never leave, staying put, and defying anything that tries to uproot them. Why is it that the negative emotions are so much harder to shake than the positive ones? Their impact is deep and raw and long-lasting, becoming embedded in our bones until they eventually bury themselves so far down, that they become part of who we are, secured and fixed in our souls, an intrinsic part of us.

We had moved to a new place, Ralph and I, settled in, put our own stamp on it. We were ticking along nicely. Better than nicely actually. We were perfect. And then I ruined it. After a few drinks one evening and a particularly difficult day at work, I opened up to him, bared my soul and told him the truth about my past, about who I really was. I hadn't planned on doing it, but we'd grown so close and my judgement was blurred by alcohol. For some inexplicable reason I felt that the time was right. It wasn't. I was so wrong. The time would never be right, but it was becoming increasingly difficult to continue living that lie, carrying the burden of who I really was around with me day after day, working through the difficulties of it on my own, so I opened up to him, gave him a heartfelt explanation of what happened. I thought we had grown close enough for me to open up to him. I thought he would understand and hoped he would forgive me, see beyond the prisoner and the seriousness of the crime to the real me underneath. I had made a terrible mistake but it was too late to do anything about it. The words were out there and there was no way of taking them back.

'Fucking hell, Mary! Are you serious?'

That wasn't his first reaction. His initial comment was to ask if it was some kind of sick joke, but once he could see my expression, my tears and the trauma I felt, he realised that I was telling the truth.

'You've lied to me all this time and just expect me to accept it?'

I cried, pleaded with him to try to forgive me, but at that point, I could see that it wasn't going to happen. His horrified expression, the look in his eyes that told me he felt betrayed. It was a big ask to hope that he would just accept my story and continue like nothing had happened between us when in fact our little world had been tipped upside down and shaken about, but I hoped that given time he would soften and understand my plight. As gentle and compassionate a man as he was, those traits only went so far.

The understanding I hoped for didn't happen. He packed his bags and left that night. But not all of him. He left a part of him inside me and nine months later, my daughter was born. Our daughter. It didn't bring us back together as a couple, the fact that we had a child. I had hoped he would change his stance, realise that we were meant to be a normal happy family, but he refused to see it that way. In fact, it made things worse. He applied for custody of her, claiming I was unfit to take care of my own child, revealing to his lawyers my years of childhood shame, telling them the same story that I had told him in confidence. There was no court order out to protect my identity, just a new name. I had done such a good job of living a low-key life that the need to have a court order forbidding anybody from revealing who I actually was had never arisen.

I considered contacting my social worker, the one I had kept secret from Ralph all these years, but couldn't face the thought of having to take on another new identity, having to uproot my little girl and give up everything I'd worked for, be forced to start again in a grubby little flat somewhere, so I stayed, waited until the divorce was finalised, the house we had bought together sold, and then there was just me and my little girl. In the end we got joint custody and Ralph decided that he wouldn't disclose my true identity to anybody else. He saw sense and realised that hurting me would also hurt our beautiful little girl. I was alone again. Just me and my child. And of course, my dirty little secret. Every time Ralph and I met to drop her off, I could see it in his eyes – the hurt, the distress. The hatred. The same eyes that used to watch me undress, his gaze lingering over my naked body, were suddenly full of anger and malevolence. My actions as a child all those years ago had driven a wedge between us that was so wide, we may as well have been on different continents. Different planets even. We were like strangers, living apart from one another after years of being blissfully happy and the grief that I felt about that was immense; an overpowering inescapable emotion that ate at me like a rabid animal savaging its prey. My child kept me going, but on the days when she was with Ralph, a void opened inside of me, a dark well of misery so deep it had no end. I knew then that my past sins would never leave me. They would always be by my side, weighing me down, holding me back, fixing me to a certain point in my life and making sure I was incapable of moving on from it. Making sure I was unable to live a normal life free of the shackles of the past. It was what I deserved. I knew that. And yet, there was somebody out there who had walked away from it all and was probably living her life in blissful ignorance of how shit my existence was. I had had a taste of happiness and it had been rudely and abruptly snatched away. I was once again living a blighted life and I hated her for it. Many times over the years I had thought of her, wondering where she was, how she was doing, her face etched into my thoughts, filling my mind day after day, week after week, month after month. I wondered if she was as lonely as I was? Did that day still haunt her as it did me? When I wasn't thinking of her, I was consumed by thoughts of Ralph and how much I loved and missed him.

Better to have loved and lost than never to have loved at all.

Another ridiculously overused vacuous phrase. It is complete and utter bullshit. My life was easier when all I had known was emptiness. To come so close to settling down and living as others around me did, and then have it taken away from me was so deeply distressing, so horribly painful there are no words to fully describe it. For once in my sorry little life, I had begun to emulate how others lived. I had found true love and was on the path to a normal existence. And then I relaxed, opened my stupid mouth, let the bad words out and the sorrow and the horror in.

So please forgive me if from time to time, I sound bitter and so full of bile that it seeps out of my pores, poisoning everything and everyone around me, but that's because I am bitter. I'm a deeply unhappy woman with nothing to lose. And it's the people who have nothing to lose that are the ones who are more likely to do the most damage.

13

___

She is everywhere and nowhere. I keep thinking I can sense her presence, feel her eyes boring into my back; that cold calculating glower, her rigid posture and pale complexion, but when I turn, she is nowhere to be seen, the memory of her face just that – a memory. A phantom who exists only in my thoughts. Already she has got me jumping at every tiny movement, every flicker and motion at the edge of my vision. If I carry on like this, trembling and shaking at any and every noise, then she's already won. And I won't let that happen.

I put my hand in my pocket, feeling for the letters she left me last night and then remember about throwing them in the fire. After finishing a bottle of wine and then opening another, my thoughts are still jumbled. I also took my medication which has a nasty habit of knocking me off kilter.

A pulse kicks at my throat. I'm tired. Even though I took my meds, I still didn't sleep so well, waking every hour to check on Whisky, each creak of the floorboards, every groan of the central heating system sending me into a near meltdown. After shoving the chest of drawers up against the bedroom door and settling the poor dog down, I spent a fitful evening tossing and turning, falling into nightmares that were so terrifying, I woke up trembling and coated in sweat. I should have hung onto those letters. Kept them and presented them to her to let her know that I'm onto her. It was a stupid move burning them both. I panicked, let my temper get the better of me and now I have nothing to show that she was ever in my house.

I straighten up, look around at everybody. Still no sign of her. A small crowd is gathering. Far fewer attendees than the talk I gave at the library. Maybe that's why she isn't here this time; she is too afraid to show her face. Or maybe she has realised that she took things too far with Whisky, overstepped an invisible boundary and that I'm now taking her threats seriously and am considering getting the police involved. Perhaps she is toying with me, playing mind games, putting me on edge. If that is the case, then it's working. She is winning this game. So far anyway. I need to stay calm, show her that I'm not afraid, even though I am. Maybe afraid isn't quite the right word. Anxious. On edge. Panicky. I clench and unclench my fists, my jaw locked tight. After what took place last night, knowing what she is capable of, what lengths she will go to, to unsettle and unnerve me, I think that afraid is probably a closer fit. I'm prepared to kick back, however. I won't go down without putting up a good fight. I hope she knows that and is ready for it.

I glance down and read through my notes one final time, the size of the room seeming to shrink around me. A buzz takes hold, a feeling of positivity emanating from the audience. This is the bit I enjoy. I clear my throat in readiness and am on the cusp of speaking when I see her. She walks in and takes a seat on the back row, those eyes already doing their utmost to unnerve me. Her hands are placed on her lap, her spine ramrod straight like a porcelain doll, her glowering stare sharp enough to cut through stone.

I can feel her watching while I prepare for my talk, those dark pupils boring into me. Once again, I shuffle papers unnecessarily to try and deflect the nerves that are creeping in now that she has made an appearance. That's her intention – to attempt to frighten me, to usurp me and throw me off balance when this is my place, my arena. I won't let her do that. After this is over, I am going to approach her, keep my wits about me, remain sharp and mindful of her wily ways, and I'm going to ask her outright what she wants from me and why she thinks she knows who I am. Even I don't have the answer to that particular question. I am an enigma. A blank slate. My previous life rubbed out by the speeding wheels of a thoughtless driver, 3,500 pounds of sharp metal knocking me aside and leaving me for dead on a dark country lane.

The room tilts when I start to speak. I blink repeatedly, take a sip of water, and pull myself together. This is what she wants. She is desperate for me to fail, for me to make a fool of myself and lose face in front of my audience but I won't let that happen. I won't let her succeed in her attempts to unravel my confidence, so instead I inhale and exhale, counting the breaths, using tried and tested techniques, and I begin.

'Welcome, everybody. I'm delighted to be here. It's lovely and reassuring to see some familiar faces.' I pause and glance her way. Wait for her to react. She shifts in her seat then quickly readjusts herself, straightening her posture, fixing her gaze ahead. Sitting statue-like. A cold hard shell of a person. 'Can I ask a question?' A lull descends as people wait. 'I'd love to know how many of you have been here before? A quick show of hands if you're comfort-able doing that would be great. Then I can feed back to my agent that there are people out there who like me and are prepared to buy more than just one of my books.'

A quiet ripple of laughter spreads around the room. I smile, try to look non-threatening. Approachable and affable. Two or three people whose faces I don't recognise raise their hands. They turn and nod at one another as if they are old friends. She remains mute, unsmiling. Unmoving. Nobody glances her way and she doesn't turn to look at anybody else. The seat next to her is empty. She sits alone. Fitting I think, for someone so solemn and brooding.

'Okay, that's great, thank you. I see some of you are a bit shy to own up but that's fine. I'm a bit of an introvert myself. I totally understand.' I catch her eye, holding her gaze for as long as I can before looking away. She doesn't respond. Not a flicker of recognition. Nothing at all.

The talk goes smoothly. I'm able to block out all thoughts of her and concentrate on reading out a couple of chapters of my up-and-coming release. I feel calm and in good spirits, ready to speak with her once everybody leaves but when I look up, her chair is empty, the door closing behind her with a swish, her shadowy figure sailing past the window. It's as if she hasn't been here at all. I have failed again. She is always ahead of me, pulling the strings. Controlling this situation and leaving me feeling like a helpless angry child every time she makes her exit.

I spend some time talking and signing books and feel flat and underwhelmed once everybody has gone and I'm left standing on my own, the prepared barrage of questions I had stored in my head for her now completely unnecessary. I feel useless and cut adrift. Just me and the sales assistant, the two of us wondering what to say to one another. I thank him for organising the event and head outside, darkness beginning to descend, disappointment stabbing at me.

My car is parked just around the corner; down a back alley, one of the few places in town that doesn't have double yellow lines or need a permit, and one of the few spaces that doesn't require a bank loan to park there for just a few hours. I pull up my collar to keep the brisk wind at bay and stop as soon as I spot my vehicle and see the damage – the flat tyres, the note jammed under the wipers. The smashed windscreen. The deep gouge that runs across the side of the driver's side door and over the wing. My throat thickens. I step forward, pull out the piece of paper and open it, my vision blurring, my heart crawling around my chest, a sharp clawed animal slithering and skittering over and through my ribcage.

I'm not the murderer. You are. Ask yourself what you did...

I lean on the bonnet for support, the world swimming around me, my head pounding.

I'm not the murderer. You are.

This is a reference to my books. It's the only explanation. I write about fictional murders for a living. Somebody has decided to stalk me, to take it upon themselves to follow and terrorise me. What other explanation is there for this warped behaviour? I think about the vast hole in my memory, the missing years of my life. The decision I made to live in isolation, sheltered in the woods and surrounded by high trees and shrubbery. Why did I make that choice? Why did I move to a secluded area and live alone with no family or friends to call upon? The world swims around me, a possible dawning beginning to take shape in my mind. I bat it away. Nonsense. That's what it is. Absolute nonsense, the possibility that I did something terrible many years ago, something so bad that all this time later somebody has decided to impose themselves in my life and ruin everything I have worked hard to achieve. Besides, if I had committed a terrible crime, surely there would be some sign of it in my current life? It's a frankly ridiculous idea that I did such a dreadful thing and it left no trace. People would recognise me. My image would be splashed all over the newspapers and on the internet. I would be able to find myself at the click of a button. There would be no escape. My face *has* changed, however; a large scar now visible after the accident. I am no longer the person I used to be, but what if she has a stellar memory, a good head for remembering people and has recognised me from many years back?

Perspiration coats my neck and back. A crunching pain gripes at my lower abdomen. Vomit burns my gullet. I lean into the gutter and throw up the contents of my stomach until there is nothing left and I end up repeatedly dry heaving. I try to fool myself into thinking that I haven't the first clue what is meant by this latest poisonous missive even though a host of grubby ideas and images are filling my head, telling me that there is a grain of truth in her words. I shake those thoughts away. I'm not a bad person. My past is over with and I refuse to believe that I have ever harmed anyone. It simply isn't possible. Besides, she is much younger than me. Had I done something terrible many years back, how would she even know about it?

I reach into my bag. My phone refuses to dislodge itself, trapped beneath a pile of detritus – packets of tissues, notepads, a hairbrush – they all conspire against its appearance until eventually it topples out onto my palm and crashes to the floor. I snatch it up, its screen as cracked as my car windscreen, and punch in the number for the emergency services. Words bounce around my head, how I'll relay this to them when I get through.

A female voice answers but before I can say anything, I feel a pressure at the back of my head, my body being pushed forwards into a nearby brick wall. The phone once again clatters to the floor and I watch horrified as a dark hooded figure smashes it with the heel of their foot, grinding it into a dozen tiny pieces. And then I'm alone. Their departure is rapid. It's as if they haven't even been here at all. Apart that is, from the damage to my car and mobile phone. Blurry-eyed, I watch them run down the alley and around the corner out of sight. I'm too stupefied, too fearful to do anything but lie on the floor and weep. I now have no phone and no means of getting home. My car is undrivable and I am lying here in a crumpled heap on the cold concrete.

'You okay there, love?'

I glance up into the face of a kindly-looking old gentleman, his bushy eyebrows crinkled together in concern. He holds out a hand and helps me up, pulling me towards him. Humiliation ripples through me. Once again, I have been knocked over and left alone.

'Thank you. I'm fine.'

'Did you fall or did somebody attack you?' He shakes his head and tuts. 'Hooligans, that's what they are round these parts. Bloody vandals and hooligans. Bring back the birch, that's what I say. Wouldn't have dared do anything like that in my day. Might sound far-fetched and cruel but it's a deterrent and it worked, I can tell you.'

I stand stock still, unsure how to react. 'Never mind,' I find myself saying a little too loudly, my voice a ghostly disembodied echo in my head. 'I'm fine and the insurance will sort it.'

'Insurance? You need the police, never mind those idiotic useless insurance companies. Did those reprobates push you over and try to take your bag? Have you still got your purse?'

I shake my head. 'No, I fell. It's fine, really.' I don't know why I'm saying such a thing. I'm not fine. I am anything *but* fine. One light push and I will shatter into a million pieces. 'I'll flag down a taxi to get home.' I need the police but want to get back to my cottage first, sort myself out. As kind as he is, I'd rather not have this man hanging about. I don't want him knowing my business. Not that there's anything to know. At least I don't think there is. This whole episode is one big grotesque mystery.

I'm not the murderer. You are...

The memory of her most recent message drills itself into my

brain. Do I really want anybody investigating this? Do I want to expose myself to any bad publicity and risk a slump in the sales of my books? Right now, I need the money. That's the only reason I'm doing all these talks, to boost sales. My health is failing, my future uncertain. A sense of hopelessness bears down on me. I feel hemmed in, useless and impotent. What if it's true? What if in my previous life I did something terrible. Something unspeakable. Surely, I would know about it? I lost the recollections from the first half of my life. I didn't emerge from a chrysalis, new and rejuvenated, a completely different person. I'm still me. If I had done something dreadful, I would know. Wouldn't I?

'Well, if you're sure? I can walk you back out onto the main road. 'Ere,' he says holding out his hand. 'Link your arm through mine. I'm not so good on me pins. We can stagger up the street together, eh? But as I said, you really need to call the police or they'll just do it to somebody else.'

I want to tell him that they won't, that I'm being targeted for reasons unknown, but remain silent, knowing an explanation would unearth more questions than answers.

He lets out a low, soft sigh and I find myself doing as he asks, placing my arm through his as we walk out of the alley together, back onto the main road through town, the rush of the passing traffic a constant growl as it hurtles past.

'Thanks,' I murmur, the sight of a passing taxi heading towards me, a welcome reprieve from this unexpected and slightly awkward moment in my life. Being helped along by somebody twice my age feels unseemly, like a child relying on its parents for assistance. 'I can take it from here. Thank you again for your help.'

'Aye, well don't forget to let the police know about what happened otherwise whoever did it will only go and do it again. No respect for anybody or anything. Trying to mug people down back alleys and trashing their property. Who do these people think they are?'

'Honestly, it was nothing. I slipped and over-reacted. I'm totally fine, but thank you so much for helping. Many wouldn't.'

A flush spreads over his mottled cheeks. He smiles and takes my hand, tapping it lightly. 'Well, as I say, make sure you call somebody and report this. I only did what anybody else would do.'

He gives me a wave and we part. I watch him hobble away; his limp more pronounced now we're no longer leaning into each other for support.

I stick out my arm and the passing taxi screeches to a halt beside me. It's empty. Thank God. I lean down and open the door, grateful for the warmth, for the fact I still have money and a means of getting home. I give my address to the driver who narrows his eyes, his confusion evident in the shake of his head and the way he sucks at his teeth as if I've just given him a difficult equation to work out.

'Don't worry,' I say, leaning my head back onto the rest. 'I'll direct you. It's only a mile or so off the main track that runs parallel to the river and then we take a left down through a little lane. Closer to civilisation than you realise.'

It's not. I'm saying that to reassure myself more than him. I live in a little cottage in the middle of nowhere, with limited visibility due to the nearby woods, and poor phone reception. If anything untoward happened to me, I would struggle to get help. I'm completely and utterly alone and I'm almost certain now, that whoever she is, this Chalk White Woman, she knows it and is using it to her advantage, preying on my vulnerabilities. She knows more about me than I know about myself. Time to put an end to it, to get my life back to how it was before she showed her face and disrupted my lonely, methodical existence.

I close my eyes and heave a sigh. I'm tired. More than tired. I'm exhausted. I think of Whisky at home on his own and am suddenly imbued with an urge to see him, to make sure he's warm and safe. This is how she has got me: twitchy and unsettled, jumping at shadows. Constantly looking over my shoulder. No more of it. I've made up my mind. From this moment on, I'm going to flex my muscles and I'm going to fight back.

14

SUMMER OF 1976

They became inseparable that summer, the three of them spending every day together. Unwashed clothes and a lack of food were relegated to the back of Heather's mind. Besides, with all her newly acquired goods, she had begun to slowly alter her lifestyle. Not so much that her parents would notice – the odd bottle of shampoo that she hid in her bedroom, new underwear that she washed and rinsed out herself in the sink each night – but enough to make her life a tad more comfortable. More appropriate for the new friends she had acquired.

It was clear to Heather that Irena didn't steal because she was short of money. She stole because she wanted to, because it was trendy and cool and made her look good. That was Heather's take on it. Why else would she do it? And if it was good enough for Lesley and Irena then it was good enough for her. They were her friends. The three of them together no matter what. Besides, she had started to enjoy it. She liked the buzz it gave her every time she slipped something in her pocket without anyone noticing.

The sun beat down on the back of her neck. She rubbed at it

with hot swollen hands, her fingers sticky with sweat. They were sitting on the grass, their bodies lethargic with the heat.

'So, you've never met your grandparents?' Irena was staring at Heather, her eyes wide, mouth set in a glossy pout, the fleshiness and shine of it mesmerising Heather, the way the sun caught her full lips and blemish-free skin. Irena was everything she wanted to be. She had thought that Lesley was glamorous with her curly hair and long eyelashes which gave her a look of Marie Osmond, but Irena was on a different level. Grown up. Confident and full of poise. Everything Heather wasn't. She did her best to put on a show but underneath it all, her impoverished upbringing would always be there, nipping at her ankles. Threatening to bring her down with a sickening crash.

'When I was little, I saw them. But I was too small to remember.'

'They live in a big house in York. Heather told me.' Lesley pulled at a handful of grass and spread it on her palm, looking for clover, tugging at the leaves before discarding them over her shoulder, the small green petals scattering in the gentle breeze like confetti. 'And she never sees them even though they're millionaires. *And* she doesn't even like them, do you, Hev?'

A rosy glow settled in the pit of Heather's belly. She liked it when they called her Hev. Nobody had ever given her a nickname before. It made her feel important. Wanted and part of a proper group of friends. They were a gang now and nothing and nobody could come between them.

'Yeah, that's right. Never see them even though they've got loads of money.' She leaned back and stared up at the sky, her tone flippant. Unconcerned. Which wasn't how she felt at all. She would love to be able to visit her nana and grandad, see how they lived, whether they had a nice house with posh furniture and food in the fridge. Other people's nanas baked chocolate cakes and cooked casseroles, gave them pocket money, and took them out to the park. But for some reason she knew it would be better if she kept up the charade of nonchalance. Acted as if she wasn't bothered by their absence. 'Not that I really care that much. They don't mean anything to me.' A small worm of shame burrowed under her flesh. She ignored it, kept on talking. 'Pair of useless fucking arseholes.' She had heard her dad call them that and seen her mam grimace whenever he said it before joining in and laughing like a drain. 'Anyway, Lesley's nana lives down by the stream in a broken old house, doesn't she, Lesley? And Lesley said she's an old cow.'

Fire licked at her face. She had to say it, to deflect the attention from her own failing family. The family she loved and hated in equal measure.

'Really?' Irena turned and looked at Lesley who shrugged and stared off over the field, tipping the blades of grass out of her palm and rubbing her hands together.

'Yeah, but she's old and stupid and my family don't like her. They say she smells as well.'

'Is that because she pees herself 'cos she's old?' Irena laughed. 'Because old people do piss their pants you know.'

The flames behind Heather's flesh raged even hotter, the thought of her night-time bedwetting crowding her mind. That was one of her dark secrets, one she would always keep to herself. God knows she had plenty of nasty things skulking in her background, but that one would never be revealed or spoken about to anybody, especially Lesley and Irena. They were both too advanced in their years, too clean and mature and wealthy to ever understand her predicament. She was aware that there may come a time when the girls would start visiting one another's houses, asking to go up into each other's bedrooms. The thought of showing Irena and Lesley around her room made her shudder. The thought of either of them ever stepping foot over her front door was enough to make her feel nauseous. She would feign illness when it was her turn, tell them anything but the truth, a whole host of excuses already formed in her mind.

It's being redecorated. I'm sleeping on the sofa till it's finished.

My dad accidentally spilled gloss paint on the carpet. It's still wet so we can't go in.

Deep down she knew that they knew. Not about the stinking damp sheets but about her family. Everybody knew – all the neighbours, her new friends. Everybody in the area. They all knew about the Oswalds. Heather wasn't stupid. She was poor and hungry and lived in a smelly old house with a mam and dad who preferred the beer and the gin to their own child, but she wasn't an idiot. Piss-poor kids still had a brain. And hers was a good one. The teachers had told her so on more than one occasion.

'Like Heather just said, it's because she's an old cow, that's why.' Lesley sniffed and stood up. 'So what we gonna do today then?'

Irena smiled, her voice low, almost a whisper. A hint of menace to it. 'We could go to a certain broken old house down by the stream. See who's about?'

Heather watched Lesley's face colour up, could practically feel the heat of it from where she was standing, and knew she had betrayed her. That was their secret. She'd done it again. Caused loads of damage. Hurt people. Something foul-tasting crept up her throat. She swallowed it down, rubbed at her neck once more with hot clammy hands.

'Nah,' Lesley replied, her back turned to them while she faced the sun, her head tipped upwards. 'That's boring. Why don't we go into town? See who's about.' Heather hadn't known her for very long but recognised forced flippancy when she saw it. The angle of

Lesley's head, her flushed skin and puckered expression; they were all signs of a contrived pose and manner in a bid to disguise her growing anguish.

'I'm up for going down to the stream.' Irena nudged Heather, a twinkle in her eye as she pointed at Lesley's back. 'What about you, Hev? You up for it?'

Heather shrugged, her scalp prickling as she spoke. 'I'm easy. I'll do whatever you two want to do.' She tried to sound non-committal. Disinterested even. Her voice was higher than usual, her throat tight.

Irena's laugh was loud, her tone cutting. 'Come on, Hev. Make a decision. Why'd you mention Lesley's nana's house if you don't wanna go down there?'

Another shrug, her shoulders hunched. She didn't know why she had mentioned it. No, that was wrong. She did know. She'd mentioned it to draw attention away from the failures and fiascos of her own family. And now she had humiliated Lesley, her first-ever real friend. Made her a target, made her feel embarrassed and small. And God knows, Heather knew how that felt. How demoralising it was. She thought they were all friends. Their gang together. Not apart. And yet here Irena was, suddenly dividing them, driving a wedge between them. Making her choose, making Lesley feel embarrassed. Making her feel how Heather felt whenever the subject of her own family cropped up.

'Well, I'm going down there.' Irena stood up, her cut-off jeans and cream T-shirt tight against her budding womanly frame. 'You two can either come or not.'

They would go. They all knew it. They would all traipse down there, following Irena like sheep, too stupid to go with their own minds and thoughts. Too weak to break free and go their own way without her.

Heather stood first, brushing tiny blades of grass off her shorts, followed by Lesley who sighed heavily, her expression lazy and apathetic as if getting up and walking were inordinately strenuous.

Irena linked her arm through Lesley's and Heather's and they set off towards the stream, the sun beating down on them while the soft breeze caressed their faces.

It wouldn't be so bad when they got there, Heather felt sure of it. She could sense it. Nothing bad would ever happen. They were friends after all. The three of them together. As solid as stone. Smooth and unfractured.

'You never know,' Irena said quietly. 'Maybe there'll be some lads down there.' She threw back her head and laughed. 'Or maybe there'll be a mad old woman who stinks of pee. Who knows, eh?'

Heather felt a tug on her arm, the sensation of Irena's strength and solidity compared to her own stick-like limbs both surprising and reassuring. It was like having a friend who was a fully grown woman. And yet sometimes, like only a few seconds ago, she was forced to question Irena's behaviour, the way she seemed intent on being the leader, telling others what to do. Throwing barbed comments their way. Heather shrugged it off, dismissing those thoughts. Irena had a different way of doing things, that's all it was. She was a maverick. A trailblazer. A born leader.

The small bones in Heather's neck clicked and groaned when she bent forwards to look at Lesley. There was no smile on her face but neither was she frowning. 'You okay, Les?' She liked calling her that. It solidified their friendship, brought them closer together. And anyway, she needed to make up for her slip of the tongue, for telling Irena about her nana's rundown old house by the water.

Lesley turned and smiled at her, her features back to their usual self. Something unfolded inside Heather's stomach, a spread of happiness and contentment. She was forgiven, her earlier misdemeanour already forgotten. She and Lesley had been friends way before Irena came on the scene. She would do well to remember that, to keep that bond going, keep it as strong and durable as it could be. Not say something ridiculous that could sever it forever. Lesley was her first and best friend. And best friends never really left one another or fell out, did they?

15

Luck played a huge part in finding her. Luck and an ordinate amount of planning and upheaval in my own life to get closer to her. But I'm here now and that's all that matters.

She looks happy enough. Happy but damaged. That part makes me smile. Even with that scar, she shows no obvious signs of distress, living her best life, giving talks, signing books. Smiling. Acting as if everything is so easy and effortless. I guess that was always the difference between us – her confidence. Her charm and poise. There is no doubt that she looks different; a broken version of herself. It should serve as a reminder to her that life doesn't always go as planned. That things materialise. Unplanned things. Dreadful things. I hope she thinks of that accident every single day. I hope it frightened her, made her realise that somebody out there hates her.

As far as I can tell, she never married and lives alone. Alone and lonely. That's what I hope. Who would want somebody like her in their lives? Or somebody like me, because we're not that different, she and I. Ralph certainly didn't. I paid a hefty price for what I did. It looks like she has continued through life with ease, carrying no embarrassing baggage that will hinder her progress, putting up barriers and determining who

*and what she can be. What she can achieve. No stints in prison. No
awkward silences and attempts to recreate another fictitious life when
asked about her childhood, the one she spent with me. A couple of weeks,
that was all it took for our lives to spin out of control. For everything to
come crashing down around us. People died that day, their futures
snatched away from them. They were caught up in the wreckage of our
actions and I'm still being punished all these decades later while she is
free to do as she pleases.*

*There were three of us that summer. That memorable hot summer
when the world held such promise. We were young, carefree. Stupidly
naïve. Blind to what was about to happen. Blind to our own capabilities
and wickedness. Would I have stepped away had I known what we were
about to do? Of course I would have, but none of us knew what levels of
atrocity we were capable of until it was too late. I've blamed lots of
people over the years – my parents, neighbours for not reporting to social
services how useless my mother and father were, teachers even, who
didn't spot the signs of neglect, and of course, myself. But without a
shadow of a doubt, I also blame her.*

*I knew who she was as soon as I saw her picture in the paper
announcing her career as a writer, and was certain there and then that I
had to do something. I had spent years letting my hatred of her eat away
at me and could no longer contain that anger. Had Ralph still been in my
life, I would have softened. He kept me on an even keel, kept me balanced.
I was happy and had a life with him; I was able to ignore those negative
emotions, keep them pressed down out of sight but in the end, the life I'd
had with her, spilled over and ruined the one I had with him. I couldn't
shake it off, that day. Those deaths. It would follow me for the rest of my
life. So I made a decision there and then to revisit my past and confront
her, tell how fucking horrible things were for me and that she could have
helped me; we could have faced the consequences together but she didn't
and as a result I lost everything.*

I moved house to be closer to where she was based, taking my daughter with me. She was older and understood my story about having to move because I had been offered a new job. She was quietly excited, truth be told. We searched for a college for her to attend and she picked out the subjects she wanted to study. My lovely young daughter who is now a young woman with a life of her own. Ralph wasn't happy about my move but I had a new job and he still saw her on a frequent basis, collecting her off the train whenever she visited him. It worked. I made sure of it. I wasn't going to let this next chapter of my life fail the way all the others had. This was my last chance to right a terrible wrong.

I waited a while before putting my plans into motion. I didn't want any occurrences to be immediately connected to my move here. I gave myself a settling-in period, following her career from a distance, finding amusement at her low-key existence. No online profile. Just endless write-ups about her books. To many she is an enigma but I know who I. L. Lawrence really is. Had it not been for that article, that grainy photo, I may never have found her. I would still be living on the west coast, wallowing in my own misery, but I'm not. I'm here and so is she.

I did see her once. I followed her in my car after attending a talk she gave at a bookshop in town to celebrate her foray into writing. I saw her house, and waited in a layby in the darkness. I hadn't planned on doing anything. I just wanted to watch her, see how she lived, but I got lucky. She was walking in a lane that led off from where I was parked up. It was an impulsive manoeuvre; dangerous and foolish, but I had to do something to release my pent-up anger. And so I put my foot down and drove at her. I wasn't going that fast. Her body hitting my car felt like the tiniest of bumps, but I could see as I drove off that she was unconscious, her body limp and twisted.

My initial reaction was panic. I didn't mean for her to die and I definitely didn't want to go back to prison. That was the last thing I wanted. I had my daughter to think of. But at the same time, knocking her down gave me a buzz, made me feel alive. Maybe I was evil, bad through and through. Maybe those tabloids were right and I couldn't ever be redeemed. But then I thought of my daughter, how wonderful and funny and kind she is. Surely if I was that bad, I wouldn't be able to give birth to such an amazing human, would I?

That thought kept me going, made me realise that being served a deep injustice at a critical point in my life was the thing that fuelled me, not the fact that I was born evil or had a warped desire to hurt people just because it gave me a thrill.

I read every newspaper I could after that day, scanning online news channels for reports of a local author killed in a hit and run, and saw nothing. Relief coursed through me. Relief because there wouldn't be a murder enquiry, and anger because once again, she had fallen in a pile of manure and come up smelling of roses. The accident did change her, however. She didn't come out of it completely unblemished. She now has a face people will never forget, her scar a ghastly reminder that every sinner must pay. A reminder that every crime and transgression comes at a price. I paid for mine many years ago, my childhood crushed and warped beyond recognition. I'm not saying I shouldn't have been punished. I just don't think it was fair that I was punished alone. But her moment of reckoning will come. I will make her see how easy her life has been, existing in a bubble while my life imploded around me, rupturing beyond all recognition. Then she will know. Then she will wish she had remained a nobody, lived her life in total seclusion away from the prying eyes of the likes of me. Her scar is visible but my scars are tucked away inside me. They still fester and I don't think I'll ever be free of them.

My daughter is the main thing that keeps me going, forcing me out of bed every morning, making me face the world and be the best I can be. Which I am for her. Aside from my small business, which I opened after my last job fell through, the company folding after I had been with them for only a few months, she is all I have. That's because she doesn't know who I really am. What I did. And as long as there is breath in my body, I'll make sure it stays that way.

16

A pulse thrums at my throat. I wish to God I had kept those other notes, not thrown them into the flames. Fatigue and anxiety had muddied my thinking and skewed my logic. I should have kept them. But I didn't because she caught me off guard and is now making me doubt my own mind. Making me think I'm going insane. Maybe I am. Maybe this whole thing is a bad dream. A nightmare.

My hands are trembling, my fingers clutching at today's note. The image of her cold dead-eyed stare is branded into my brain. I place the piece of paper down on the table and snatch up the land-line phone, the temptation to call the police diminishing every time I recall her words.

I'm not the murderer. You are.

What if I am? I'm torn between laughing and crying. This whole thing is beyond ludicrous. The fact I'm even considering it is risible. It's the emptiness in my brain that is fuelling this whole bizarre episode.

I swallow, rub at my eyes and slump down onto the armchair. How would I even begin to explain this to the police? How would I tell them that I have no memory of my previous life? That the first note disappeared, morphing into something different. That I disposed of the others. That I have no idea if it was her who damaged my car and no, I didn't see her do it, it's just a hunch. I would have to tell them that I've not seen her do anything untoward. Nothing at all. All she does is stare at me and put me on edge. It would make me sound unbalanced. A crazy woman. And what if any of this gets out into the press? How damaging would that be to my reputation as a writer? I already know the answer to that question and push the phone away, frustration and anger building in my gut, bubbling like hot bitumen. Had there been CCTV in the area, I could at least take this further but I know for sure that it's a blind spot, a place that few people know about.

Whisky stands by my legs whining to be let out. I march into the kitchen, grab at his lead, and pull on my jacket. A walk is probably the best thing for me. I need to clear my head. My chest feels tight, as if my lungs are made of cast iron. My thoughts are muddled, blurry and full of jagged edges.

'Come on, old boy. Let's go for a tramp in the wilderness.' Whisky complies, striding up beside me, his head cocked to one side, his tongue lolling out of the side of his mouth. 'We'll blow off those cobwebs, shall we?'

Outside, the wind is sharp, the sky clear. We walk through the woods, twigs cracking underfoot, the susurration of the leaves above us a familiar sound. Comforting. There are times when living here feels so damn lonely and then there are other times, like now, when I feel blessed to be here.

'Fetch, Whisky. Fetch it!' His dash into the shrubbery is more of a hasty stumble as he forages for his favourite tennis ball amongst the fallen leaves and dense undergrowth, his nose twitching, suctioned to the ground as he searches.

I watch how his back end sways from side to side, the view of his wagging tail a sight that always warms my heart. We play the same game for the next few minutes until he tires of it and crashes down at my feet panting, small misty orbs emerging out of his mouth.

'Time for a rest, eh?' I ruffle his ears and lean down, kissing the fur on the back of his neck. 'Let's just go for an easy walk, shall we? Let you get your breath back, give your legs a rest.'

We make our way out of the woods and head for the lane that leads to the main road, the tip-tap of his claws on the thin strip of concrete, a reassuring sound. It's narrow on this route, the towering foliage a reminder of how dense the woods are, how inaccessible we are. I hardly ever walk it alone. Nobody comes this way and I always have a tension of opposites pulling at me as I amble along; mild apprehension at the solitude and loneliness combined with a sense of deep relaxation, as if I'm the only person in the world.

I feel it as we head farther along the lane, a cold and uneasy sensation, as if I'm being watched. As if somebody is lurking somewhere deep in the woods, hiding amongst the trees and shrubbery. Waiting to step out and confront me. Her face catapults into my mind – Chalk White Woman. I ignore it and continue walking, looking down to Whisky for comfort and protection. I'm not alone while he's with me. Never alone. He could hardly be described as a vicious guard dog but who's to know that? He's big and looks the part.

A crunching sound from nearby makes me twitchy and nervous. I turn back the way we came and pick up my pace, poor Whisky struggling to keep up, his elderly body and ageing limbs causing him to stumble over the uneven cracked tarmac.

'Come on, old boy. Let's head for home. You'll be ready for a nap by now, won't you?'

He looks up at me, his rheumy-eyed gaze tugging at my heart-strings. I shouldn't walk him this far but he always seems happy to keep going. He'll have a long sleep when we get back, snuggling up in his bed and dreaming of chasing tennis balls while the fire roars in the hearth.

Another sound from close by. The unmistakable thud of footsteps, the rhythmic rustling of somebody walking towards us, twigs and foliage being trampled underfoot as a person appears from behind the trunk of a large oak tree.

She looks startled to see us, the woman who steps into the light from the shadows, blinking and looking around as if lost.

'Hi,' she says after a second or two, her hand cupped at her temple, curled fingers shielding her eyes from the sudden glare of the sun.

I smile and nod, less than eager to become engaged in a conversation with her. She's a stranger. An unknown entity. A possible threat. I'm wary and rightly so after the past few days.

'I think I'm a bit lost.' She waits for me to say something, a silence stretching out between us, only speaking again when I say nothing in return. 'I was hoping to get to the walkway that runs next to the river.'

I glance down at her sandal-clad feet, her lack of proper walking attire and feel my skin pucker. 'You need to head back through the woods and follow the track that way.' I point behind her and watch as she turns and stares into the darkness of the woods, into the knot of branches and towering shrubbery that will tear at her exposed flesh. I think of the giant hogweed that will sting and burn her arms and legs and the rush of the river, how even the most experienced of walkers can struggle along the narrow track.

'Right. Okay, thank you. Not sure how I managed to stumble off the path.'

Neither am I.

A smile then a series of blinks, her eyelashes fluttering repeatedly before she looks away.

'Have we met before?' I wish I hadn't spoken. I'm prolonging this moment, this awkward contrived moment.

'I don't think so?' She turns once more and watches me, her eyes boring into mine.

There is something about her mannerisms, her stance and gait that causes a stirring inside of me, fingers trailing through the still waters in the deepest recesses of my mind, making ripples and dredging up dirt and silt.

I know you. I definitely know you.

My flesh turns cold. I empty my mind and reply, my voice cold and sharp. 'Right. Okay. Sorry, I see lots of people and often get confused.' I need to stop talking, to put a halt to the stream of nonsense that is coming out of my mouth. I don't know her, I can't. But there is something...

A wave of heat travels over my skin, a feeling of dampness gathering around my neck and hairline. I tighten Whisky's lead, my fingers clasped around the leather leash. Her presence initially doesn't register on his radar. But then he lifts his head and stares at her, his dark eyes assessing her. Sizing her up. I feel him pull on the lead and see his tail wag. If there is one thing I know about Whisky, it's that he trusts everyone. He isn't able to pick up on the fact that her sudden appearance is peculiar and out of keeping with our usual routine. He's a dog. All he sees is a smiling stranger, somebody who at first glance doesn't appear to pose a risk to us.

I turn and start to walk away, relieved to be leaving her behind. Whisky resists, whining to go to her. I yank at his lead, eager to put some distance between us. There is something not quite right about this woman, the way she stepped out of the woods in front of me, the way she is dressed – ill-prepared for this type of topography and terrain – that is making me treat her sudden appearance with caution.

'I take it you live around here, then?' The temperature of my blood drops a few notches at the sound of her voice, my skin growing cold and clammy despite the trickle of sweat that is running down the side of my face from my hairline to my jaw.

'I hope you find your way back to the walkway,' I say, spinning around to glance at her. 'Follow the route of the river and you won't go far wrong.' I click my tongue at Whisky and walk off, indicating the conversation is over. Whisky's tired legs slow him down, his resistance on the lead pulling at my arm and dragging me back.

'Maybe we have met at some point, eh? In another place or another life. Maybe that's where you recognise me from. Or maybe it was more recent than that. Who knows.'

The tone in her voice sets off alarm bells in my head. I have an urge to run and to keep running until I'm back in my cottage with all the doors locked behind me. I tug at Whisky's lead again, clicking my tongue to hurry him along but he stubbornly refuses to speed up, lolloping along at his slow pace like a death march, turning every couple of seconds to glance her way.

'Have a think about it. Maybe we do know each other. Maybe we've met before.' She smiles and for a second or two, I feel something, the jerk of a dusty old memory as it hauls me to another time in the past but, as always, it's gone before I can hold onto it and study it in forensic detail. 'And thank you for the directions.'

Her voice fades into the distance. I don't turn back to look. My heart pounds. My gums are dry, my tongue sticking to the roof of my mouth. I take a deep breath. A pain shoots through my collarbone. My shoulders are hitched up to my neck and my spine is taut and rigid, bones crunching and grinding across the upper part of my back as I walk away.

By the time we get home, my head feels as if a hundred fireworks are exploding in there, thudding and bashing against my skull. I take off Whisky's lead, a painful red welt sitting over my knuckles where I wrapped the leather around my hand to speed him up and get home as quickly as possible.

He pads over to the corner of the room, flopping onto a soft rug and closing his eyes almost immediately. He'll be asleep within seconds. I envy him, the way he is impervious to what is going on around him. I wish I could be more dog and not feel so frightened. It's as if there's an invisible enemy out there who means me harm. I thought I was alone living here, just me and my dog in our cottage in the woods with only the birds and local wildlife for company. I know now that that isn't the case at all. Whoever she was, she wasn't out for a ramble. She hadn't accidentally lost her way and stumbled off the walkway. That was a lie. She deliberately stepped out of those trees having strategically placed herself close to me. Or at least that was how it felt at the time. Now she has gone, I am questioning myself. I also think of somebody who reads my books. Somebody who has become obsessed with them. Obsessed with me. A stalker. And yet, there was unquestionably something familiar about her that resonated with me, evoking a long-since forgotten incident. It was her manner, her walk. Her voice. And what about Chalk White Woman. Are they associated? If so, what is the connection and what does it have to do with me? I wish I had followed her, asked what she meant by that last sentence.

Have a think about it. Maybe we do know each other.

I empty my bureau where all my papers and documents are stored, where the few photographs I have are kept. I tip them all out onto the table and spread them out. My birth certificate is there. I pick it up and type my birth name into Google along with the address where I was born. Nothing. Not a damn thing. I search nearby schools and am faced with a flood of school websites and Ofsted reports. I try again, this time using my name and the town where I was born. A site pops up and I click on it, a small amount of anticipation beginning to grip me. I know before I even read it that it's not about me. It's a site written by somebody with my name who has composed a blog protesting against local planning decisions in the town.

I have another rummage through the papers, scrutinising the grainy photographs. I look very different to when I was a child. My face, even without the scar, has changed shape. My eyes have gone from pale blue to green. My once long hair is now short and curly. Although I still live in the north east, I don't live anywhere near the place where I was born and grew up. I live closer to Whitby than Teesside, in an isolated area off the moor road near the River Esk.

My head begins to thud, a sudden painful twinge pushing at my temple and spreading across my forehead, small bony fingers pressing against my skull. I need a break from this. I'm tired of thinking about it. Tired of second guessing every bloody little thing. Tired of *her*. It's been a long day. I hope that woman finds her way back to the walkway and keeps on walking, never to return. I feel like I could sleep for a decade or more but know that once I lie down, my brain will spring to life.

I reach for my medication, popping a zolpidem out of the packet and into my mouth, swallowing it down with a mouthful of water. Now I'll sleep. I can close my eyes and let it all fade into the background, then wake in the morning, rested and ready to fight another day.

17

SUMMER OF 1976

'There's nobody in. Come on, let's get the bus into town instead.'
Heather picked up a pebble and threw it, watching as it skimmed
across the surface before disappearing into the stretch of dark
water leaving behind only the tiniest of ripples. She stepped closer
to the edge of the stream, her reflection a distorted image of her
real self. The water was lower than usual but still deep enough to
make her shudder at the thought of falling in. Swimming had
never been her forte. Lessons at school made her want to run and
hide, the thought of stripping off in the communal changing rooms
in front of all the other girls making her blood curdle and shrivel-
ling her insides.

Irena was standing by the window of Lesley's nana's house, her
hand raised against the glass, palm flat on the surface. Every now
and then, she would push at the pane as if trying to force it out of
its frame. Heather watched as her friend peered through it, eyes
squinting into the dimness, her face so close that her breath left
small steamy spheres that grew and dissipated in rapid succession.
Heather's stomach clenched. Irena was enjoying this. She grinned

and pushed at each window in turn, hoping to find a way in before kicking at the wall and swearing.

'Fucking stupid house. C'mon, Hev. You have a go and try one of the windows.'

This was a bad idea. The worst. Every fibre of Heather's being was screaming at her to turn and leave, to get as far away from this place as possible and to do it as quickly as she could. She didn't know what Irena had planned but knew by her behaviour and demeanour that it was something bad. Something dark and unpleasant. The rumble and swish of Heather's gut told her so. The look of dismay on Lesley's face told her so. Irena was an unknown quantity, her penchant for troublemaking spreading out over them all like hot oil. Dangerous and unmanageable.

She wanted to move, to turn and run until her muscles ached and her lungs burned, flames of exhaustion singeing and charring her breastbone. But she didn't. Anxiety reduced her to a useless coward, unable to do anything except smile and nod as Irena spoke, her voice carrying across the area, powerful and unavoidable. Taking charge of her small group of friends with an air of authority that made Heather wilt with dread. The traits she had only recently venerated and envied in her friend were now an unstoppable force, something she no longer saw as admirable. Confidence had made her perilous, pushing her along a dark and unsteady path.

'We're not going to town. We're staying here. We're gonna have some fun, aren't we, Lesley?'

It crept up Heather's throat, the panic. It pulsed in her neck and throbbed in her temples making her dizzy and nauseated. She had no reason to feel this way. Except for the timbre of Irena's voice, the influence she had over the pair of them; the way they did whatever she commanded. Those things were enough to turn her insides to water. Even her dad's drunkenness and her mam's rages didn't scare her the way this situation did. There was something different going on here. A feeling she couldn't quite put her finger on, as if the earth was about to spin off its axis, their lives and everything around them about to be hurled into oblivion.

In her peripheral vision, she saw Lesley nod, her face pale and waxlike, her eyes downcast. She watched her walk over to where Irena was standing, the low thud of her footfall a sonic boom in Heather's ears. That meant that she would have to do the same, to follow and stand next to Irena and Lesley and then wait to see what would happen next. It was out of her control now. There was no going back. Her own steps felt heavy and unwieldly as she kicked leaves aside and headed towards them, a frisson of annoyance at her own cowardice nipping at her innards. Why couldn't they just play in the stream or go back to the park or take a bus into town? All those things felt better than hanging around an old woman's house just for the sake of it. Just because they could.

Heather stared in the window to get a better look at the place. It was dark in there, the glass smeared with grime, cobwebs meshed into the corner. A dead spider was lying on the sill, its long brown legs curled up under its body. She shivered and stepped away. It was too difficult to see anything. Too dark to tell whether anybody was inside. What was the point of all of this anyway?

'Maybe she's out. She's probably in town shopping. We should just go.'

Irena gave a derisory snort and slammed her hand against the wall. 'Go? We've just got here. I'm not going anywhere. Are you going anywhere, Lesley?'

There was a long silence. Heather could hear her own heart-beat. Was able to feel it banging beneath her shirt, the heft and momentum of it like a huge pendulum, making her hot and woozy.

'Lesley? Are you going anywhere else?' There was no escaping the ice in Irena's tone. The pointedness of her question. The aggression springing out of her. She seemed to grow in stature, her presence an unavoidable barrier that neither of them could scale.

Heather wanted to grab Lesley's hand, to run out of the woods and back to their usual hangouts where the world was a softer, easier place. Where the sun shone down on their backs and neighbours shouted over garden fences, hollering at kids in the street to come in for their tea and to stop kicking the ball into the garden and ruining the flowers.

They're already dying of thirst! Go and play in the park and stop hanging round here, ya little buggers.

Heather longed to hear those voices, those angry commands. It was better than being here. Anywhere was better than being here.

'No. I s'pose not.' Lesley bit at her lip, her usual grit and feistiness gone, her confidence and customary dignity now overshadowed by Irena's strength and iron will.

'Right, well what we waiting for? Let's go inside, see if anybody's home. Let's give the mad old bitch a shake up, eh?'

Without waiting for an answer, Heather watched as Irena twisted the handle while pushing at the door with her hip. It stayed put but not for long. Another hard push from her resulted in wood splintering as the door gave way. Flakes of dried paint stuck to her clothes. She flicked them away with long slim fingers and smiled. A deep groan filled the near silence as the door slowly opened and Irena stepped inside, turning to look at them, her mouth set into a wide manic grin. 'Come on, you two. What you standing there for looking gormless? Let's go and meet Lesley's mad mean old nana. The show's about to begin.'

* * *

The darkness swallowed them. Heather blinked, dragged her fingers through her tangled hair and looked around, waiting for her vision to right itself. They were standing in a small vestibule, the three of them huddled together. She wanted to reach out, take Lesley's arm, let her know that she was there for her, standing close by and on her side, but couldn't. Everything was muddled, her thinking and emotional reactions distorted by fear. Warped and distorted by Irena's impulsive imperious ways. Later when they were out of here, she would whisper to Lesley that she was sorry, that it just slipped out of her mouth, those words rolling off her tongue, telling Irena about this place. It should have remained a secret between the two of them. She knew it now. Had known it then but somehow it just came out. She had wanted to protect her own family's reputation by dragging Lesley's down to her level and now it had come to this. They were here, standing in an old woman's hallway with no idea of what was going to happen next. She thought of her mam and dad's reaction and what they would say if anything bad took place. How they would shout at her for breaking into an old woman's house, smacking at her bare arms and legs while yelling that she was always ruining their lives, that she was rotten to the core. An idiot. A bloody nuisance. A mistake.

'Hello!' Irena's voice ripped through her thoughts, a screech in the darkness that creased her skin, making the hairs on the back of her neck and her forearms stand to attention.

No answer, but then seconds later, a noise came from upstairs. Heather glanced up at the ceiling and listened. A low shuffling sound. Movement. Somebody walking about. The dull erratic thumping of a person struggling to move. Somebody who used a stick or a walking frame. More bile built in Heather's gut. Her parents' drunken ways she was used to. Even shoplifting didn't scare her any more. She had grown accustomed to it, liked it even. It had given her a buzz like no other, but this – this was different. This was tantamount to breaking and entering.

'Come on, Nana. Show yourself. You've got visitors.'

The power and disdain in Irena's voice siphoned every last pocket of air out of Heather's lungs. She took a step back, dust motes swirling in the dim light in front of her face. She wanted to look at Lesley, to touch her arm, feel that connection that they had; to feel it like a bolt of electricity running through her veins or feel it as a solid smooth stone she could hold in her hands, something weighty and tangible. But she didn't. Instead, she stood, motionless, watching Irena, her ears attuned to the noises coming from above, her eyes fixed ahead at the staircase, waiting for somebody to appear. Waiting for the moment when Lesley's nana would materialise out of the darkness and realise what was going on, that three young girls had broken into her house when she was on her own. She would possibly shout at them, wave her walking stick about in the air, screaming and hollering for them to get out before reaching for the phone and calling the police. And then that's when everything would really begin to unravel.

18

I have my writing to take my mind off other things. At least I have that. That's what I tell myself as I sit at my desk, fingers tapping away at the keyboard, eyes roving over the text, mumbling aloud while I search for plot holes and typos. My books are the things in my life that remain static and predictable. They're a steady, reliable thing and a good form of distraction when the real world gets me down. My agent and publisher are only ever a phone call or an email away. They fit well with my needs and requirements, they're not difficult people I dread dealing with, the type who cause me interminable problems. They are solid and dependable and that works for me. I know where I stand with them and what is expected of me when I speak to them. I prefer those fixed points in my life, people I can turn to should times get rocky. For now, that is. I'm not an idiot. I know how ruthless the world of business is, and that's what I am to them – a commodity. Somebody who helps keep their business afloat. But that's fine. It works for me. I don't want for much. My world is small. My books are still selling well. I daren't look too far into the future and feel glum about the possibility of a slump in sales and the carnage that would inevitably follow, because it could happen. I'm not stupid. Right now, my books are a consistent source of income and with my recent diagnosis, I need them to stay that way. That's why I keep writing and giving talks, to get my name out there. There may come a time when my body fails me and my mind follows suit. What will I do then?

I write for another hour or so then lean back in the chair and close my eyes, thinking back to yesterday's incidents. The encounter with the woman in the woods and the car and the attack have all left their mark on me. Last night I dreamt I was drowning. I was paddling in the river and felt somebody push me under the water. I woke up spluttering and coughing, hardly able to breathe, my chest concertinaed with fear and exhaustion. It was 2 a.m. and the darkness both outside and in was absolute. I got up and stumbled to the bathroom, gasping for air, convinced it was real and not a dream. It took me over an hour to calm down and get back to sleep, fear and a terrible sense of foreboding filling my mind every time I closed my eyes. It was as if there was a memory there that I couldn't quite reach. Something from my past that danced elusively in my mind, taunting me, refusing to reveal itself, but when I did eventually fall asleep, I woke this morning with no idea of what it could have been. Something to do with a stream. That memory and the bottle I found all that time ago all point to something connected to water.

I sit for a short while, thinking, wondering. Out of curiosity, I bring up a map of my childhood home and try to see if there are any bodies of water close by. I sigh and rub at my eyes. There are at least four becks and then slightly farther afield there is the River Tees. I slam the lid down on my laptop, weary and all out of ideas. Who was I with in the water? I stand up and pick up the bottle off the windowsill, my fingers wrapped around it, hoping for something – anything to spark to life in my brain. Nothing happens. Not a damn thing. My brain is empty. I feel like throwing the bottle against the window and watching as it smashes into a hundred tiny pieces. It's useless. What was the point in hanging onto it?

It slips though my fingers and hits the bottom of the bin with a dull thud as I drop it in, then in a moment of weakness, I bend down and pick it back out, fearful that without its presence, I'll lose the few memories I do actually have.

I stare outside at the empty space where my car is usually parked. It's been towed away for repair and a hire car will be getting dropped off tomorrow. As for my mobile phone – that's a problem for another day, the idea of spending an hour or more on the landline phone trying to request a new one is too much to bear. I'm all out of energy and patience, my strength sapped. Things have changed lately. I have changed. Whether it's my general health or my mental health playing up, something is definitely awry. Up until a few months back, I always used to wake early, ideas for my manuscript forcing me up. By 7 a.m. I would be showered, breakfasted, and sitting at my computer. Just recently, I find I haven't the impetus to do anything constructive. Except read that note over and over, trying to find some hidden meaning in it, hoping it will jog a memory, shake up my thoughts like a snow globe – flakes of old images and recollections falling around me. Parts of my old life shredded beyond recognition. Pieces of me waiting to be put back together.

There are things I need to know. Like are Chalk White Woman and the lady in the woods connected? The fact that they have both appeared at the same point in my life makes me think that they are. But if so, how? Maybe she really was just a woman who was walking in the woods and got lost, and I'm putting two and two together and coming up with five. An inability to sleep without taking medication, and stress are playing their part in this. I'm certain of it. Coming across a rambler wouldn't usually concern me. So why is it? I can't seem to get her face out of my mind. There's a memory there; I know it. Some connection to her. And she felt it too. Her answer, that sarcastic tone. I didn't imagine them. Her accent gave nothing away. She had a northern twang but beyond that, it was hard to tell where she came from.

Like a knife slicing through butter, the fog in my brain suddenly lifts. I grab at the landline handset and punch in Alicia's mobile number with more force than is necessary. I've done numerous talks at the library lately. Chalk White Woman has been there for at least three of them. Alicia will have some idea who she is. She knows everyone who goes in the place. A small surge of excitement pushes up into my chest, a rush of relief at having somebody close by who might have the answers.

'Hello?' A cool voice as she picks up and speaks.

Hearing her reserved timbre, visualising the distance between us both physically and emotionally, is like having cold water poured over me. This is a stupid idea, calling her like this. We're not friends. We're barely even acquaintances. She'll be wondering why I'm ringing her on her mobile phone out of hours, probably even regretting giving me her number. She will be at home. I should have checked the time, waited until she was in her work-place. At times like this, it's a sharp, painful reminder of how insular my life is. How alone and isolated I am. How alone and isolated I made myself. This is after all, my choice. I live my life like this for a reason. I just wish I knew what that reason is, why I became a hermit. It must have been an active choice. It's a frightening concept when you don't even know or understand your own brain. I think back to my last hospital visit when the consultant told me that I just had to give it some time. I don't want more time. I want to know what is happening to me.

'Alicia? Hi, it's me. I—'

'Yes, I saw your name and number come up on my phone.' She

cuts in before I can finish what I was going to say. Did I detect a hint of irritation? Or am I being paranoid, looking for nuances in her voice that aren't actually there?

Shame and humiliation burn at my flesh. My reason for ringing her now seems trivial and unimportant. I could have waited until tomorrow, called her at the library instead of doing this. My vulnerabilities coupled with paranoia have put me in this embarrassing position and now it's too late to back out. I can't put down the phone. I've got her ear and need to use this time constructively, regardless of how silly my question sounds or how ridiculous it makes me look. And it does make me look ridiculous. Petulant and petty, like a small child demanding that their needs are met. Hanging up, however, would make me look even worse, like somebody who is losing their grip.

Maybe I am.

I swallow and clutch at the phone with such force that my fingers begin to ache. 'Really sorry to call you at such a daft time. I should have waited until you were back at work.'

A deathly silence at her end. I stare out of the window at the line of trees, at the birds perched on the outer branches, their heads tilted, eyes darting everywhere, watching out for predators. I know how they feel, to be constantly on the lookout for nasty surprises. A grey cloud passes overhead, darkness suddenly swamping everything, coating the landscape and the woods in a murky shade of grey.

I bite at the inside of my mouth and continue, swallowing down my misgivings, telling myself that in a few seconds I'll have the answer to my question. Alicia will know for sure who Chalk White Woman is. Then I can hang up and let her go back to her day.

'I'll make it quick, I promise.' I inhale sharply, cold air traversing down my throat and into my lungs. 'I just wanted to ask if you knew who the pale-skinned lady is who's attended quite a few of my talks at the library?'

'Pale-skinned lady?'

I'm overcome with relief. At least she's replied. She hasn't snubbed me or sighed loudly down the handset. She's prepared to speak, to politely converse despite being interrupted at home and asked inane questions out of office hours by a sad old author she barely knows.

'Yes. She doesn't ever speak. She is thin and has long reddish-brown hair. She's nearer your age than mine. Younger actually, maybe in her late teens. She sits and watches but never says anything. She's been to quite a few of my talks now.' I don't give her the number of times. It would make me look pedantic and desperate. Which is exactly what I am. A desperate woman who can't remember anything and is frightened by an eccentric young female who has shown her face more than once at the local library. In the cold light of day, my worries seem silly, bordering on ludicrous.

Another short silence. Then, 'No, that description doesn't ring any bells with me, I'm afraid.'

Shock ripples through me. I expected, or hoped, that she would know straightaway who she is. It's obvious she doesn't. At least her voice sounds softer now, less abrasive. I decide to ask again, find a different way into this conversation. She must know. She has to. All it will take is the mention of a few incidents to jog her memory, to put her in the picture properly and then she will sigh and say, 'Ah yes, I remember her now'.

'Actually,' I say, emboldened by a thought that has just jumped into my brain, 'the last time I saw her in the library, she handed me a note. I dropped it and you and I both bent down to pick it up.'

'Yes, I recall the piece of paper,' she says, a slight inflection of humour in her tone. 'We banged heads.'

'We did. Really sorry about that. I got rather flustered and dashed off. Very rude of me.' I stop, aware I'm beginning to gabble.

'It's fine. No lasting damage. Just an accident.'

'Right. I'm pleased to hear that. So, you do recall the woman who handed it to me just a few seconds prior?' My heart begins to patter, my chest tightening in anticipation. This is it. The moment when I can stop doubting my own sanity. The moment when Alicia tells me that she too, has seen her, that I'm not the only one who has given thought to the strange-looking woman in the audience. That I'm not going mad, losing my mind and my tenuous hold on reality. Perhaps she will also add that the original piece of paper fluttered under the table or the bookcase and was retrieved by the cleaning staff and is currently sitting on her desk waiting for me to collect it. Except she doesn't say any of those things. There is a moment's silence that seems to go on for an age. Then, 'Ah, I'm really sorry, I don't recall seeing anyone.'

Disappointment and confusion stab at me. She must be mistaken. How could she not remember? There were only three of us in the library that evening after everyone else had left. She couldn't have missed her. I think back to that time. I was anxious. Alicia was otherwise occupied. Is it possible she could have not taken any notice of what was going on? Chalk White Woman's presence was obvious to me but to Alicia, she was just another attendee at the event. It was getting late. She was tidying up, her mind on other things. Other places. Probably dreaming of home. A hot bath, glass of wine in hand. Why would she take any notice of a pale wisp of a thing who slipped away into the night when her back was turned?

A wave of humiliation creeps up my throat, burning at my cheeks. Instead of thanking her and putting down the phone, I continue with the same old line.

'Are you sure? Really pallid-looking creature. Very slim. Hard to miss, actually.' The words are out before I can stop them. I want to bite off my own tongue.

Tears burn at my eyes. Why am I doing this? Calling up Alicia and forcing her to think back to a day that to her, was not unlike any other day she spends at her workplace. She sees lots of people every day, every week. Why would she remember this particular person? Just because Chalk White Woman is haunting my thoughts doesn't mean that she is taking up space in Alicia's head.

'Absolutely certain. Pretty sure I would remember her with that stark description. Why do you want to know?'

The buzzing in my head increases; a swarm of wasps slamming into my skull. Why *do* I want to know? I was so caught up in making this call that having a pre-prepared answer for this question hadn't entered my mind.

'Oh, I just wanted to get in touch with her to reply to the note she gave me.' I'm shocked at how easily the lies pour out of my mouth, at how easily deceit comes to me. Maybe that's who I actually am – a perpetual and brilliant liar.

A flash of a distant memory briefly punctures my thoughts but is gone before I can pin it down. A butterfly flitting around my brain. No, not a butterfly. A dark moth, full of peril and fury. Lies. Deceit. Anger and hurt. They are pinpricks of memories, gone in an instant leaving behind a residue of grime that makes me feel tainted. I shiver, sigh, and try to muster up a smile, for that smile to find its way through the handset. For Alicia to pick up on it and see that I'm not a bad person for telling a little white lie, that I am actually just tinged with desperation and fear, my need to find out who Chalk White Woman is, an all-encompassing force. A force that is driving me on, making me do silly things like calling the local librarian on her mobile while she's at home.

'Anyway,' I say a little too breathlessly, blood pounding in my ears, 'I've kept you on here for too long. Just thought I would ask the question. I'll let you get back to whatever you were doing.'

I don't give Alicia any time to reply, her words abruptly cut off as I end the call and place the phone back in its cradle with a clatter.

19

I don't live a completely hopeless and aimless life. It's not all bad. It's not all good either. It could have been so much better. I never expected or asked for a trouble-free existence or a perfect one; that would be unrealistic. All I have ever wanted was an ordinary one with a husband and a home. A family. Not much to ask for, is it? And I almost had it. It was within my reach and then it was gone. I have never struck up a relationship with another man since Ralph's departure from my life. I couldn't bear the thought of opening up to somebody else, to construct a life for myself only for it to be torn down again. So I remained alone. Not completely alone. I had my daughter. Still do. Of course, she is a grown woman now. A young lady with her own life, her own interests and pastimes. She has a partner, a career. She is everything I'm not – carefree and confident. Successful and happy.

I can't remember the last time I felt carefree. It's an alien emotion. A foreign concept. I've allowed my hatred and resentment to eat at me like acid, stripping away layers of flesh. One day I will wake up and there will be nothing left of me except cartilage and bone.

Damaging her car was easy. It was parked down a back alley.

Nobody around. Until she arrived, that is. I panicked, pushed her to the ground and fled. That part wasn't planned. It was a bonus. A small gift.

She hasn't seen me or recognised me at any of her talks, of that I'm certain. I would know if she had. I would see the slow dawning, the recognition in her eyes. All I ever see there is indifference and on occasion, a small amount of fear. That usually happens at the larger venues where a hundred or so people attend. I wonder if that's because of her scar, the zigzagging welt that runs across her face. The one I gave her when I took aim and drove at her on that dark cold night. I kept that small pixelated picture of her. I cut it out of the magazine and tucked it away in my purse to keep for comparison.

But even the accident didn't stop her. She's still writing, making a good living, residing in her own piece of secluded paradise close to the North Yorkshire moors. Far enough away to live her life in anonymity but close enough to civilisation. I'm willing to bet that that's why she moved there. To be alone. To make sure nobody ever picked her out in a crowd. Not that many people knew who she was. She escaped all the tabloid attention. She was saved from the abuse and death threats that came my way. I absorbed it all on her behalf, took the blows and did what I could to not let them affect me.

Neighbours and friends knew who we were. Tongues wagged incessantly. About me that is. Not her. Never her. She got the pity while I took the blame. She walked away unscathed. I will never forgive her for that. Ever. My bitterness runs deep. But not as deep as the spite and hatred that was directed towards me when it happened. Pictures of my face splashed all over the local and national newspapers, stories of how wicked I was, how damaged and depraved I was. How my family were a band of useless alcoholics who cared about nobody but themselves. The shock of those words cut as deep as any sentence that was meted out to me.

I've taken a chance moving back here, closer to where the crime took place but it was one I was willing to take just to be able to see her again up close, to watch her career take off and then sit back and plan. I need some form of retribution. My day of reckoning. I've bided my time, waited around for many years and put my dreary little life on hold. I'm not back living in the same town – the conditions set out by my probation officer wouldn't allow it, and besides, I'm not that stupid. But I am back in the north east which with a population of just over two and a half million, is enough to give me a degree of anonymity. I'll probably spend the rest of my life looking over my shoulder but with my changed appearance I'm hoping I can relax a little. With each passing year, the chances of me being recognised lessen. I look different, people forget, more crimes are committed, pushing mine to the back of people's minds. They'll never forget, the people who were alive when it was committed, and neither will I, but unless something drastic happens and I accidentally bump into an old neighbour who happens to have a photographic memory and the extraordinary ability to see the once child in my features, then I think I'll be safe. After all, she hasn't recognised me, even when I've stared her right in the eye. Standing so close to her and seeing no recognition in her expression has made me more confident.

My most recent meeting with her was a close encounter. I was nervous and felt sure she would recognise me but at the same time, couldn't help but push it a little, asking her pertinent questions, throwing the odd weighted statement into the conversation to see if it resonated with her. I longed to see the recognition in her eyes, the quickening of the pulse in her neck when she realised who I was. I had parked my car up on the main road and walked down into the woods. I had no idea why I took such a chance but as I stepped out of the trees, we were almost face to face. I went there ostensibly to simply watch her, to wait for another opportune moment to frighten her. The dog nearly gave the game away. I think he recognised me from the last time I took him. He made it an easy thing to do. It was effortless. Such a soft gentle boy. All it took was a *few kissing noises and the promise of a snack and he was mine. I didn't plan on doing anything bad to him. After all, I'm just a middle-aged woman with a past I'm not proud of. I'm a mother and a daughter. An ex-prisoner and an ex-wife. I'm not a monster. Am I?*

20

SUMMER OF 1976

She was even smaller than Heather imagined. Tiny actually. Hunched over and frail- looking, a walking stick clutched in her hand. She stood at the top of the stairs, face pinched, back arched, ready to do battle.

'Who is it? If it's money you're after, you've come to the wrong place. I don't have any.' Her voice was deceptively strong for somebody so small. A boom in the darkness, like a punch to the gut.

Heather felt her legs weaken, her muscles watery with trepidation. They'd done it, got inside and frightened the old lady. They could leave now, turn right around and just go. But they wouldn't. She could see it all before it happened, the trouble that lay ahead. She could hear Irena's voice echoing in her ears as she shouted up the stairs, her caustic domineering words, the barrage of insults she would fire at the old lady. The pensioner would wave her walking stick around, threaten to call the police if they didn't leave. Which they wouldn't. Fear of Irena, fear of losing her friendship would root her and Lesley to the spot. They would stay and witness it all, be a part of it, and when the police eventually arrived, she and her friends would be led out by their arms, manhandled into the back of a marked police car, and taken home where she would be given a sound beating by her mam and dad for bringing more shame to their family and marking them out as villains. Being feckless lazy alcoholics was one thing but getting into trouble with the police was another thing entirely. The Oswalds lived above the law. They still had a certain amount of pride. It was wafer thin, that pride and dignity, a flimsy thing with little substance but it was there all the same. It was all they had left. If she took that from them then it would leave them completely worthless. Rudderless and alone. Ostracised from the rest of the neighbourhood.

'We've brought somebody to see you.' Irena's perfectly white teeth gleamed in the darkness as she grabbed at Lesley's hand, pulling at her, and propelling her forward. Lesley stood at the foot of the stairs, head lowered, her voice a hiss, low and pleading. 'We need to go. Now.'

'Eh? Who is it? Wait till I turn on the light. I can't see you.' The old woman's words pierced the air, a shrill cry in the darkness.

More movement overhead, loud breathing and shuffling before they were flooded in a spread of ochre that tore at Heather's eyes. She lifted her hand, cupping it over her brow, blocking out the glare and the sight of the old lady. The shocking sight of a woman so bent and frail that Heather felt sure she must already be dead. Her hair was sparse, the old lady's scalp visible. What few strands she had sat atop her head like a mop of silver candy floss, wispy stray tufts sticking out at divergent angles. A threadbare nightgown covered her stick-thin body, her legs poking out from underneath, ankles so painfully slim they looked as if they would snap in a sharp breeze. The flesh wrapped around her skeletal frame was almost translucent. Heather suppressed a gasp, shocked at how grey she looked. How close to death she appeared to be. Was that what happened when you got older? Your body simply shrivelled up until there was nothing left of you except a heap of wrinkled skin and a pile of worn-out dry old bones?

She couldn't swear to it, but she thought that perhaps she heard a sob coming from Lesley, a small hiccup that was quickly disguised as a cough.

'Lesley? Is that you down there? What you doin' here then, our Les?' The old lady's voice was suddenly gentle, no longer a grating shriek but softer, welcoming even.

Her features slackened as she stepped closer to the top of the stairs, a smile spreading across her face.

'I thought you said she was an old battle-axe?' Irena turned and stared at Lesley, shoulders hunched, her backbone a ridge of perfectly formed sharp mounds beneath her T-shirt. Anger creased her face, a deep furrow cutting her brow in half. The words were fired at Lesley, shards of ice frosting the air between them.

Heather could hear Lesley's sudden rapid breathing, was able to detect her shifting mood. Her apparent fear. Had she lied about her nana? The lady before them didn't fit the description Lesley had given her. She was frail and looked close to death. She was also smiling, her voice laced with kindness when she spoke Lesley's name. Something wasn't right here, a piece of the jigsaw not fitting into its rightful place.

'Eh? Speak up down there. I can't hear you. I haven't got my hearing aids in. Can't seem to find them anywhere.' The sharp voice was back. Not laced with anger this time, more of a plaintive cry. The plea of an old woman who was struggling to survive in a rundown house that was working against her, the elements continually eroding the walls and the roof that kept her safe and warm and dry. Even with her limited knowledge of how life worked, how difficult it was to pay for things and keep everyone housed and happy, Heather could see that something wasn't right here. This wasn't how Lesley had painted things. This old lady was helpless.

She wasn't an old cow and she wasn't a witch. She was just a vulnerable old woman who lived alone in a scruffy rundown house that was dropping to bits.

Heather had so many questions at the ready but before she could say anything, Lesley barged past her, grabbed at the door handle, and ran outside. It all happened so quickly, what came next. Too quickly for her to do anything, to intervene and make a difference. Too quickly for her to change the course of events that would alter her life irrevocably, damaging it beyond repair. It filled her head night after night as she lay in her grubby bed in the prison that she was forced to call home month after month, year after year, what she could have done to change things that day, how if she had acted differently, her life would have gone down another path, a smoother one, with fewer ruts and potholes. A path that was less likely to cause her ongoing, untold pain.

But it was all too late once it had happened. What was done was done and could not, no matter how hard she tried or wished, be undone. Her future was set, all mapped out in crystal-clear formation. There was no going back from that horrific murderous day. Everything was just too damn late.

21

It's still in my head when I wake, the dream from last night. Not a dream. A memory. Or at least I think that's what it is. I didn't think they would ever return, any of those images and recollections. I always hoped they would, but after months and months of wishing and waiting, I had all but given up hope but last night proved that they're still there, trapped somewhere in the dark confines of my damaged brain.

I rub at my eyes, letting my thoughts wander back to the dream. I'm a child playing in the water. I can feel it lapping around my ankles. Except I'm not playing. There is no laughter. No feelings of happiness. Just a pit of darkness. A feeling of heaviness. I think hard about that body of water. It's not the sea. Too small. Too dark. One of the becks I saw on the map. Not the River Tees. It's not wide enough to be a river. Something presses down on me when I think about that water. Something dark and unpleasant.

I lie back, rest my head against the headboard and close my eyes, waiting for more images to emerge. There were voices as well. Shouting. Not the sort of happy commotion associated with splashing about in a stream, more of a hollering. A command from somebody nearby. A scream even. Anger. Definitely anger.

I shiver. My eyes snap open. I sit up, my heart pounding, a deep well of rage opening in me. So much fury and ferocity. And then they're gone, those images, the accompanying feelings. They vanish, leaving behind a filthy splatter of dirt in my brain that clings to me like poison ivy.

I grab at my robe and jump out of bed, eager to shower, to scrub my skin until it burns. If these are the memories I've been longing to return, then I don't want them. They're ugly and oppressive. As craggy and as shocking as the scar on my face.

After speaking to Alicia yesterday, I spent the day wandering around in a haze, my final attempts to work out who Chalk White Woman is, destroyed by her words. Writing was impossible. I took Whisky out for a final walk, came home, and curled up in bed, too tired, too miserable and despondent to do anything except sleep. I took another tablet, felt myself falling, and then came the dreams; the memories that resurfaced with a vengeance. I longed, or at least hoped for happiness or a degree of contentment once they made an appearance. I didn't expect desperation and doom. And yet something inside tells me I should have expected it, that my move here and lack of contact with the outside world happened for a reason, that it was a deliberate manoeuvre to protect myself. From what, I don't know. What I am now certain of, however, is that there was something – an incident or an event – that was traumatic.

I make a coffee and stare out of the window, trying to dismiss the imprints of the dream, refusing to spend yet another day wrapped in a mantilla of misery.

I need to take back control of my life, show these women, whoever they are, that I'm not unsettled by either of them. Even though I am. Didn't some wise person once say that only when we are no longer afraid do we begin to live. I'll make that my mantra, the thing that keeps me afloat amidst a sea of uncertainty.

People would be forgiven for thinking that my scar has eroded my confidence, but if anything, it's had the opposite effect. I was lucky. I survived that hit and run. My scar is an outward sign of how lucky I was to pull through. Not once has it ever stopped me from appearing and talking at any of my gatherings and yet the sight of that pale-faced young woman is enough to turn my insides to water, for my knees to tremble and my head to pound. I just wish I knew why.

* * *

I carry my breakfast through to my study and sit at my desk, the faint scent of shampoo mixed with coffee a heady combination. I showered for as long as my skin could stand the searing heat. It felt good to scrub away the remnants of that dream. By the time I stepped out onto the cold tiled floor, my fingertips were wrinkled, my flesh mottled and pink.

I take a sip of the coffee and leaf through my diary, scanning the pages for bookings. My next talk is in two days' time. Another stint at the library. Alicia anticipated large numbers so we split the talk into two separate sessions. I really need to stay focused and get my mind sorted otherwise I could fall behind with deadlines and miss bookings that have been pencilled in for months. I sip at my coffee and take a bite of my toast, crumbs spilling onto my lap. In many ways, I hope Chalk White Woman is sitting there in the crowd at the library. I've got a couple of days to work out how best to approach the situation. What to say to her. How to catch her before she slips away. I need to let her know that she is no longer welcome. I can't prove it was her who damaged my car and pushed me over but every part of me is screaming that she was the one who was responsible. Nor can I prove that it was her who took Whisky and left him alone in the dark. I don't have any evidence for any of those things but common sense and a strong instinct tells me she is behind it all. I'm being targeted. I just don't know why. Perhaps she's a stalker, a reader of my crime fiction books and the lines between what I write and how I live my life have become blurred in her unbalanced brain. Or perhaps it's linked to the flash of memories I've been having. That can't be possible. She's younger than me; much younger and I'm a child in the dreams.

I'm not the murderer. You are.

That's got to be the most rational explanation. The obvious one. That she believes my stories are somehow a reflection of my life, that I do really murder people for a living. I smile. It feels unfamiliar, my mouth stretched into a tight line. I've been so sure that I was the one who was losing my grip when in all likelihood, she's the one who is teetering on the brink. She's a reader. A stalker. A dangerous individual. That thought is a sobering one. And worrying. I don't know who she is but I do know that she is clearly mentally unstable and it's the people who are out of balance that are capable of the most dreadful deeds.

I ignore the small voice in my head that is reminding me about the incident with the woman in the woods. Her appearance is just a bizarre coincidence. An unexplained occurrence. They're not connected. They can't be.

Today, in between writing and walking Whisky, I'll work out what I'm going to say to her when she arrives at the library. I won't wait until the end and watch her disappear like she has in the past, leaving me feel discombobulated and frustrated. I want this sorting so I can get on with the rest of my life. I'll catch her early; watch and wait, delay my opening gambit if I have to so I can speak with her. I'll do whatever it takes to bring this shambolic episode to an end so that I can get on with the rest of my life. As sedate and boring as it was, I'd like to have it back.

If this whole debacle has taught me anything, it's how close we all are to unspooling and coming undone at the slightest provocation. Or maybe that's just me. Maybe my mental state is so fragile that all it takes is one unexplained presence in my life, one person to radiate hatred towards me and in no time at all I'm a gibbering wreck. I hope that isn't the case but how well do we really know ourselves and understand our own minds? With no memories of my formative years, I'm an empty vessel. I don't know myself. Not really. I'm a stranger to those around me and I'm a stranger to myself. There's no escaping that fact. Not once has anybody approached me and recognised me. Not once. I no longer live on Teesside but surely somebody must know who I am?

Maybe I've always been alone and maybe there's a reason for that. Maybe I salted myself away here in the woods because I'm trying to hide from something.

I'm not the murderer, you are.

No. I refuse to believe it. One day in the near future, my memory will come back. Like the doctor said, I just need to give it time.

I press the heel of my hands into my eyes and rub furiously. Time. Something I may not have lots of, and I do want to know who I am – who *she* is – before my illness gets any worse. I need to put all the pieces together, to see the whole picture. That's not too much to ask, is it?

22

Today is a busy one. Easier to blend into the background, remain anonymous. Which is good. Because despite knowing that the odds of being spotted are slim to non-existent, I've still got it – that dread of being recognised. Weight gain, haircuts, the general ageing process do little to alleviate that feeling. One day, I'll be an old lady and there will be no resemblance to the child that I used to be, but until that time comes, I will continue to carry around the weighty burden of anxiety. I've changed. Of course I have. Whether or not I'm still recognisable as that young girl from all those years ago is debatable. I don't think I am but I have no photographs of myself as a child to compare. I threw every single one of them away, keen to sever that link to my past, and I kept no newspapers that carried the story, so the image I have in my head of how I used to look back then is all I have to go on, and even that has faded with the passing of time. Most people give scant thought to how their faces have changed over the years, how our features define who we are but I think about it all the time. And we were a well-known family – the Oswalds. Well known and notorious, our levels of poverty and my parents' drinking habits talked about in neighbourhoods far and wide. Few were surprised when the story of what happened broke. They expected something to happen but nothing quite as bad as what took place that day. Nobody was more surprised than me. I was trying too hard to be part of a gang, led along by a need to be needed. To belong. There was also the fear that I felt, a lack of impetus to break away and make a run for it. Who would have thought that two simple emotions could lead to such a catastrophic turn of events. I realise it sounds like a terrible worn-out old cliché, but I wasn't a bad child, just misunderstood. I was in a bad place with a bad person. And look where it got me. It took away my childhood. Stripped me of a normal life. Stripped me of **my** life, the one I should now be leading.

Today might be the day she sees me. Or maybe not. She seems to be blind to what is right in front of her. Her mind is so entrenched in her fantasy fiction world that she can't see the important things. The real things, like how I can take a wrecking ball to her life and smash it to pieces with one swift blow.

I hope that today will be the day that she will finally see me for who I am — who I used to be — and a flicker of recognition will cross her face. I want to see the fear in her eyes, that look of sheer hopelessness, like a cornered animal awaiting its fate. At some point it must happen. We can't go on like this, being together in such close proximity yet acting as if we're total strangers. Something has got to give. I just need to be patient, to give it time. If I can endure her ignorance for just a little longer, it will make the final dawning all that much more pleasurable. Just to be able to see the horror on her face, the way her expression will change from professionally pleasant to one of complete dread when she realises why I'm here.

I lean back slightly, raise my face to the ceiling, questioning my own motivations for doing this. What **do** I really want from her? I've waited so long for the opportunity to do this that I haven't given a great deal of thought to the outcome. Is it revenge I'm after? Or is it something more than that, something more complex than a simple poke at an enemy that I've hated for nearly all of my life? I've been driven by my emotions, a need to get back at her forcing me on, and now that I'm here, I realise that I don't actually have a plan. My endgame is so close and now a vacuum has appeared. A big black hole that needs filling. Hunting her down has been so pleasurable, that I got caught up in the chase, forgetting about how it will all conclude. And there will be a conclusion to this. I haven't gone to all this trouble to let her slip away unscathed. She needs to see the trouble I went to, to find her, but I need to be careful. I'm not about to risk being outed by the local press. This is between me and her. There is no way I am going to end up back in jail. Not a hope in hell.

For now, I'm content to sit and watch. Observing her from afar gives me some thinking time, a chance to be meticulous, to get everything just right. If she thought that the damage to her car and her phone getting smashed were distressing then she needs to buckle up because those things were just the beginning. Already, as I'm sitting here, waiting for her to notice me, ideas are flooding my mind, ways in which I can upset the delicate equilibrium of her well-ordered little world.

A voice drags me out of my reverie, dulling the sinister thoughts that are sluicing around my brain. I briefly close my eyes to gather myself, opening them again to glance around the room. A few spare seats. Not a complete sell-out then. That will chip away at her ego, make her realise she's not quite the superstar she thinks she is.

Her voice cuts into my thoughts, forcing me to sit up and take notice. Even the sound of her speaking irritates me, makes me want to scream at her, to ask her if she knows how fortunate she is.

'Good afternoon, everyone. It's lovely to be here. It's also great to see some familiar faces. I'm always grateful that people take time out of their day to come and see me, especially since the weather is so awful today.' Her voice carries around the room, everyone attentive, hanging onto her every word. She gesticulates outside to the driving rain and howling wind that is currently battering at the windows and pounding on the skylight above us with such ferocity that many glance up and shiver, *wrapping their arms around themselves as some sort of protection, even though it's so warm in here, I could close my eyes and drift off to sleep.*

Her eyes sweep across the rows of seats, taking in the sea of expectant faces, readers who are eager to soak up her words of wisdom, eager to listen to her read an excerpt from her latest book. I try to catch her eye, to see if her gaze lingers over my face for longer than is necessary. I think that perhaps she does see me, stopping for a short while, her flesh taking on a different pallor as she narrows her eyes and stares somewhere close to where I'm seated. I turn and look at the few empty chairs nearby and stare at the people around me, trying to work out if it's them she is assessing, or me. I pray it's me, hoping she is doing her best to avert her gaze, not make it obvious she has recognised me, but it's too difficult to work out. Even now, after all these visits I've made, everything I have tolerated and the effort I've gone to, to make contact with her, she still has the upper hand and I am that sad little child, tagging along, following her around like a lost puppy, desperate for any scraps of attention she deigns to throw my way. My stomach feels hollow, desperation worming its way into my chest. Nothing has changed. After all these years, she still has me dangling on a string like a fucking puppet.

Look at me!

I want to scream it out loud, to say those words, see what sort of reaction it provokes, to take great delight in seeing her quiver with fear. Maybe she already is. Maybe she has seen me and is a damn good actress, covering up her nerves with an even soothing tone and the mask of contentment that she wears in public. It's possible. I just wish I knew it for certain. Some sort of benchmark would help me, keep me buoyed up knowing I'm heading along the right track to scaring her and dismantling her life.

There is, of course, another way to speed up the process, to expedite my plan and make it known who it is the public are dealing with without exposing who I really am. Excitement heats up my blood. I reach for my phone and log on to the site. A film of perspiration rests on my top lip. I wipe it away with a shaky finger. My body feels as if it's vibrating, electricity flowing through me. I need to focus, not lose my track of thought. I'm here for her, to show her that my will is as strong as hers, that the fortress she built for herself all those years ago, that purportedly impetrative fortress she created to protect her real identity, is about to come tumbling down around her. And I will be stood by watching and smiling when it happens.

23

She's here. Part of me hoped she wouldn't turn up, the frightened cowardly part of me, that is. But then the determined side of me was glad to see her sitting there.

I push back my shoulders, clear my throat. Do all the things that people do when they want to appear confident. My gaze rests on her, deliberately making eye contact. Showing her that I'm not scared. It's as I'm watching her that it happens. Another flashback. A dark memory resurfacing, needling its way into my brain.

I'm in the same place, down by a stream or beck. I hear those voices again. Shouting. A scream. Then a glimpse of a face. Not mine. Somebody else's. A young girl. Too quick to get a close look. Just a misty snapshot of a young, terrified female, her mouth wide open as she lets out a piercing scream.

I snap myself out of it, the hairs on my arms upright, my scalp prickling with fear. I stare out at the crowd, at those eager waiting faces. Row after row of them. The weather seems to be working against me, the elements drowning out my words. The wind howls through the rafters, the rain thunders against the skylight, echoing around the room. A handful of the audience shiver, glancing upwards, their bodies tight, arms wrapped around themselves for protection, watching and waiting as if the roof is going to fall in or the walls are about to split open and crumble to the ground, trapping us all and turning us to dust.

Despite the heater blowing hot air onto me, I shiver. My fingers are like ice as I place my hands on the lectern and look down at my book, the page I'm about to read held open with a small paperweight. An image grips me – me brandishing the paperweight, holding it over the top of Chalk White Woman's head and bringing it down with force over and over again; blood running down her cheeks, pouring out of her ears and streaming from her nose, a scarlet river of it. I swallow, rub at my face, and clear my throat. I look around for Alicia to ask if I can have a glass of water but she's nowhere to be seen. A sudden panic that I will cough uncontrollably and not be able to continue seizes me. I can't let that happen. The humiliation would kill me. I take a deep breath and tell myself to stop it. I'm being stupid. Soft and pliable. Somewhere hidden in my brain is a younger, more confident me. I want her back. The only thing I feel confident about right now is my books and even that is starting to wane, my equanimity dissolving by the minute. Maybe I'm the one who will turn to dust, everyone else sitting, rigid and made of stone. How easy would that be? For me to crumble away, to disappear and escape from everything. From everyone.

I count to three, pull myself together and continue speaking, reading an excerpt of my latest novel without a hitch. No coughing, no stumbling over my words. Not a single error. All that worry for nothing. I feel somebody beside me and look up to see Alicia place a cup of coffee beside me before scurrying off again. My smile is aimed at her back, my words lost in the noise of the raging wind and rain that is still battering at the window as I give her a quick whispered *thank you*.

The rest of the talk, despite my initial fears, goes smoothly.

Once again, I scan the audience. She's still there, watching me. I gaze at the rest of the people and stop, a certain other face catching my attention. Do I know her? She's smiling at me. Not actually a smile. It's a sneer. There's something familiar about her. I can see her features, her expression in my mind's eye, the way her mouth moves when she speaks, even the timbre of her voice. And yet I can't place when or where we've met. Another of my talks. It must be. They're the main sources of contact I have with the outside world, aside from my shopping trips into town every couple of weeks. And my visits to the doctor. She could be a receptionist at the surgery or a cashier at the supermarket. Or she could just be a reader of my books. She's here, listening to what I have to say, giving me her full attention. I don't know her from anywhere else. I'm being paranoid. Oversensitive, desperate, and neurotic. Like one of the characters in my books.

People file up to where I'm standing, their fingers gripping copies of my novels. It still gives me a well-needed boost, seeing those paperbacks in their hands. I'll never tire of it. I wonder if other writers who have a fuller life than I do get this buzz, or are they too busy simply living? Socialising with family and friends and generally doing all the things that ordinary people do while I spend day after day holed up in my cottage with only my faithful old dog for company. I'm happy. I repeat those words over and over in my head.

I'm happy. I'm happy.

It's my life; the one I chose.

'I love your latest book! Can you dedicate this to Muriel please?' I nod and take a hardback copy of *The Memory Man* from an elderly gentleman. It's about a person who is tried for a murder he can't remember committing due to a bout of amnesia. I thought that writing a story about somebody with memory loss would be therapeutic. I was wrong. I sign the book and thank him for attending.

'Where do you get your ideas from?' He grins at me, his ill-fitting dentures glinting under the glare of the fluorescent light. 'This one really spooked me. It's very different from your other ones, isn't it? I'd love to see inside your head, try to see how you come up with such an original idea. Clever, that's what you are. Very clever.' He taps his temple with a finger and smiles again.

I want to tell him that inside my head isn't a place that anybody would want to visit, and that I'm anything but clever. Paranoid, possibly. Suspicious, maybe. Insecure, definitely. But not clever.

A tic takes hold in my jaw. I rub at my face and press my palms into my temples. I can feel a headache coming on.

'Oh, I'm not that clever at all. My ideas come from here and there. I'm a magpie. I hunt around and take a few concepts from TV programmes and films, a little bit from other books and then the rest comes from real-life situations.' My head buzzes at the sound of my own voice, a ghostly noise that doesn't sound at all like me. *Real-life situations*. Why did I say that? Am I being truthful? Or am I simply using a well-worn trope to answer a question I get asked on many occasions?

'Well, wherever you get your inspiration from, it's worked. This one is a belter!' He points at the open page where I have signed my name. 'This is for my wife. She's out shopping with our daughter and she doesn't know I'm here getting this signed for her so will love this. Your books keep her going. Give her something to look forward to. She says that if ever she commits a murder, she'll pretend she's lost her memory as well to avoid prison.' His laugh is a rumble of thunder, loud and relentless.

Heads turn to look. The heat around me rises. Perspiration breaks out on my face; my palms are clammy with sweat. I hand back his book, give him a wide smile and he leaves the library looking contented, happy with my response. Was I lying – giving a reader the answer he wants to hear? Or is there a grain of truth in my words? I rub my palms on the side of my clothes and clear my head, readying myself to speak to more people. Don't dwell on things. Move on. I have a job to do, people to see.

A line of smiling faces queue up, waiting to speak with me, to get their books signed and to chat about the world of crime fiction. I remind myself that I can do this. It comes easily to me, isn't overly taxing and as long as I smile a lot, my readers are always extremely polite, telling me how much they love my books and how they can't wait for my next one.

I sign another book, chat for a couple of seconds and thank them for turning up, then move onto the next person and then the next, all the time keeping a close eye on Chalk White Woman. She's still there, sitting alone, everyone around her now gone. A lone face in the emptiness of the seating area. Why? Why is she still there?

The queue of people seems longer than ever, the interminably endless wait to speak with her, torturous. If I could just sign my name and usher them along, then maybe I could—

'Hi, can you dedicate this one to my daughter, please?' The woman standing in front of me makes my pulse race. My legs weaken, turning to water.

'Yes, if I—'

I speak but she cuts in. It's her. The lady who was stumbling along close to my cottage in unsuitable footwear and clothing. I remember. That's where I know her from. A breath catches in my throat. I peer over her shoulder and see that Chalk White Woman has left her seat. It's empty. I'm torn between quizzing this woman who is standing watching me, and shouting over to try to find out where Chalk White Woman is. I want to run towards the back of the library to catch her before she leaves. Again. I want to bar all the doors and shake her until she is dizzy and falls to the ground. I want to scream at her to either tell me what she wants or to leave me alone.

The woman in front of me twists her head, following my gaze to the other side of the room. Chalk White Woman is standing next to a small huddle of people who are chatting to Alicia. Her face is turned towards us. Alicia stops talking and looks my way. I attempt to catch her eye in order to send a subliminal message that the woman standing near her is the one I described the other day, that she needs to get a good look at her but instead she grins at me and gives me a little wave. I wave back and smile. So does the lady standing in front of me. I want to shake her as well, to tell her that this is my arena, that she needs to go away and leave me alone. Instead, I grab her book, open it, scribble my name on the first page and close it with a snap to indicate that her time with me is over. No dedication. Nothing else to be said. She smiles, her face the picture of contentment. If she is disturbed by my rudeness, she doesn't show it, tracing a line over the cover of the book with a long slim finger, caressing it even, her nail looping in small circles, outlining the shapes on there – a house in the distance, a shadowy figure on a hill, dark clouds overhead – a generic crime novel image.

'Lovely cover, isn't it?' she says, her voice low and husky. 'What do you think it is that makes you so good at writing crime novels?'

She smiles again. I don't return the gesture. Irritation builds in my gut. I need to get away from this woman. She is making me impatient and bad mannered.

'I'm sorry,' I reply. 'I need to speak to somebody.' I don't try to mask my annoyance. I want her to leave.

Beyond her is a movement. Somebody opening the door. Lots of people are still milling about the library, chatting and mingling. A small crowd stands patiently in a line, waiting for me to sign their books. The heat in the room rises again. I shiver, a wave of cold passing over me, glazing my skin, burrowing into my bones. I think about my medication, trying to remember if I took too many last night. Or not enough. The floor feels spongy under my feet. The walls lean in. I try to look over to see where Chalk White Woman is but everything is blurred, my eyes misted over, the people on the far side of the library cloudy and indistinct, no more than hazy outlines.

I feel something close to my face and try to brush it away. Heat filters into my ear. Warm breath. Somebody moving closer to me, a soft low voice saying something. Whispered words. I blink, rub at my eyes with hot fists. It's her, the woman with the book, the one who now knows where I live. The woman I tried to put off only a few seconds ago. It's not Chalk White Woman. She's gone. Disappeared once again, escaping before I can corner her. Before I can ask her why she is here.

I try to move away but am trapped between the lectern and the wooden bookshelf behind me. Soft words spoken again. The same woman leaning into me, almost touching me. I recoil. The room starts to spin. I hear her words. Feel them boring into my brain, sharp and unforgiving.

'Ask yourself what you did.'

I wince, try to step back but am trapped. Nowhere to go. No means of escape. My head pounds. My heart is racing. A murmur of concern from those around me. Darkness begins to descend, bleeding into my brain like tar, coating everything, blocking out the light.

I feel myself falling, stars bursting behind my eyes, the heat of my body leaving me, seeping out of my pores, replaced by a rush of cold that sits on my flesh like a sheet of ice. The last thing I see when I look up is her face. Not Chalk White Woman. *Her*. And she is smiling down at me, her voice soft and honeyed.

Ask yourself what you did.

A sudden pain shooting behind my eyes as my head hits the tiled floor with a dull thud. Then nothing.

24

SUMMER OF 1976

A sob erupted out of Lesley's throat like the bark of an animal: a primeval howl. She was bent over, kneeling at the water's edge, a weeping wreck of a thing, her slim body crumpled in on itself.

'I lied. It was all a stupid lie. I don't know why I said it. It's not her, my nana. It's not her fault. It's them, my mam and dad.' She looked up at Heather, eyes glassy with tears. 'I was messing about when I said what I did, being stupid and saying stuff I shouldn't have said. They're the ones who hate her, not me. They fell out with her years ago. She doesn't see them.' Lesley hiccupped, wiped at her eyes. 'They won't come and see her.'

Something inside Heather's head clicked into place. She knew then; she didn't have to say anything else because she recognised the signs, was able to see beyond the mask of normality and self-assurance to the frightened girl underneath. Maybe that was why Lesley initially gravitated towards her. Maybe that was why they got on so well. Two damaged people together, that's what they were. Two kids who gelled because of their broken home lives. Lesley's confidence, her poise and finesse had all been a desperate lie.

'But I thought your mam and dad were okay? Your dad has a job and a car and your mam always wears lovely clothes and has nice hair.' Heather knew it was a façade but had to say something. It was a carefully constructed façade that fooled everyone. Even her. Especially her. She thought it was only poor people like her mam and dad who hated their own family, the grinding poverty driving them to drink and resenting anybody who added extra pressure to their sad little lives. That wasn't the case at all. Even well-to-do people fell out with each other, saying terrible things about family members regardless of how weak and frail and alone they were. And Lesley's nana was frail and weak, and living here in that sad-looking, broken-down old house, she was definitely very much alone.

Lesley shook her head, tears running down her cheeks, dripping onto the ground in great wet splodges. 'They hate my nan. Won't let me see her. I've asked and they said no, said she's an old cow. I once tried to visit her when I was on my own and they found out. And then...' She shuddered, her hands clasped together as if in prayer. 'I wanted to see her when I came here with you but...'

Heather waited. She held her breath, counting how long she could keep it there, stuck in her throat. Lesley looked away, chin trembling, too upset to say anything else. Not that it mattered. Her friend didn't have to find the words. Heather understood all too well. They were kindred souls, her and Lesley. Kindred souls.

It was still hard to swallow, the idea that Lesley's family fought like hers did. She had always thought the Oswalds were the only ones. Well-off people didn't argue and fight, did they? Her eyes scoured Lesley's face, travelling down over her slim body, her gaze stopping when she saw them – the fingertip-sized bruises on Lesley's arms. The small welt on her collarbone. The scratches. The tell-tale signs that all was not as it seemed. The signs that Heather recognised and knew so well.

'So, she's not an old cow at all, then?' Heather didn't know why she was asking. It was just something to say, words to fill a silence.

Tears flew from Lesley's cheeks, a spray of saline spreading around them in a tiny arc as she shook her head. 'No. And now Irena is in there saying all that horrible stuff to her.' Darkness settled behind her eyes, anger descending. A sudden fury that was impossible to ignore. 'And it's all your fault, Heather! You did this by telling her. If you hadn't opened your big fat mouth, we wouldn't even be here.'

The words took Heather by surprise, punching a hole in her gut, smashing her intestines to pieces. No more being called *Hev*. No more terms of endearments. Just hatred. Despair howled in her head. She should have known that it would come to this. It always did. Nothing positive lasted for long in her world. The nice things always came to a juddering halt. She wanted to shrink away to nothing, to disappear into the ether. Be as small as a fleck of dust and float away into space. Her mouth was dry. She ran her tongue around her teeth, trying to find something to say to make everything right again, yet knowing deep down that nothing would work. Their once close friendship was fractured. Once again, her loose words had rolled out of her mouth, damaging everything. Crushing their friendship and turning it to ash.

'I'm really sorry.' It was a feeble attempt to heal the hurt she had caused. She sounded pathetic. Lesley's companionship had lifted her out of her drab gritty home life, giving everything a touch of glamour and sparkle. And now she had ruined it. Maybe her mam and dad were right. Maybe she was rotten to the core. A useless child. A hopeless nobody.

'Sorry?' Heather didn't recognise the voice. It was a different Lesley. Not the happy, shiny one that she knew. This version of Lesley was a fierce, angry person. Her voice was laced with bitterness, venom evident in every word, every syllable. 'Bit fucking late for that now, isn't it?' Lesley's arm appeared in front of Heather, her outstretched palm knocking Heather to the floor as it connected with her shoulder.

The push took her by surprise., knocking the breath right out of her. She landed on her back, a pain shooting up and down her spine. Her first reaction was to scurry away but then a sudden rage took hold, white-hot flames combusting in her veins. In a matter of seconds, the dynamics of their relationship had changed, the scales oscillating wildly. For weeks, Lesley had been the leader, taking charge. Until Irena came along, that is. Maybe that was where her anger stemmed from? She had been usurped, pushed out and demoted. Heather understood Lesley's distress over her nana, but this? This was an overreaction. Gratuitous and unwarranted.

'What was that for?' Heather stood up and brushed herself down, dusting flakes of dry mud off her shorts. She stood over Lesley, staring down at her tear-streaked face. 'I said I was sorry, didn't I?'

'Yeah, and as I've just said, it's a bit late now, isn't it? You've made me look like an idiot and you've upset my nana, made her scared in her own house.'

'Scared in her own house? It's dropping to bits! And I wasn't the one who upset your nana. Sounds like your mam and dad did that all on their own. Sounds like you need to sort out your own family before you start blaming me for everything.'

'Yeah well, maybe my family are useless and horrible, but it's your fault we're here. You made us come to her house. We'd be somewhere else if it wasn't for you.'

There was a wobble in her tone, as if she was softening. But then it happened again. A sudden and unexpected push. Heather stumbled, falling backwards, landing on her backside with a crack. The pain rendered her immobile for a few seconds, the world spinning around her. A surge of heat travelled up her neck into her face, flaring across her cheeks and ears. She scrambled up again, her body angled and undignified as she slipped about on the incline that led down to the stream. Mortification filled every inch of her, slithering under her skin, beating and thrumming in her throat. Enough was enough. What did it matter if Lesley was her friend? It was over now. She had nothing to lose. May as well fight back, show her that she was an Oswald and wasn't about to be bullied and pushed around. She had apologised, tried to make everything better, back to how it once was but Lesley had decided to ignore her apology and fling her about like some sort of ragdoll. Whatever took place next wouldn't be her fault. Lesley had brought it on herself with her refusal to accept Heather's heartfelt admission of guilt. Saying sorry didn't come easy to her but she had managed it, thinking it would solve this situation that she had created, get them back on a firm footing, and Lesley had thrown it back in her face, shouting at her and knocking her over. Hurting and humiliating her. And nobody hurt and humiliated Heather Oswald. Nobody.

She curled her hand into a fist and hit Lesley as hard as she could, the ridge of her taut knuckles striking the other girl's face with a crunch. The sensation of the soft cartilage of Lesley's nose beneath her hand felt satisfying. She could feel it shift and break. The jet of blood was instantaneous, shooting out of both nostrils, spraying Heather's clothes, turning them a deep shade of red. Nausea swept over her. She stared down at her bloodied shirt, lip curled in disdain.

'Oh my God, that's disgusting! *You're* disgusting. Look what you've done to my clothes, you stupid bitch!'

Grabbing at handfuls of grass, Heather swept the small green tufts over her T-shirt, dragging clumps of foliage over the stains, making it worse. It didn't remove the blood; it mingled and became a dirty smear, streaks of lime now combined with sticky splashes of scarlet. Heather wanted to scream, to rip off her top and stamp on it over and over. Dealing with her own blood and bodily fluids was bad enough, being covered in somebody else's was more than she could bear. It made her sick to her stomach. More reasons to hate Lesley. More reason to want to pummel her face into a pulpy bloody mush.

Heather dropped the clumps of grass, determined to hit her again but a quick glance told her she didn't need to do any more. She had hurt her enough, blood still dripping from her nose in great long globules. Lesley's hands were cupped beneath her chin, catching the scarlet strings that ran out of each nostril. She should have felt guilty, she knew that, but was too angry to feel anything other than fury and resentment. All the effort she had put into being Lesley's friend and it had come to this. It felt like such a waste. Like everything in her life. She had come full circle and was once again that stupid smelly kid from Tunstall Street, the one who lived in the tiny terraced old house that stood out from everybody else's because of its peeling paint and grimy windows. If dirt could penetrate bricks and mortar, the exterior of her home would be as black as tar, the filth from the inside clawing its way out. Nothing had changed. She was back to where she started. Unwanted. Undesirable. Stuck on the outside looking in.

She started to walk away, determined to head home alone. But then something stopped her. A sound. Not a sound. A scream. A scream coming from the house.

Lesley was up on her feet, congealed blood covering her face and her hands. Heather couldn't tell and wasn't an expert, but thought that her nose was probably broken. It was badly injured – swollen and bent to one side. She looked down at her hands, unaware of her own strength. It had just come out of nowhere – all that rage and frustration – a lifetime of it. A lifetime of being beaten and ignored and shoved to one side. She wanted to calm down, to feel remorse for what she had done, but adrenaline was still pulsing through her and no matter how hard she tried, she couldn't summon up any feelings of regret. And she certainly didn't have it in her to apologise again. Twice was enough. It was more than enough for her. Too much.

Heather watched Lesley run towards the house and stalled. This could be her chance to leave it all behind. Leave Irena and Lesley to it. Let them sort out this mess. It was nothing to do with her. She could make her way back to the park, sit on a swing. Be on her own for a while and think things through. Going home didn't appeal but neither did following Lesley into that house.

Another loud shout. It banged against her skull. A lonely echo. A blood-curdling scream.

Her legs carried her at speed over to the open door of the rundown old house in the woods; that house, that moment forever emblazoned on her brain as the time that changed her life forever, tearing it to shreds with no chance of it ever being put back together.

25

My eyes snap open. I'm aware that something is wrong, that my surroundings are unfamiliar. Everything hurts when I attempt to pull myself upright from whatever it is I'm lying on, my body resisting and slumping back down. I'm not at home in bed, or on the sofa. It's a different sensation, the surface beneath me not like any of my own furnishings. It has a leather-like feel to it. A sticky vinyl texture that forces me to sit up.

I think about my medication, its side effects, the worry of being transported to hospital. A pain ricochets through my head, pounding behind my eyes and making me woozy as I shift about and move. Dust motes swirl in the dim light that is filtering in from a nearby window. A hand is placed on my arm, heavy fingers pressing me back down. Then a voice, soft and comforting.

'Don't try to sit up. You need to rest. The ambulance is on its way.'

Panic cuts me in half.

An ambulance. No hospital. No more doctors.

'I'm fine.'

I'm not fine. I feel anything but fine. Sickness swills in my stomach. My throat is tight and painful. My head hurts like hell. I am anything but fine but the last thing I want is to be taken away by a team of medics and ferried into the hospital where specialists will prod and poke at me, shining lights in my eyes and sticking needles in my arms, discussing what is best for me. Making decisions about my body and my illness when all I want is to just go home. I need to see Whisky, to let him out. He'll be ready for a feed and a walk. A lump is wedged at the back of my throat. Tears burn at my eyes. I visualise my cottage, the daylight slowly vanishing, leaving Whisky plunged into darkness, and want to open my mouth and scream that I need to be left alone.

'You need to rest up.' I recognise Alicia's voice, a quiet and gentle sound, reassuringly familiar in a frightening and unfamiliar place.

I feel her strength, the pressure of her fingers on my shoulders as she tries to pull me back into a lying position. I resist and carefully remove her hands, realising where I am.

'Honestly, I feel loads better.' As I'm saying it, the whole sorry debacle comes flooding back to me. I don't feel better but I do need to go home. 'My dog,' I say, swinging my legs off the makeshift couch I'm lying on. 'I need to take him out for a walk.' I think about the distance to where the hire car is parked on the other side of town. It's not far at all. I made it this morning in just over five minutes but with a swimming head and weak legs it may as well be on the other side of the world.

'I really think you should stay here and get checked over. That was quite a hit you took on your head when you passed out.' Alicia is next to me, watching my every move with wide concerned eyes, holding my arm when I wobble to my feet with as much grace and dignity as a baby elephant. Shame heats up my face, burning at my throat and ears with such ferocity I almost flop back down onto the recliner chair, the place they put me when I made such a fool of myself in front of so many people. I sigh and shut my eyes. I don't think I can bear to think about it.

'No, honestly. I really am okay. If I could just get a lift to my car, that would be helpful. My legs are still a bit shaky and I'm not sure I can walk there on my own.' I quickly add, 'But honestly, I'm really okay. I don't feel ill.'

She bites at her lip, then seeing how determined I am, relents, pasting a smile on her face. Poor Alicia. The consummate professional. Always helpful. Apart from when she receives telephone calls at home from a near-hysterical author. I swallow and run my fingers through my hair, wishing I was a million miles away. 'Of course! I'll get somebody to cover for me while I take you there. If you give me a minute, I'll cancel the ambulance and get my keys.'

Relief doesn't come close to how I'm feeling. No interference from hospital staff. Nobody asking me questions about my failing health and deciding whether I can go home on my own. Whether or not they deem me fit to leave even though I'm an adult and have full control of my faculties. Aside from the big black hole in my brain, that is. Aside from not knowing who I really am.

I glance around the room and spot my coat and bag laid on a desk. The floor feels insubstantial and springy under my feet when I stand up and walk over to where my things are placed. I need to put my mind at rest, to make sure that my brief moment of inelegance isn't already being talked about online. I'm aware that it makes me sound egotistical, that people don't have better things to do than spend their precious time chatting about me, a pathetic lonely old writer who dropped to the floor like a stone whilst doing a book-signing event in her local library, but until I can be certain that nothing has reached the papers, I won't be able to settle.

I turn on my iPad and scroll through the usual local news sites, perusing for anything that looks suspiciously like an article about me passing out in a public place, and thankfully see nothing. I'll check every couple of hours. The clock tells me that it only happened fifteen minutes ago. I shouldn't feel too relieved at the absence of the story just yet. There is still time for it appear. Local papers love stuff like this.

I continue browsing through the usual sites, relieved that nothing untoward jumps out at me. A feeling of release unfolds in my chest at not seeing my name mentioned. No stories or articles. No feeding frenzy at my expense. Not even a passing mention of an unnamed author falling into a swoon at the local library. My relief is short-lived. I click onto a national site for book reviews and see it there at the top, the most recent review for my novel. My name is above it in bold, the title of my latest book beneath, highlighted in yellow. Impossible to miss. And then the words underneath, each one like a knife slicing into my jugular. I feel like I'm bleeding out, my veins emptying, leaving me feeling weak and dizzy as I read each word.

The Memory Man by I. L. Lawrence

Well, what to say about this book? Where do I even begin? A story about a main character who suffers from memory loss and cannot remember murdering somebody. When the lines between fiction and reality become so blurred, then this is the result – a book that attempts to remove all culpability from the person who carried out the crime. Perhaps the author needs to take a long hard look at her own character, ask herself what it is she is hiding from. She needs to glance in the mirror and ask herself how she is so well versed in the minutiae of murder, knowing enough to actually make a living out of it. Not all writers are killers and not all killers can write a decent novel but in this case that is exactly what has happened. Step forward out of the shadows I. L. Lawrence and ask yourself what you did. Ask yourself why you use a pseudonym instead of your real name but more than that, ask yourself what you did. I think that maybe this book needs a different title, a more attention-grabbing one. How about this? *I'm Not the Murderer. You Are.*

I can't seem to breathe properly. Every bone, every muscle and sinew in my body feels as if they are vibrating. What the fuck is this? What the hell is going on here?

Already, half a dozen people have liked the post. My whole body is a heartbeat, my mind fogged up with terror. Who put this here? Which warped person did this to me? I look for a name but it's been done anonymously, under a silly alias with an avatar as a profile picture instead of a photo. I don't know why I'm even checking. Already, I know who wrote this libellous post.

Behind me, I hear a click followed by a creak. It's Alicia coming back into the room. I need to pull myself together, act normally and show her that nothing is amiss. Except I can't seem to control the shaking, my hands trembling like a leaf in the wind, my skin freezing cold.

'Really sorry to bother you, Alicia, but I don't suppose I can ask for a drink of something? Just an orange juice or something sugary to get my strength back.'

'Of course. I'll just be a minute.' Another bright smile, eyes sparkling with innocence.

She disappears again, scurrying away and closing the door behind her. I need more time to pull myself together. If she sees me like this, she will want to call an ambulance again and I can't let that happen. I'll be checked into a ward and pumped full of drugs when all I want to do is go home to the safety of my cottage where Whisky is waiting for me. I think of him snuggled up in his bed, his bladder beginning to twinge. Another reason for me to leave here as soon as possible. His needs are far greater than mine and way more important.

I put my iPad in my bag and get my things together ready to leave. The sooner I get out of here the better. Another creak of the door behind me once again alerts me to Alicia's arrival. She hands me a glass of orange juice. I thank her and take it, drinking it down thirstily then give her back the empty glass, surprised and pleased to see how still and controlled my hands and movements are. To an outsider I look like a normal woman in control of her emotions. That's not how I feel. I feel limp and useless, my legs weak when I stand and gather up my belongings, my head stuffed full of cotton wool.

'Here, give me those. I can carry them for you.'

Before I can protest, Alicia has taken my bag and has it slung over her shoulder with the practised ease of somebody half my age. Somebody who isn't troubled by any aches or pains or a debilitating disease that could incapacitate or possibly kill her.

'Right, let's get you back to your car. The long-stay one next to the church you said?'

She takes my arm as if I'm an old lady incapable of walking properly. I don't shrug her off. It does feel rather comforting to have somebody by my side helping me. My pride is screaming at me to push her away but my aching body is telling me to keep her close, take as much help as I can.

There are so many questions I want to ask as we walk along together out of the library and down the main road that leads to the car park, like who helped me up? Who laid me out on the recliner chair in the staff room? How long was I unconscious for? I want to ask if Alicia spotted Chalk White Woman, but more importantly, I really want to question her to see if she knew the lady who whispered those dreadful words in my ear that caused me to fall into a swoon, those awful cutting words.

Ask yourself what you did.

In the end, I don't say anything. It's all too raw. Too recent. I'll save it for another day, maybe give her a call or better still, send an email. Put some distance between us. I'm not sure I'm in the right frame of mind for her replies. I need to brace myself, be prepared and ready to digest her answers. Because if once again, she claims to have not seen anybody, then I won't know what to think.

'Right,' she says softly. 'We'll head out to the car park out the back. It's only a short walk but let me know if you need to stop for a rest.' She turns and smiles at me. 'And don't you dare collapse on me again. My first aid certificate may just lapse on purpose if I have to deal with anything like that again. My heart was in my mouth seeing you lying there like that.'

I return the smile, unsure how to respond.

'And I don't know who or what you were calling out for but you soon stopped once we moved you to the back room.'

My blood stills. I stop walking and try to appear unperturbed by what she has just said.

'Calling out?' I laugh, my voice hollow and contrived.

'Yes. I couldn't quite make out the name but it sounded something like Eena.' She stops and taps at my hand. 'Anyway,' she says, her grip on my arm tightening as if I might try to escape from her clutches, 'it doesn't really matter. As long as you're okay. That's the main thing, isn't it?'

'Yes, I suppose so,' I reply, the words I say disconnected from my body, a ghostly sound that booms in my head, a distant memory looming in my mind, an ethereal hazy thing that is just out of reach. 'That's the main thing. As long as I'm okay.'

26

It was a thing of beauty, seeing her fall like that. Being able to stand so close while she collapsed onto the floor in an ungainly heap. The fact she hit her head when she went down was a real bonus – the icing on the cake. It was everything I could have hoped for. She always was a little too dramatic for my liking. Some things never change. A small bruise is all she will have when she wakes in the morning. A small bruise and the memory of what I said to her. Those words that I whispered into her ear, a delicious barbed phrase that I've had stored up in my head for months and months. I hope it's firmly fixed in her brain, chiselled right in there, and I hope she now realises that I'm not going to go away. I only wish I could know whether she has seen the review. It's been a slow build up but I feel like I'm finally starting to get the message across. By now, she must know who I am, why I'm doing what I'm doing. Her face, the look in her eyes showed nothing when I was standing right next to her. I refuse to believe she doesn't know who I am. But then, I've gone to great lengths to change my appearance. I suppose I should count it as a positive, the fact she hasn't recognised me. If she doesn't know who I am then it's highly unlikely anybody else will remember me. I won't spend so much time terrified I'm going to be outed, my face pasted all over the internet and labelled as a deranged murderous psychopath. I'm none of those things. I made a mistake and I've paid for it a thousand times over. What I am is angry. And she needs to know that.

I have to say, I'm impressed with the numbers she draws in at her talks. There's no denying she has done well for herself. I imagine her wealth will be extensive. Large cottages in the woods don't come cheap. The fact that it's remote only adds to its appeal. Not so far from the main roads but far enough to leave everything behind. To hide away and pretend she is somebody else, not that young girl from a small town in the north east where money was short, tempers often frayed and children were hungry.

If she hasn't already woken up to the fact that I'm about to expose old wounds, to watch her bleed to death in public, then maybe she isn't as intelligent as we all think she is. But I'm too far down this path to put a halt to it all now. I might not have a plan for how this will end but I do know that there will **be** an end. I'm not stopping until everyone knows the truth of what happened that day. Ideas will come to me. I'm on a roll now. I refuse to go through this alone any more. Carrying the burden of blame for all these years has been a long and lonely road, the weight of it pressing me deep into the ground. I'm old before my years, the lines on my skin, the grey hairs that I regularly cover with hair dye, a constant reminder that my life has been tough. I'd like to share some of that worry and angst with her, to let her know how it's been for me. Giving her that scar on her face wasn't enough. I thought it would stem my anger and resentment. I thought it would alleviate the hatred I feel for her, but it hasn't. I want more.

27

The world feels like a dark and lonely place when I awake the following morning, the room too big for my bed, the bed too big for just me. Having a partner to share things with has never been my goal but at times like this, it feels as if there is an emotional void in my life, something more than my missing memory. A person-sized hole that needs filling. Somebody to share my troubles with. Somebody who would simply listen, ease my worries, and let me know that I'm never truly alone. She would know all about my problems. I would talk to her about my lack of memory, the constant nagging worry I have that somebody is stalking me, trying to unnerve me, pushing me off balance and then standing by to watch me fall.

And fall I did. Publicly. I rub at my head, my fingers gently tracing over a lump on the side of my skull that is hidden beneath my hair. It hurts like hell but at least I'm here, at home in my own bed, with an egg-sized protrusion on my head and nursing a huge dent to my pride. I'll mend.

Alicia's words were firmly in my mind when I first woke up. What I said while unconscious. Who or what is Eena? I shake my head. It's probably nothing. Just a collection of sounds with no meaning. It certainly doesn't resonate with me, it's no more than an utterance from a semi-conscious woman who had passed out and was rambling wildly.

I take a bath and get dressed then carry my usual breakfast of toast and coffee through to my study. Only one slice and half a cup. Anything more would be too much for my still queasy stomach. A sickness swirls in the base of my belly when I think about Chalk White Woman. Sickness when I think of the other lady, the one who whispered those words in my ear, but most of all a deep fathomless sickness that makes me shaky and fearful when I recall the things that entered my head last night while I slept. Bit by bit, it feels like it's all coming together; fragments of my broken memory finally finding their rightful place and slotting back into position to form a complete picture of the jigsaw puzzle that is my disparate shattered life. They're connected, the two women. I know that now. I should have known it from the start. I don't know how I know they're connected; perhaps it's common sense telling me so, or perhaps it's a real and solid memory, pushing my brain in a certain direction, making me think in a way that will help me get to the truth.

She was there in my dream – the woman from the library, as was Chalk White Woman, her pale skin almost translucent under the unabating glare of the burning sun. Except it wasn't a dream. I woke up with the memory still in my mind. It was as real as my other thoughts, a vivid inscription embedded deep into my subconscious. We were standing shoulder to shoulder by a stretch of water. I was overcome by a desperate need to run away. I had no idea why I felt that way, I just knew that I had to go. She spoke to me, Chalk White Woman, her voice not the soft flowing sound I had expected but a caustic grating command that made the hairs on the back of my neck stand on end. She told me I had to follow her, which I did. We walked into a house and almost immediately, I could smell something that made me want to retch. An overpowering metallic smell. I just knew that I had to run – to get away from the place as quickly as I could. Except I didn't. I stayed, waiting there in the darkness, my heart galloping about in my chest. A huge swinging metronome helping to keep the rhythm of my breathing and every beat of my heart in synch. There were other people there too but it was too dark to see their faces clearly, just an eerie presence that made me nervous and agitated.

When I woke up, the sensation of being there with them was so real, I felt as if I could hear the low rasp of their collective gasps, was able to reach out and touch them, my fingers meeting with their cold flesh. It happened. I know it. I was a child and it was one of the becks or streams I saw on the map. Something happened there. Something hideous and terrifying.

My fingers type furiously. I search online for clues using the name of the town and the words, *beck, stream, children* and *crime,* plus the nearby areas of Ormesby and Marton, in case it was farther afield.

Nothing matches. The internet throws up recent articles from local newspapers about anti-social behaviour from young kids hanging around the area. I add the words, *woods, house,* and am presented with endless sites of properties for sale. I try again, starting afresh with the keywords, *children, crime, water, woods, murder,* and then the name of the town.

A story flashes up from 1976. A write-up of a crime that shocked and horrified both the locals and the nation at large. My eyes skim over the text, looking for images. There is only one photograph and a black-and-white image of a young stick-thin girl with short dark hair and pale skin. I study her features, trying to see something that will kickstart my memory. Something that will spark some life in my useless malfunctioning brain. Nothing. I read the article, my eyes blurring over. It's horrific. This cannot be it. It just can't. This event is too disgusting for words. I could not have been involved in something like that. It simply isn't possible.

A tic pulses at the side of my face beneath my eye. I swallow, rotate my jaw and press at the side of my cheek to stem it, then slam my laptop closed before tentatively opening it again. I use the same keywords then add my real name into the search bar. Relief doesn't come close to how I'm feeling when my name isn't recognised. I read the article in full, hardly able to breathe, disgusted at how such a thing could happen. And yet it did. And although I daren't admit it, even to myself, I think that somehow, I may have been involved. One young girl went to prison, her face shown to the public, the judge believing it was in the national interest to reveal her identity. I say it out loud – Heather Elizabeth Oswald. Does it mean anything to me? I'm not sure. Perhaps. Or perhaps not. The setting fits the image I have in my brain, the one that haunts my dreams – next to a stream in the woods. But had I been there at this awful crime, would I not have evidence of it in my home? Or was I so ashamed and disgusted that I discarded anything that linked me to it. That's what most people would do. It's what innocent, horrified people would do. And I do feel horrified and I am almost certain that I am innocent.

I sit for a short while, staring out of the window, trying to bleach that dreadful story out of my head. I feel dirty, the content of the article clinging to my flesh and seeping into my pores. I push my laptop away, as if it's contaminated. I wanted to remember my past and now that it's finally coming back to me, I don't want it. If I could, I would reach inside my brain and pluck it all back out.

Seconds pass, turning into minutes as I sit, looking at nothing in particular. I should focus on my writing but my brain is devoid of ideas. Too many distractions. Too many other horrors taking up space where my thoughts and concepts should be. I can't think which route my current story should take anyway. It feels pointless sitting here, waiting for something momentous to happen. Waiting for inspiration. I grab Whisky's lead and clip it onto his harness. A walk will help, blowing away the cobwebs. Emptying my mind of the sordid details I've just read.

'Come on, old boy. Let's go for an amble in the woods.'

The wind is brisk, the rain still coming down in spurts but the weather is less ferocious than yesterday when it did its utmost to break into the library, unnerving people and hammering at the windows and skylight, small wet fists relentlessly beating at the glass.

I pull up my hood and tighten it around my face with the drawstring to stay warm. Whisky hates dog coats which isn't surprising. He's a big dog with plenty of fur to keep off the chill. I ruffle his ears. He'll be fine.

I pat at my coat pocket, feeling out of sorts without my phone to hand. Silly really. People managed quite nicely before we had mobile phones. I shrug and set off, determined to walk off my breakfast and get my strength back after yesterday's embarrassing occurrence. I'll plod on and lose myself amongst the foliage, pretend me and my dog are the only living creatures around. Just me and Whisky, safe in our own little patch, our very own corner of paradise.

I've only taken seven or eight steps when I hear it – the distinctive crackle of disturbed gravel. It's coming from round the back of my cottage, the rhythmic *crunch, crunch, crunch* an immediate giveaway. I steel myself, ready to confront whoever is skulking there. It's too early for the postman and I'm not expecting any deliveries.

My throat is constricted, my fists curled at my sides by the time the offender emerges; their face tucked away inside a dark deep hood.

'Can I help you?'

The hood is pulled down and a bedraggled-looking Alicia

heads my way, her hair mussed up and glasses sprayed with rain. I'm torn between feeling relief and being angry at her for making me anxious and twitchy. I envisioned an intruder or perhaps that awful woman from last time, but while I'm going over all of those things in my head, I am also thinking one thing, a notion full of sharp corners and serrated edges – how does Alicia know where I live?

'Hi! Sorry, I parked around the back as there was more space there. I hope you don't mind?' She doesn't wait for my reply, continuing instead with her prepared spiel. 'I just wanted to check that you're okay. We were all really worried about you and since I was passing this way to drop off some leaflets at Whitby library, I thought I'd call in, see how you were getting on.'

She holds out a scarf: my grey and turquoise satin wrap. 'You also left this behind. It must have fallen off when—'

'Ah,' I whisper, because I can't think of what else to say. 'Thank you.' I take it from her, the memory of passing out in the middle of the library, utterly mortifying.

She stops and bites at her lip, watching me closely, as if I'm made of glass and about to explode into a million pieces.

'Thank you. And thanks for yesterday – for driving me to my car and helping me out. I couldn't have managed without you.'

She dips her head and removes her glasses to wipe them dry, eyelashes fluttering, small drops of rain landing on them like tiny crystals. 'It's no problem at all. I hope you're feeling better today.'

'I am, thank you. Just off for a walk with my trusty old pal.' I look down at Whisky who is sitting patiently by my side waiting for me to finish my unplanned conversation, the rain doing little to dampen his enthusiasm for foraging in the woods. His tongue is lolling out, his eyes fixed on the trees ahead of us.

'Ah, okay. He's a big lad, isn't he?' There is fear in her stance as she watches him, anxiety at his lumbering frame stamped all over her face. She takes a few steps back and shoves her hands in her pockets. 'I'll let you get on with your dog walking then. He looks like he's all ready to go.'

I feel Whisky move as he stands up and pulls on his leash, his head angled away from us, towards the trees and the darkness beyond.

'Right. Thank you again, Alicia. For everything.'

She smiles and begins walking away.

'Just one thing, Alicia.'

When she stops and swings around to stare at me, I can't decide whether her eyes are narrowed against the rain or narrowed at me, glinting with suspicion at what she thinks I'm about to say. I wait. She shivers, her shoulders hunched over, spine curved into a narrow ridge.

'Do you want to come inside for a coffee?'

Coffee isn't the reason I'm asking her to come into my house. It's a gradual introduction, a way of softening her up, keeping her sweet if I am to get the truth out of her.

'I really need to get back.' She sounds determined. And yet she has stopped walking. Not so sure of herself after all.

'The rain's getting heavier. Why don't you wait until it eases up? That road up to the top is a bugger in this weather, full of potholes.'

The holes have never bothered me in bad weather but Alicia isn't to know that.

'What about your dog? I thought he was ready for his walk?'

I glance down at Whisky, guilt rippling through me. 'He can wait. I'll let him have a run around the back garden on his own. We'll go out later once the rain eases up.'

There's a short silence, just a few seconds, and yet it feels like an age before she responds.

'Well, if it's not too much trouble?' She spins around and holds her upturned palms towards the grey, cloud covered sky. 'I'll head off once this downpour clears up. I've left Charlie on his own in the library. The local primary school are visiting this afternoon and we need to prepare so I don't want to be gone for too long.'

I smile at her and shrug my shoulders. 'Just one coffee. I'll need to walk this old chap at some point anyway and then settle down to some writing.'

We walk together to the front door like old friends. I unlock it and step inside. Whisky brushes past me closely followed by Alicia who sidesteps him, her fear of dogs now plain to see.

'Come on through to the kitchen and take a seat.' My smile feels forced when I catch her eye, my voice taking on an ethereal quality, as if there is somebody else inside my head directing my speech, forcing out the question I'm about to ask. 'And I might even be able to stretch to a slice of cake. Chocolate and raspberry sound okay to you?'

She nods, her shoulders dropping when she takes off her coat and lowers herself into the chair. 'It sounds perfect, thank you.'

I pour us both a cup of coffee each and lift the cover off the cake.

'Shop bought, I'm afraid but tasty as hell. And it'll give you enough energy for dealing with those schoolkids this afternoon.'

She laughs and watches me cut into the sponge, buttercream and scarlet jam spilling out of the sides. I hand her a slice and cut a smaller piece for me.

'So,' I say softly, sitting down opposite her, 'it's really kind of you to come all this way to bring back my scarf. You definitely caught me on the back foot because my address is a closely guarded secret, so I have to ask, Alicia, and please don't think me rude or take this the wrong way, but how did you find out where I live?'

Her attempt at covering up her shock at my question is futile. She tries, bless her, the white lies pouring out of her in a hot rush, telling me how she just somehow knew and that it was probably on their system or maybe it was on the bottom of my email. I don't stop her, letting her ramble until she eventually runs out of steam, her face flushed, her fingers trembling when she pushes her plate away, thanking me for the cake. I watch her swallow repeatedly, the lump in her throat bobbing up and down, her eyes fluttering like the wings of a small bird about to take flight.

'I really need to get back. Charlie is new and he isn't quite sure how to...'

Alicia makes no disguise of her need to make a hasty retreat and I don't try to stop her. We both know she is lying. We both know that she has been caught out and is desperate to flee from both the house and this horribly uncomfortable situation, but neither of us says anything. Instead, we nod and smile politely, waiting in silence as she pulls on her boots and trudges back out into the rain.

I won't get the truth out of her at this juncture, and now isn't the time to push it any further, but I will find out. One way or another, I will find out. My home is my sanctuary, the only place I feel completely safe in a changing and often turbulent world. Alicia is the second person who has found her way here in a matter of weeks. The second person who has arrived on my doorstep uninvited. And after yesterday's troubles, I'm going to make sure she is definitely the last.

28

She was lying at the bottom of the stairs, her walking cane swishing about in the air, thin fingers clasped around it like a bird's claws curled around a perch, her yellowed nails hanging onto it for grim life. It cut through the air like a whip, the long wooden stick, now being used as a weapon as it caught Irena on the side of the head. A sudden yelp. The hit broke the skin, blood running down her face, long red rivulets dripping onto her shoulder and soaking into the fabric.

'Bitch!' Irena staggered back, palm pressed to her cheek, stream of expletives filling the air of the dim dusty hallway. 'You fucking mad old bitch!'

'Get me up, our Les.' The old woman held out her free hand, the underside of her palm creased and dry as parchment, deep grooves running the length of it from forefinger to wrist. 'I slipped down the last few steps. Think I might have broken something.' She was unperturbed by the situation and the fact that her stick connected with Irena's face, her voice calm and measured as she spoke.

'Here, let me help you, Nana. Take my arm.'

Heather watched it unfold in cinematic clarity, their actions dulled and sloppy as if in slow motion. Her insides leapt when she detected a movement to her right. Irena stepped forward, standing ominously in the shadows, visible only to Heather; fire in her eyes, ice in her expression.

'Come on, Nan. Let's get you a nice cup of something warm for the shock. It's just bruises, I think. Nothing broken.' Blood was smeared over Lesley's face, her nose swollen and red as she tried to get her grandmother up off the floor.

Heather watched a large ruby globule fall from one of Lesley's nostrils onto the floor, splattering and spreading out into a shiny ragged orb. She thought of star shapes, red lipstick. Death.

'Oh my God, our Les. What happened to your face, eh? Who hit you?'

'Come on. Let's just go home, get out of here and forget about all of this.' It was something to say to break the moment. Heather's voice was reedy, her desperation to negate all responsibility, obvious to even the most dim-witted.

She didn't have to turn to see Lesley's eyes on her. She could feel the burn of the gaze, the heat of it travelling up over her arms and neck. A wave of hatred resting somewhere just above her jaw.

'Nothing, Nana. I fell, that's all it is. I'll be fine. Let's get you sorted instead, shall we?'

'I don't think so.' Irena's obtrusive statuesque form filled the space between them. Two long strides and she managed to wedge herself between Heather who stood motionless, and Lesley and her nana, two small figures who were huddled together on the floor, their limbs working feverishly as Lesley tried to haul the old lady upright.

'I need to get her up. Can I have some light around the place, please?'

Heather winced. Either Lesley was too absorbed with the task of lifting her grandmother up off the floor to see the obvious, or she was being clever, ignoring Irena's acerbic tone. Heather couldn't decide which and waited for the fallout, fists clenched hard, her ragged nails digging into her palms. Because there would be a follow on from this, an aggressive riposte from Irena. A toxic comeback. That's how she was. The leader. Answerable to nobody.

The dull scrape as the walking stick was snatched out of the old lady's hand and dragged along the floor turned Heather's skin cold, the hairs on the back of her neck standing on end. She knew what came next, could see it before it happened – the swish of the length of thin, yet hefty wood as it cut through the air, the dull thud when it connected with flesh and bone – the vision she had in her head as bad as anything she would ever see. Except it wasn't. It didn't come close. The scream came before the hit. Or maybe they both happened together, a collision of sounds. A clashing collective of pain and horror. And then the broken flesh and thick syrupy blood that pooled on the floor.

Heather stood, frozen. Unable to do anything except breathe. *In, out. In, out. In, out.* Blood pounded in her ears. Her head throbbed. It was a battle to force herself out of her torpor, her limbs finally catapulting into motion, cartoon-character style, hands clutching at nothing but air while the cane swished about over her head, coming down across Lesley's back, the sound it made, the breeze that tickled the back of her neck as it passed close to her, making Heather retch. Her chest convulsed. She swallowed, hands flailing, fingers suddenly wooden and semi-dextrous while trying to grab the cane out of Irena's hands.

Beneath her, two bodies writhed, arms and legs snaking about in a puddle of blood. Her own feet slipped and slid, becoming tangled with Irena's, their legs suddenly entwined, their bodies suctioned together, arms raised high above their heads, the long cane held in the air just out of Heather's reach.

No time to think or to plan. To be rational or thoughtful. Another hit, this time with greater force. She tried to look down, to see who had taken the blow, check to make sure they were still alive but out of nowhere a hand grabbed at her ankle, knocking her off balance and onto the floor. She landed on her knees, palms spread out to try to break her fall. The blood beneath her hands was warm and sticky, the bodies below her, wet and bony. Bile rose. She gulped it down, a trail of burning acid that snaked past her gullet and into her stomach. A pair of eyes stared at her. Rheumy fish eyes, unseeing. Unmoving. A quick blink; thin sparse lashes fluttering. She recoiled, scrambling away, the damp slimy surface hindering her escape. She was still alive. The old woman was still alive.

Then the whack that knocked everything out of her, her lungs shrinking, reduced to two pinheads as she gasped for air. Stars burst behind her eyes, a flare of pain that ricocheted up and down her spine, each nodule, each disc popping and exploding beneath her freezing flesh.

The fingers holding her leg pulled tighter. A hiss in her ear.

'Get it off her. She's going to kill us both if you don't.'

Heather scrambled up, a rush of adrenalin masking her pain, injecting a flash of energy into her ailing body. She could do this. She could grab at that walking stick, wrench it out of Irena's strong hands. Make her stop. Make *this* stop, this violence. This growing insanity.

Blood swilled at her feet, so much of it. Too much. Sticky and slippery as she tried to get her balance. A metallic meaty smell rose, circling and swirling, a thick fog of it filling her nostrils, lining her throat and gums. She gagged. Her tongue felt thick and swollen. She ran it around her mouth, swallowing down her terror, trying to stem the rising nausea.

The floor swayed and tilted; her head swam. The walking cane.

She needed to grab it, hide it. Break it in half if she could. Anything to stop Irena. Anything to stop this sickening scenario. She rose to her feet phoenix-like, standing on her tiptoes, arms outstretched, fingers almost touching it. And then a push, a hand from below shoving her forwards, closer to Irena. They toppled, she and Irena, the cane still firmly encased in Irena's tight fist as she fell. Heather turned, staring at Lesley, at the hand behind the push, at Lesley's wide-eyed expression, unable to determine whether it was innocence and panic that had made her do it, or whether it was sheer bloody-mindedness and retribution for their earlier fracas and her subsequent injured nose. Lesley's beautiful alabaster skin was still splattered with spots of crimson blood. Heather's foot was made of concrete as she kicked back at Lesley, a sharp thrust to inflict more damage. She had been so close to grabbing that stick and now she was lying on the floor, the four of them locked together in a messy heap, gluey pools of dark fluid hindering her progress. They were swimming in it.

'Stupid cow! I nearly had it then. I nearly had hold of that walking stick!' She felt her heel connect with something solid, the satisfying thud of her rubber sole hitting the side of Lesley's face and then the soft vibration of a vacuum of air being created as Lesley rolled away before clambering to her feet and disappearing out of the door leaving the old woman on the floor, her skeletal frame resembling nothing more than a pile of old bones.

Two voices merged. A cacophonous screech as Irena and Heather hollered for her to come back, screaming insults at her. A moan from the old woman. She was still alive. Heather watched, chest compressed with dread as the near-lifeless bag of bones reached forwards and sank her teeth into Irena's ankle. A rustle of clothing as Irena pulled away and dragged herself upright, walking stick held aloft over the old woman, her face twisted into a grimace, eyes dark with fury. Floorboards creaked and groaned. Heather could hear the rush of her own blood as it swelled in her veins, hurtling up her neck and roaring in her ears. Later that day, when the police arrived at Heather's door, she would question how differently things would have turned out had she feigned injury, just stayed immobile and unmoving. But she didn't. One more swish of that stick and the old woman would die. She could feel it in her bones, could see it in her mind's eye. One more swish of that stick and *she* could die. The glint in Irena's eye made her flesh wither, compelling her to move. She couldn't recall her shift in position. It was instinctive. A desperate act of self-preservation but before she could think properly, she was on her feet, grappling for that walking cane, the angle of it low enough for her to snatch it out of Irena's grasp. The angle of it too low, their combined strength forcing it downwards closer to the old lady's face. Only when Irena finally relented and let go did it happen – the snapping of the wood, the splintering of it, Heather falling forwards and the final blow, that hideous final moment when the shattered sharp end was driven into the old woman's face, Heather's fingers still clasped tightly around the makeshift weapon, her fingerprints determining her future, exposing her part in the crime.

Then a deadly silence, the lack of anything human coming from the body that was lying at her feet; that was the thing that propelled her towards Irena, her body catapulting to where the taller girl was standing, her face expressionless.

'You did this! This is all your fault. She's dead and you murdered her!'

A crooked smile. Then, 'I wasn't the one who killed her. You did it. I wasn't even holding the stick when it happened. This is all your fault.' Irena's voice was calm, a whisper almost, any panic she may have been feeling, cleverly concealed. Any regret or empathy she may have been feeling, absent.

A roar from behind. A flash of somebody rushing past then a

scuffle and a crash as Lesley grabbed at Irena's legs and pulled her to the floor, dragging her by the ankles towards the open doorway behind them as if possessed by a superhuman strength. The strength of the furious. The strength of somebody bereaved.

By the time Heather left the house to track them, they were both thrashing about next to the stream, their limbs locked together in a struggle.

'Stop it! Both of you just stop it!'

No response from either girl, their minds angled towards vengeance, their faces lowered towards the ground.

The darkness from inside the house crept out, wrapping itself around Heather's throat, tightening and tightening until she couldn't breathe properly. Her neck was hot, her temperature feverish. Sweat ran down the side of her face, gathering between her shoulder blades and running down her back. The shrieking from the stream continued. A scream to the side of her then a sudden splash of water. And something else. Gurgling. Somebody struggling underwater, unable to catch their breath. The sound of somebody who was drowning.

She couldn't remember running across to where they were, time losing all meaning, her actions, her mind out of kilter, limbs and thoughts working against each other in an uncoordinated frenzy, but found herself at the water's edge all the same, witness to the spectacle of the two females caught up in a fight, water spraying around them, their saturated clothes clinging to their bodies, features contorted with anger.

Irena's face was a blur beneath the stream, her body bucking as she fought for air, Lesley's hands holding her down under the water. She was already dead by the time Heather knocked Lesley aside and dragged Irena out and onto the patch of grass. Except she wasn't. She was still very much alive. Her eyes sprang open, a scream ringing out that reminded Heather of the death throes of a

wild animal gasping its last. It pierced the warm summer air. It
drowned out the sound of the birdsong. It deadened the rush of
water that glided over the pebbles beneath their feet. She needed it
to stop, that scream. She had to do something. Inside that house
was a dead body. People would hear. They would come running to
see what was going on. She just wanted to stop the noise, that was
all it was. She just wanted it to stop.

29

We're close now. So close to the moment of discovery. So close to her realising what is going on. But we're not there yet. Not quite. I lay awake last night, thinking about what comes next, the sacrifice I'm going to have to make to let her know that she ruined my life that day down by the stream. I will gain a sense of triumph – that goes without saying – but I also risk losing somebody I love dearly. And I don't want to lose that person so I have to come to a decision about how I'm going to approach it. How I'm going to make sure she knows who I am without her blowing my cover, revealing to everyone who I really am. The person I used to be. I've thought about it a lot over the past few nights and each time, have come to the same conclusion. I've pondered over it again and again and again, picking it apart and dissecting it, studying it in great detail and the conclusion is this – I am going to kill her. May as well be hanged for a sheep as for a lamb. All those years spent behind bars. I may as well do something worthy of those years that were taken from me. The years she spent wandering freely, building up a decent life for herself while I was incarcerated, being forced to shed my old skin and emerge as another person. An embittered resentful person. Prison didn't rehabilitate me. It soured me. Made me vengeful and hateful.

Ending her is the only way out of this mess. And all I have to do is make sure I do it without leaving any incriminating evidence. A clean murder. That's what I'm going to do. End it all for her and slip away unnoticed. Not like last time on that country lane when it was messy and unintentional. This time I will mean it. It will be pre-meditated, a sort of atonement for that summer when an accident turned into a murder and I was left to pick up the pieces. I've killed before. I can do it again.

I need to time it, to get everything just right. Preparation is the key to success and all that. Her dog already knows me. He recognises my scent and has taken a shine to me so isn't likely to set off barking when I make my approach.

The last time I checked, there were over a hundred likes for my comment online about her books being close to her real life. Nobody really knows who she is but everybody loves a bit of scandal, don't they? All those people sitting there in the safety of their homes, wedged behind their keyboards, enjoying watching somebody being dragged down, their life exposed and torn apart while they sit and salivate, relieved it isn't happening to them. The negative comments always outweigh the positive ones. It's just how it is. It's how people are – mean and spiteful while painting on a smile and pretending they care about one another. I've learned that particular lesson the hard way, been on the receiving end of it and it's now time to turn the tables, let her see how it feels to be on the bottom rung of the ladder, desperately trying to work your way up while attempting to escape the kicks that are aimed at you in a bid to stop you rising to the top.

I'm nervous. Of course I am. Murder is a huge step. The biggest. And after all, I'm just an ordinary woman trying to live an ordinary life against all the odds. I'm not a monster. But as I've already said, I've done it before. The first one is the most difficult. It gets easier after that. Or so I've heard. And anyway, all I'm doing is evening things up; redressing a balance that has been asymmetrical for far too long. Only then will I be able to sit back and really feel as if my life is back on track, safe in the knowledge that the person who has fuelled my bitterness and held me back for all these years is finally dead.

30

SUMMER OF 1976

Heather felt herself being pushed aside, Lesley's slim body knocking her into the water, her face hitting the sharp edge of a rock. She could feel its rough angular contours, the cragginess of its surface as it tore at her skin, grazing and cutting her cheek and damaging the thin flesh beneath her eye. A trail of pink flowed past. Her eyes were drawn to it. It reminded her of a length of ribbon, the line of her own smoky blood twisting and turning before gradually fading and disappearing altogether. Then she felt the sharp sting that ran up and down the side of her face, the cool water doing little to stem the burst of pain. She scrambled to her feet, the surprising power of the stream slowing her down, weighting her feet to the silt at the bottom and weakening her. The throb that took hold on the side of her face made her dizzy, sapping her strength and slowing her down. She didn't like being injured or unable to defend herself but it hurt so much, the intensity of the wound making her eyes water and her nose run. She ran a hand over her face to clear away the tears and snot, sniffing loudly and stifling a sob.

Next to where Heather was standing, body bent over, hands

outstretched whilst she attempted to steady herself, Irena continued to roar. As if driven by an invisible force, Lesley grabbed hold of Irena's sodden hair and pulled her head backwards before lunging herself at Heather, Irena's wet hair still bunched up in her fist.

'You killed my nana. You both fucking well murdered her!'

A bolt of lightning spiralled from one side of Heather's skull to the other, white-hot rage combusting inside her brain and soaring through her veins. The pain of her bashed cheek receded, nudged aside by a tidal wave of anger at Lesley's accusation.

Body still bent double, Heather retaliated and launched herself at Lesley, sending Irena careening off to one side, her taller frame making a splash before disappearing under the water. Staggering as if drunk, Lesley's limbs flailed and flapped, her legs rubbery and lacking rigidity as she tried to right herself. Another push and she fell backwards on top of Irena's submerged body, their spines fused together by the water, the weight of Lesley's sodden clothes rendering her a lead weight on top of the other girl.

The rough twine of anger that was tightly bound around Heather's skull refused to loosen itself. Even the sight of Irena's struggling body locked beneath Lesley's did little to lessen her fury. Viewing it all as if from behind a pane of glass, her unbridled anger was unleashed. Jaw locked and teeth clamped firmly together, Heather threw herself down on top of both girls, all three bodies sucked lower into the water, their collective mass pressed awkwardly on the gathering of rocks at the bottom of the stream.

At some point, Irena's limbs fell still, her lungs and vital organs succumbing to the weight of both bodies, but the heft of Heather's fury blinded her to it. She would plead later that she didn't know, that she hadn't realised the enormity of her actions, how her childish need to vent her rage had become an all-encompassing emotion, obliterating everything else. Her defence would claim that after years of starvation, mental abuse and neglect, her survival instincts took hold and that she wasn't responsible for her actions that day and shouldn't be held to account in the same way an adult would, that she had acted out of ignorance and fear. But it didn't matter how many arguments they put forward, how hard they pleaded, asking for clemency and understanding due to her impoverished background, her destiny, her future was carved out that day by the stream.

Somehow, despite the force of Heather's anger, despite the bulk and velocity of it, Lesley was able to squirm out from underneath her, wriggling and twisting until she was free and wading out of the water. Heather watched, lungs burning, as Lesley broke into a run after clambering up onto the dry grass before disappearing altogether into the nearby woods. The sight of Lesley's shadowy figure lumbering out of view and the sensation of Irena's slim unmoving body beneath her own dulled Heather's anger, a sickening realisation dragging her back to reality, forcing her back into the cold unforgiving harsh present where two dead bodies lay. One of them pressed under the water and down onto the layer of stones and rocks by her own flesh and bones, and the other lying on the floor of the nearby dilapidated cottage, her sagging flesh now cold and lifeless, her own splintered walking stick protruding from her face.

And Heather was left with it all, with the horror and the blood and the inescapable awareness that she would be held to blame even though it was an accident. That's what it was – a horrible accident. A terrible mistake. It was Lesley who fell onto Irena. She was the one who started all of this, dragging Irena out here into the stream. It wasn't just Heather. She didn't do this alone.

Her mind raced, flesh both hot and cold with fear and fury. She could run away, take herself off up into the hills, eat leaves and berries and drink from the small rivulets that ran down the side of the rocks. She would sleep beneath the trees and cover herself with foliage. It was warm enough. Who needed a bed when the weather was this dry and hot? Besides, her bedroom was hardly a conducive place to rest her head with its mould-covered walls and filthy stinking sheets. Outside would suit her just fine. Anything was better than what she knew would lie ahead for her. The beating she would get from her mam and dad. The relentless name-calling and slaps and kicks that would come her way. All because of what happened down here by this stream. All because she didn't turn and leave.

The water made barely a ripple when she backed out of it, her eyes lifted heavenward, gaze averted from the sight of Irena's life-less body. Maybe it would float away. If she gave it a push, it might just vanish and never be seen again. It happened. People drowned and their bodies were never found. She'd read about it in the news-papers, seen it on the TV. There were ways and means of making sure Irena disappeared forever.

Rocks.

Sometimes bodies were weighed down with rocks to stop them bobbing around on the surface. If she stuffed Irena's pockets full of rocks and stones and pebbles – anything heavy she could find – it would drag her body deeper and deeper and people would just think that Irena had run away, gone to London like teenagers sometimes do to find a better life for herself. She was the type to do it. It wouldn't be so out of character for her. Irena was confident and sassy. Heather could visualise her getting the bus from Middlesbrough to a place farther south, then hitching rides from town to town, navigating her way around the big cities with ease, chatting to strangers like they were old friends. By the time the police had scoured the nearby area and checked to see if anybody had seen her on public transport, her body would have been carried downstream and be on its way out to sea.

The fist of anxiety that had been clutched tightly around

Heather's throat loosened. She gasped, sucking in air until she was able to breathe properly again. She had a plan, a way of getting out of this. If Lesley told anybody what really happened, she would laugh it off, tell them she was being stupid, that Irena had got up out of the water after Lesley left and walked away and that that was the last Heather had seen of her. She would say that Irena was embarrassed by what had taken place – being overpowered by her two less well off, socially inept friends – and that she had probably disappeared because of it. That line would carry some weight. Everybody knew that Irena was the leader of their gang, the cool one. The person who never ever wanted to lose face.

Scrambling around for anything small and dense, her hands sweeping the bottom of the stream, Heather gathered up a small pile of pebbles and stones. There wasn't enough to weigh anybody down. She needed more. A large rock, something that would drag Irena to the bottom of the water, make sure she was never seen again. Heather's knees hurt, the welt on her face a hot streak of pain when she bent down at the water's edge and swept her arms backwards and forwards, dredging and sifting. Her fingers clawed and grasped at anything solid, eventually coming up with half a brick. It could work. All she had to do was stuff it into Irena's pocket and she would sink to the bottom, her dead, staring eyes sinking beneath the surface. That was the worst part, the part of this task that made her feel as if her chest was being squeezed by a hundred pairs of hands, fingers bent into tight claws as they clasped and kneaded at her heart. She didn't want to turn Irena over. She didn't want to have to look at her pale face and those lifeless eyes but she needed to get the brick into her pocket, push it deep in so there was no chance of it ever coming out. She took a couple of deep breaths, trying to prepare herself. All of a sudden, she felt horribly sweaty and anxious. It was as if an army of angry ants were crawling under her skin, a million of them scurrying and darting beneath her flesh. They bit and nipped when she reached forwards and pulled at Irena's clothes, searching for pockets so she could shove the brick in. Despite the warmth of the day and the intense heat, despite the perspiration that coated her flesh, her fingers were icy cold and lacking in dexterity as she tried to grapple with the tight sodden side pockets of Irena's cut-off jeans. The gap was sealed shut, held fast by the weight of the wet fabric, the opening too tight and too narrow. The water rendered the denim as tight and strong as a length of taut rope. It wouldn't fit in. The pockets were too small, the brick far too big. No matter how hard she tried to manipulate it into place, it simply would not fit. All she could manage was a handful of small smooth stones that were as light as air. Panic took hold once again, her breathing erratic, fear roiling in her stomach and undulating across her clammy skin. There wasn't enough time to gather more stones because behind her she could hear it, the distant angry chattering and hollering of approaching adults. Grown-ups never came down here by the stream. This was the place where the kids came to play. The place where they spent long hot summers running wild in the woods and splashing about in the stream. The place where people died.

This was Lesley's doing. She started all of this and then ran, leaving Heather to fend for herself. Leaving Heather to take all the blame. And now she had told somebody instead of pretending that nothing had happened. They could have walked away and forgot that they had ever been here but now everything was going to be turned on its head. Lesley had ruined everything. She would never forgive her for this. Ever. Deep down, Heather knew that her word held no sway, that denying everything was futile. Getting rid of the body had been the only way out of this horrible mess and she had failed. Her mam and dad were right. She was pathetic. A good for nothing idiot. She could explain away the death of Lesley's nana, tell them that Irena had done it, but this – this was too difficult to escape.

She had just a couple of minutes to get going, to get a head start and take herself off. She was faster and fitter than any of the adults round these parts, their smoking and drinking turning them into a load of wheezing old farts that could barely run a bath let alone a mile up into the hills.

Skirting around the edge of the woods was easier – no breaking of twigs underfoot to give away her location. She ran and ran until her lungs felt fit to burst, not stopping to look behind her, certain that she would make it without being seen except that as she approached the bridle path that led up the hills, she saw them – a gathering of ramblers, backpacks on as they stood chatting and swigging from their flasks. Her cheeks were red. Sweat coated her neck and hairline, running down her back. Her hair was a mess and although she couldn't see it, she knew that her face was swollen and bleeding. Slipping past them unnoticed would be impossible and unless she went back the way she had come or crossed the busy dual carriageway, there was no other way of getting up there.

Her mind raced, thoughts whirling and colliding. She was trapped, nowhere else to go except home. It would be empty and even if it wasn't, her mam and dad would probably be too drunk or too wrapped up in their own world of misery to notice Heather slipping in. She could hide. It wasn't a big house but there were plenty of hidey-holes, places where she could salt herself away. Places only she knew about where nobody would find her.

It wasn't a perfect plan but it was the best she could think of at the time given the pressure and lack of resources she had to hand. That was the difference between her and other kids, she thought, as she turned and headed off in the opposite direction towards the back lane that led her home; they would have enough money to travel somewhere where nobody would find them. Irena or Lesley could jump on a train and vanish yet she had no choice but to scurry away and hope that nobody would know where to look for her. She was trapped. Poverty-stricken and trapped.

She headed back home and for once, luck was on her side. The gravel lane that led to the back of Heather's house was empty. No witnesses to her arrival She almost smiled at that thought but couldn't seem to summon up the strength. Nothing about this felt funny. She tried to imagine what things would be like in a week's time or even a month's time, hoping that everything would be back to normal, her life back to how it used to be. Being piss poor and grubby and having to sleep on urine-soaked bedsheets was better than this. Once she was inside the house, she would throw away all the stuff that she had stolen and shove it in the bin and if anybody found any of the items, they would think that her mam had taken them. She was the local drunkard. It was believable. People didn't go to prison for stealing shampoo and lipstick. She would probably just get a telling off from the local police officer. They might even make her take it all back. That's the worst that could happen, she felt sure of it. And all the while, Heather would be hidden away, everyone thinking she had run off. Another missing person, that's what she would be. Yet another teenage runaway. She wasn't a teenager just yet but she was mature and clever and soon they would get sick of looking for her.

Already she knew where she was going to hide. Slipping through the back door that was always unlocked, she grabbed a cup of water and a handful of stale biscuits and made her way upstairs, ready to be the invisible child. The missing one. The one who got away.

31

It's still there, that review, those blistering words. Every phrase, every sentence still there, garnering more interest and even a few rogue comments written underneath.

Is this true?

Who is she?

Give us her real name!

I shiver and slam my laptop closed. At times like this, I feel like I want to give up writing completely, lock all my doors and never see or speak to anybody ever again. But I know that that isn't going to happen. All I can do is keep on doing what I'm doing – be as unobtrusive as possible until the day arrives when none of it matters any more because my time has run out. How long I have left is down to me and my next appointment; whether I choose to stay alive or whether I make the decision to let everything run its course. I'm almost certain that my mind is made up. I have only half a life stored up in my head so living half a life rather than all of it feels like the right thing to do. It may not be the sensible thing to do but my choices are limited. And besides, the memories that are coming back are unwelcome ones, dark distressing images that scare and unsettle me.

In the meantime, it's business as usual. Despite everything that has happened, despite my current unease and accompanying feelings of apprehension, I need to get out there and face the world. Be my usual self. No cracks in my veneer. No outward signs that I'm coming undone and falling apart. A broken version of the woman I once was.

I've got two more talks booked in. I could cancel them both, plead illness. That's not so far from the truth. In fact, given my circumstances, I think I've done tremendously well to have kept going for as long as I have. Or I could go along, brave it out, act like I haven't got a care in the world and then head home and call it a day; continue writing and put a stop to my public appearances. My readers will cope. It's the books they look forward to. My talks are a bonus, a way of cementing my relationship with my readership base. Doing those final couple of talks could be my last chance to confront both women. If they attend, that is. For all I know, I may arrive brimming with confidence and ready to challenge them, recite my usual speech, sign a few books, and leave without ever seeing either of them again. Or they may do what they usually do – turn up, sit and scrutinise my every move, put me under enormous pressure and then disappear leaving me feeling queasy and out of sorts. Frightened even. Frightened that one of them will again do something awful to me. Frightened because I have no idea what it is they want from me. Frightened because I think that I might actually be losing my mind.

I look at my blister pack of tablets. I can't remember if I took one or two last night. Time seems to be my enemy lately, one day merging into the next.

Whisky sits beside me, whining for his walk.

'Sorry, old boy. Completely forgot about you, didn't I? Silly

Alicia and her unexpected visit have thrown me.' I clip on his lead and head to the back door.

Outside, the rain has stopped. A shimmering grey moon hangs in a pale sky. Beyond the treetops is a rainbow, almost translucent, its colours an insipid pastel wash that arc downwards, vanishing somewhere beyond the line of the hills. Suddenly everything feels bearable. A glimpse of a silvery moon, the sight of a clear sky, the cessation of a deluge of rain and life is suddenly worth living again. The scent of wet foliage and the delicate aroma of damp rose petals that wafts my way lifts my spirits. It doesn't put a spring in my step but I do feel easier, my thoughts clearer.

'Right, Whisky, you can have an extra-long walk for being so patient. You are such a good and thoughtful old dog.' I bend down and kiss the bristly fur on his snout, the slightly stale smell of his breath causing me to take a step back. 'If only dogs could eat mints to freshen up, eh? Good job you're not on the hunt for a lady friend. She'd run a mile with a stink like that coming towards her.' I swear he can understand what I'm saying, his nose twitching in response, his tail wagging madly, hitting the floor with a muffled thump. Even his eyes appear to crinkle up slightly at the corners as if in mirth, our shared humour the thing that keeps us going through the hardest of times. He is my rock, and aside from my books, has been the only static thing in my life for as long as I can remember. I collected him from the local canine rescue centre once my recovery from the accident was complete and he has been by my side ever since.

He drags me to the door while I'm still in the process of pulling on my boots and jacket. 'Hold on there, big fella!'

I laugh as we both stumble out into the fresh clean air, Whisky already snuffling the ground and bolting off towards the woods. I pull the door to and run after him. His bladder will be bursting, poor old guy. I've left it too long. After Alicia's impromptu visit, I sat and pondered over things, trying to piece everything together, still coming up with nothing despite pulling it apart and repeatedly picking at the bones of it.

I chase after Whisky, the rustling of leaves and the cracking of branches and undergrowth as he scurries on ahead, a clue to his location. Alicia knowing my address is another worry I can do without. She is hardly serial-killer material and poses no threat. Poor Alicia with her timid ways and gentle manner, having to endure my relentless questions and brusque manner.

Whisky's tail bashes against a nearby spread of shrubbery while he leans down to retrieve a stick from under it. It's a sight that never fails to make me smile, warming my heart. I try to forget Chalk White Woman and the other troublemaking female who has decided to stalk me but it's not easy. They have succeeded in their attempts to unnerve me.

We spend the next hour or so exploring the woods, Whisky chasing squirrels and foraging for anything he can play with, one of his discarded old balls that he lost over a year ago and somehow managed to locate beneath a pile of old leaves, being his new favourite. I pick it up and clean off twelve months of dirt and grime then throw it into the near darkness of the thicket, the treetops providing dense cover and almost cutting out any shafts of daylight that filter in. I stand and listen to the birdsong. No unexpected walkers. Nobody else around except for me and my dog. I'm safe here. We're both safe here, Whisky and I, nestled deep amongst the trees and the wildlife.

Everything feels easier as we head back home. Lighter. Whisky is tired and satisfied after an hour of running and chasing and sniffing at the ground like a hunting dog even though he would not know what to do with his catch should he ever be brave or fast enough to track anything down.

Yet again, my brief snatch at happiness is short-lived, destroyed and taken apart when I step out from the shade of the trees and see the door to my cottage standing wide open. I locked it. Except I didn't. I can't have. It flashes in my head, the image of me leaving here an hour ago – Whisky being too eager, dragging me out, me struggling to get on my coat and boots. And then pulling the door closed behind me and forgetting to lock it. It isn't Whisky's fault. It's mine. I left it too long to take him out. He was desperate. I was stupid. Stupid and thoughtless.

My heart thumps, my throat is constricted. I can't decide whether I am frightened or furious. Perhaps both. I've been held hostage by fear lately, terror kidnapping me and keeping me tied up and powerless and I'm sick and tired of it. So I allow anger to take over. And I do have every right to be angry. This is my home. My place of safety. My secure base. People have no right to come here and enter without being invited. Enough is enough.

'Come on, boy. Let's have a look inside, see what's going on, shall we?' My voice echoes around me. I'm being deliberately loud, doing what I can to sound authoritative.

If anybody is lurking inside, they should know that I won't tolerate this, that for too long now I have tiptoed and skirted round the edges of my own life to avoid disturbing anything or anybody but the time has come for me to show them that I am brave enough and furious enough to finally tell them to piss off and leave me alone.

I deliberately play with Whisky, ruffling his fur and dangling his treats high up where he isn't able to reach them until he becomes overexcited and yelps. He isn't a guard dog, far from it, but a loud bark should be enough to let whoever did this know that I'm not alone. Whisky is my secret weapon; he's the only one I've got.

'Good boy.' He gobbles the gravy bone down in one gulp. I plant a kiss on his nose and lean down to whisper in his ear. 'Go on. Go and sniff them out, Whisky. Off you go.'

He leaps into the house and I follow, my footsteps loud and heavy, the skittering of his claws on the wooden flooring enough to alert any unwanted intruders to our presence.

We trail from room to room, Whisky sniffing at the furniture while I inspect under beds and sofas, opening wardrobe doors like a character from a low-budget movie looking for hidden monsters, and finding nothing. Not a damn thing. By the time I finish searching, Whisky has already disappeared, flopping down onto his bed with an exhausted clatter.

I continue checking while the old boy quickly falls into a comfortable slumber, his snores loud enough to shake the foundations of the house. I am mildly disappointed to find nothing out of place or missing. Once again, I begin to doubt my own sanity. Did I leave the door ajar? Or was I in such a rush that it didn't shut properly and a gust of wind caught it and pushed it open? I have a memory of it clicking closed behind me. Could a swift breeze really force it open again? It's a possibility but while we were out in the woods, there wasn't a breath of wind.

As always when faced with adversity, doubt begins to creep in, pushing aside my earlier flash of confidence and bravery. The anger hasn't completely vanished, however. I stand up and pace around the kitchen, my eyes scanning every corner of the room, determined to find evidence of a break-in. Determined to prove to myself that I'm not unravelling and coming apart under the strain.

There is nothing. No sign that anybody has been here. Maybe I'm overreacting, seeing things that aren't there. It's understandable, I think, after recent events. A damaged car, a broken phone, strangers approaching me and whispering veiled threats into my ear. I think back to that alleyway and the push that sent me reeling, how I should have defended myself, ran after her and demanded she explain her actions. I wouldn't be at this point had I done that, had I been reactive enough and brave enough. I've rolled over and played dead.

One more sweep of the house and I'm happy that nothing has been taken. I can get back to my life. My life of doing nothing other than writing, giving talks in town and walking my dog.

I glance over at Whisky in his bed. He's already in the deepest of sleeps. He'll be there for the next few hours. Aside from his grunts and snores, the house is silent. Nothing has been disturbed. I imagined it. Nobody has been in here. We're completely alone. I sit down at my desk and begin to type.

32

I knew if I hung around long enough, an opportunity would present itself, and it did. I didn't get lucky. I wouldn't want anyone to think that. I've been patient. Very patient. A persistent presence. Nearly every day I have waited, hidden myself away amongst the shrubbery and today was the day when it finally paid off. My car is parked up on the main road in a layby. I made the journey down here on foot through the woods while it was still dark, and crouched behind a hedgerow, watching and waiting for her to leave. I'm good at keeping out of sight. I've had lots of practice over the years. Hiding from the police and my family after those deaths and then continuing to hide from those closest to me behind a new identity, an imposter in their midst. I'm a master at deception and disguise. One of the best.

When I arrived at her cottage, I initially thought that I would have to break a window to get in but she left the door unlocked making it so easy for me, her dog intent on dragging her out for a walk. I knew that today would be the day when I would get inside. I could sense it, an excited twist in my gut and the unmistakable impression of triumph lodged deep in my bones telling me as much.

I've watched her movements for some time now so I've become quite accustomed to her daily routine but this morning there was a slight hitch. An unexpected visitor. My breath became concertinaed in my chest when I saw who it was. I thought that perhaps it was all over for me at that point, that my cover had been blown as they say in espionage films. But this is not a piece of fiction, it's not a glossy Hollywood movie, what I'm about to do. It's for real. This is atonement for years and years of bitterness that has eaten at me like acid. Atonement for her denial and escaping unscathed while my life crumbled away.

As soon as she took that big old dog out, I knew my time had come. Why would I ignore such a golden opportunity? She all but handed it to me on a silver platter, the chance to get in there and find her spare key. Every household has one, don't they? A spare key in case of emergencies that is nearly always left hanging in a key box somewhere near the hallway. She may live an unconventional lifestyle but her routine and practices are the same as everybody else's. Not so unique after all. And not so clever either.

Getting hold of it was simple. It's the next part that won't be so easy. I'm going to wait until it's dark, make sure there's no chance of being disturbed. All it would take for me to be seen is a visitor turning up and I would be catapulted right back to the start. I'm not prepared for that to happen. I've done my time, paid my dues and all that.

Her cottage was a haphazard affair inside, not exactly what I expected. Lesley was always well turned out. I imagined her house would be the same way, all clean lines and modern fittings but it appears she has lost her touch for neatness and glossiness in the intervening years, her life and surroundings now a disorganised collection of random accessories with large gilt-framed paintings hidden away behind furniture and overstuffed armchairs cluttering up small spaces. And cushions. So many heavily embroidered cushions scattered along the back of every sofa. I began to wonder how she could live each day with so little light filtering in, the nearby woods and trees blocking out the sun, but then perhaps it's a deliberate move to avoid scrutiny, living there in that dusty old cottage with its heavy drapes and leaded windows while she sits like Miss Havisham, ageing and shrivelling away to nothing in a prison of her own making.

My coat smells of petrichor after the downpour. I take it off and give it a shake, tiny droplets arcing in a spray around me then stamp my feet on the patch of concrete where I'm standing to loosen the excess mud. I climb back in the driver's seat and stare at the clock on the dashboard – plenty of time before I return here later tonight. Plenty of time to think things over, make sure I've got everything sorted and my plan is as watertight as it can be. No room for error. No chance of being caught. There aren't any cameras around these parts and I've left my phone at home to make sure my movements can't be tracked. Just one little tweak, a removal of the stone in my shoe that has niggled me for quite some time now, and everything will be perfect. Perhaps not perfect but close to the mark given who I am and what happened to me. I can't remove the defectiveness of my early years but I can rebalance things, make sure she knows that the punishment I endured on her behalf hasn't gone away and that I'm ready to share it out, let her know how difficult it was for me, that her cowardly actions that day down by the stream have consequences. She may have forgotten about me, pretended that I don't exist but I'm about to change all that, let her know that I'm back and that the weight of darkness that obliterated my formative years is about to wrap its arms around her and squeeze the very life out of her.

33

SUMMER OF 1976

It was easier than she had hoped, as if life was giving her a helping hand for once, away from all the destruction and the melee, away from the hordes of people who would see her imprisoned if they could, for a crime she didn't even commit.

The stool wobbled beneath her when she reached up and opened the loft hatch with the long pole that was always left standing in a corner of the landing. She'd seen her dad do it in the past whenever he wanted to stash something that he didn't want anybody to find. She reckoned it was stolen goods but never asked. It wasn't worth the beating.

The ladder slid down with a metallic scrape; Heather was relieved that everyone was out of the house and unable to hear it. Sometimes her mam would sleep through any amount of noise but then at other times, a barely audible whisper or the faintest squeak of a floorboard would be enough to rouse her, her temper ferocious as she flew from the bedroom, hair askew, eyes wide with fury. Occasionally, a vein would bulge at her temple, a small green snake of anger throbbing and pulsating. That was when Heather knew she would have to disappear out of the house until darkness fell or take a good hiding. Disappearing had always been her speciality.

She climbed up and placed her small stash of biscuits and water on a rafter then headed back down and removed the stool, placing it in the back bedroom, making sure it looked as if it hadn't been moved. Not that housework and keeping a pristine home was high on her mam's agenda. Heather was thinking more of a police search of the house. She had watched films where the officers and crime scene investigators had taken note of every single tiny detail. She didn't want a stool that had been misplaced by only an inch to be her undoing. She was better than that. Cleverer. Not clever enough to escape this morning's occurrence though. That weighed heavily on her mind, how everything turned out. How she was left to sort it all out on her own. Except she wasn't able to make Irena disappear. Clever enough to hide herself but not quite clever enough to dispose of a dead body. The thought of Irena and Lesley's nana made her stomach do a somersault and turned her insides to sludge. The image of that broken stick protruding out of the old lady's face made her feel sick. More than sick. Her head began to spin and the floor swayed beneath her. She swallowed. She needed to stop this, to shove it out of her mind and concentrate on her movements. Make sure she got up in that loft without anybody guessing where she had gone. Time was against her, the clock ticking, its steady unforgiving rhythm a portent to her future.

Her feet slipped and vibrated on each rung as she slowly and carefully climbed higher until she was swallowed by the darkness above. A torch. She had forgotten to grab hold of a torch. It would be dark up there. The palms of her hands were slick with sweat. What were the odds of there being batteries in any of the torches she might find in the house? A memory of her dad keeping one hung up in the shed sprang into her mind. She couldn't sit in the darkness for hours and hours. She had no option. If she was fast, she might just have enough time to grab it and get back up through that hatch, pulling up the ladder behind her before anybody realised where she was. Before her mam and dad came home from wherever they were.

Her legs were still weak, her balance unsteady as she slid down the ladder and skittered downstairs at lightning speed, running as if her life depended on it. Which it did, she thought wearily, her stomach churning with despair. The key for the shed was in its usual place, nestled at the bottom of an old cup next to the back door. Her mam's housekeeping skills were predictably atrocious but at least her dad had a canny habit of storing his knick-knacks in the same place. For once, he had inadvertently made her life easier.

Her feet padded across the patchy chessboard of yellowing grass, the current drought wreaking havoc with everybody's lawns. Not that it mattered to her parents. They didn't care whether things in their garden lived or whether they withered away in the unrelenting heat, unlike their neighbours who spent hours tending to their plants, trying to keep them alive with what little water they had. The Oswalds' garden was barren in comparison, everything desiccated and dying.

It was quiet out, everyone either at work or standing on the street gossiping. Still, she crept around the perimeter just in case, staying close to the fence to avoid being seen. If it wasn't for the seriousness of the situation, the way it made her blood sizzle uncomfortably, she would giggle. Maybe it was a natural reaction to feel that way, like when people laughed at funerals even though deep down, they were really upset. It was an unexpected outburst. An uncontrolled eruption of emotion. That's how people's brains worked, how their bodies reacted when they were faced with a tense situation. She had read about it in one of Mam's magazines. Inappropriate laughter and reactions to protect themselves from a terrible occurrence; that's what it had said. Maybe that's what was happening to her now. She wasn't laughing at what had taken place earlier. She wanted to laugh because what she doing was absurd and unnatural. She definitely wasn't about to laugh because people had died. That made her feel quite sick, the thought of those bodies. The image she had in her head of all that blood and Irena's pale wet skin. Whenever she thought of it, it felt as somebody was scooping out her insides leaving her stomach wide open and empty, cold air rushing in and flooding her chest cavity, making her shiver with dread.

The key slipped effortlessly into the lock, turning with ease. Heather stepped into a face full of cobwebs, their silken webs spread over her face and hair. She spat and rubbed at her cheeks and chin, wiping her forehead with the back of her hand. An array of old plant pots, cracked and stacked as if in haste, sat on shelves on each wall of the shed. A pulse throbbed in her neck, eyes wildly scanning every dusty corner for the torch, panic blinding her to the obvious.

She stepped forward and tripped on something large. It rolled across the floor, stopping when it hit an empty paint tin with a clatter. The torch. A surge of relief pulsed through her.

Please let it have batteries inside!

Hands trembling, fingers cold and semi-dextrous, she pressed the button, her heart a deadweight in her chest, heavy and pendulous, a thumping wieldy thing until a spread of light filled the small area, her feet swathed in pale yellow. She silently thanked her dad for being kinder to his tools and gardening implements than he ever had been to his only child, making sure they were in half-decent working order, and switched it off, backing out of the shed and locking it behind her. She needed to move quickly. She had no idea where her mam and dad were. They could come back at any time and it would be heart-breaking for her to get this far and then fail when she was so close to succeeding.

Again, there was nobody about as she hurried back into the house and locked the door behind her, placing the key back into the old cup on the shelf with a dull clank. Sometimes she did get lucky, she thought. Sometimes. But not often.

Time was against her, every second, every minute that ticked past bringing her closer to the possibility that they would arrive unannounced; the all-too-familiar sound of the door being opened, the stumbling clatter of feet on the tiled floor telling her that they were back home, breaths reeking of booze, fists at the ready. Minds securely angled towards a fight. It made her blood go hot and cold, the thought of being caught, giving her enough impetus to pick up her pace and clamber up that ladder, hauling it up behind her before they discovered what she was up to. What she had done. That thought, that reminder of today's event made her shiver. In truth, she hadn't done anything, but knew that people, including her mam and dad, wouldn't see it that way. Everyone likes to apportion blame. People don't like or understand accidents or inexplicable occurrences. They want something solid to go on; something concrete so they can rest easy knowing a culprit has been caught and punished. Everything was black and white in their worlds. And yet, even as young as she was, Heather knew that grey areas existed, that things often happened for no good reason, that people made mistakes, bad unexpected things occurred and people died. That was what had happened. A terrible thing had taken place, something that nobody had meant to happen and two people had lost their lives. If anything, one of the dead people had actually caused it, but Heather also knew that blaming the dead and speaking ill of them would make her look even worse, turning everyone against her, making them less likely to believe her.

The scrape of metal as she hoisted up the ladder made her

teeth itch, the sound of it ricocheting around the house. She slipped the loft hatch squarely into place and sat in the darkness, her breath rattling in her chest, blood pounding in her ears. It was real now. She was doing this. No turning back. As much as she wished she could wake up to discover it was all a horrible dream, she knew that it wasn't. This was her reality. Her life had turned into a living nightmare. If she thought things were bad before, she knew she was going to have to ready and be brave herself because things were about to get a whole lot worse.

34

I'm always amazed at how quickly time passes, the subtle movement of the sun as it shifts across the sky, finally settling on the line of the distant hills before disappearing completely, a constant surprise to me. Having managed to convince myself that my own stupidity was to blame for leaving the door open, I settled down to write and now here I am, hours later, with over 5,000 words written and a sore back and wrists from hammering out my fresh ideas on my keyboard.

I stretch my arms and neck and crack my knuckles, freeing up my aching joints and releasing a wave of tension that has set in from sitting too long at my desk. The sound of the crack is a snap in the surrounding silence. A reminder of how alone I am. How isolated I am, sitting here in my ancient armchair in my cottage in the woods. It's a wonderful sensation though, the knowledge that the words are finally flowing again and I'm back on track. I will probably make my deadline which will undoubtedly please my agent and publisher. It also pleases me. Accomplishing something positive puts other worries into perspective.

A chill glides over my skin. I glance at my watch and realise that

Whisky hasn't been fed. As if by magic, like a mind reader, he appears at my feet, sniffing at the floor before staring up at me, his big brown eyes pulling at my heartstrings.

'Okay, okay. Come on then. Let's get you fed and walked before it gets too dark, shall we?'

He complies by padding along next to me. We head into the kitchen together. I open the cupboard where his food is kept, and fill his bowl, watching while he laps it up as if he hasn't eaten in days, my own stomach growling, reminding me that I also haven't eaten anything since breakfast.

I grab at a packet of cookies and pull one out, biting into it to stave off the hunger pangs until we get back from Whisky's walk. It only takes him a couple of seconds to empty his bowl, licking around it enthusiastically until it's completely clean and the porcelain dish shines like glass.

I don't bother putting on his lead. It will only be a brief but brisk walk. My jacket feels reassuringly warm and heavy, the ambient outside temperature plummeting once the sun makes its descent. I zip it up and this time, I make sure I lock the door behind me, tugging at it constantly just to be certain.

The wind picks up, a blast of cold air catching me unawares and making my flesh sting. My eyes water and my nose begins to run. I shove my hands deep into my pockets for a tissue and instead find something I wasn't looking for, my fingers landing on a small gravy bone. Whisky intuitively senses food is close by and snuffles at my feet. I snap the treat in half and lay it flat on my palm. He takes it from me, his long rough tongue scraping across my flesh, warming me through.

We don't stay out long, just long enough for Whisky to stretch his old legs and carry out his business. By the time we get back home, the woods are in complete darkness and more rain has begun to fall. I stand at the front door, a small amount of fear gripping me. What if it's open again? What will I do then? I grab at the handle and turn it, relieved to find it's still locked. I almost laugh at my own stupidity and the lack of confidence that I have in my own abilities. No matter how often I tell myself that I'm a successful author and have the capacity both financially and cognitively to stand on my own two feet, I am constantly riddled with doubt, insecurity being my closest friend. I'd like to know if I've always been this way or if life did indeed treat me badly, sending me scuttling off here to this cottage to hide.

Once again, Whisky falls asleep in his bed, taking only a matter of seconds to drift off, a series of loud snuffling snores emanating from his half-open mouth. I decide that after a hot bath, I will also have an early night. I have a pile of books to be read and after a day of non-stop writing, I deserve a treat. I've avoided reading the local papers online for stories of my fall at the library. And as for the website with those reviews – I made a pact to myself yesterday to never visit it again. It's a waste of my time, harming my already damaged self-esteem. If I have to live in ignorance in order to remain mentally healthy then so be it. I'll do whatever it takes to protect myself and not end up a delirious nervous wreck of a thing, unsure of which way is up.

I stay in the bath for over twenty minutes until the water begins to cool and my fingertips are wrinkled, then clamber out and dry myself off. I'm certain sleep will come quickly tonight but decide to help it along with a glass or two of red wine. Just a couple. Enough to knock me out and make sure I don't wake in the early hours, the usual round of worries whirling around my brain. I also take one of my tablets. Just in case. Because you never know.

I sit propped up against a wall of pillows after finishing my wine and popping a pill. I feel too tired to read. Instead, I turn off my bedside lamp and am carried away by the arms of sleep into a deep and dark slumber.

Water. So much water and yet only the slightest of currents. A house behind me, darkness enveloping it. It's not my house. I have no idea where I am. Or maybe I do. There's a familiarity about the place. Something that resonates with me. Something that makes me feel uncomfortable, filling me with dread.

A hammer bashes at my temple. Somebody shouting. Somebody else close to me gurgling, struggling to breathe. And then I'm falling. I hit the water, its coolness wrapping itself around me. Something soft beneath my flailing body. I'm not floating. I'm resting on an object, its solidity stopping me from hitting the bottom. I struggle to clamber up but then another weight presses down on me like a giant hand, its palm pushing me lower into the water.

I lift my head, eyes wide and stare down into the water and am met with a face. Her face. I know that expression, recognising immediately the pallor of her skin. Long wet strands of her hair are knotted around my fingers, strangling my blood supply.

Her eyes spring open. I let out a scream and sit up.

My chest is pulsating; perspiration coats my flesh, gathering between my breasts and in my clavicle. I'm sitting in a puddle of sweat. The sheets are damp beneath my thin nightgown. I shiver, goosebumps rising on my arms and across the back of my neck.

I glance at the clock. 1.40 a.m. My hands tremble when I flick on the bedside lamp, the sudden glare of light ripping through the darkness. My dressing gown is hung on the bedpost. I clamber out of bed and pull the robe tightly around my body, then set about yanking off the wet clammy sheets and locating new pillows.

It only takes me a few minutes to bundle the damp bedding into a pile on the floor and put on clean linen, fluffing up the spare pillows and replacing the quilt cover. I gather everything up then open the door and step over Whisky who continues to sleep, and I head downstairs, turning on lights, the house flooded with a clinical white glare as I move from room to room.

The hum of the washing machine kicks in as I bundle in the sheets and turn it on. Its low drone cuts through the near silence, drowning out the lonely hoot of a distant owl. And then something else. I see it – a movement in the darkness to the left of me. Something drifting past the window. There is a shadow in my peripheral vision. I swing around but see nothing. My bare feet make a slapping sound on the tiles when I quickly turn and switch off the light, peering out into the darkness, eyes wide like a startled deer. There's nothing to see. Just a swathe of inky blackness punctuated by a series of stars peppered across the sky.

I wait, my breathing a deep rasping sound, and continue staring into the darkness of the woods. I don't even know what I'm waiting for. Something or somebody? Images of the earlier dream still linger in my mind, cooling my skin, making me shudder. It wasn't a dream. It was a memory. I know that now. It was unpleasant and disturbing. I try to not think about it. Later perhaps, once this is over, I'll unpick the threads of it but right now, I want to make sure that my house is secure. I need to be certain that whatever or whoever is possibly out there, cannot get in.

It takes me five minutes or so to tour the house, pulling at windows and doors, rattling handles to make sure they're as secure as they can be, and only after that when I'm completely satisfied that the cottage is burglar-proof do I head into the bathroom and turn on the shower, a mist of steam billowing like dust and clouding up the room within seconds.

I feel clammy and grimy, salt coating my flesh. I pull off my nightclothes and step into the cubicle, the hot water cascading over my shoulders and down my spine and stomach. Even while I'm showering, I keep an ear out for any unfamiliar sounds – the creak of a floorboard, the unmistakable groan of a door being pushed open – I would recognise them all, this cottage the only thing I'm totally familiar with. I've spent long enough inside it over the past year since my accident, to know its foibles and defects, how movements from the hallway echo throughout the rest of the house. If anybody stirs or takes the tiniest of steps, I'll know.

I finish showering and dry myself off, then do one more final walk around the house, moving slowly and methodically like a death march, before climbing back into bed and falling asleep within seconds.

35

Perhaps she heard me although I think that's unlikely. I crept through those woods like a ghost, my footfall as light as air, every movement I made barely noticeable, even to the wildlife lurking nearby. I was as silent as the grave, stepping into the well-worn track I've made over the past few weeks so as not to get lost and stumble into the river. The rush of the current is a constant; a distant reminder of how important it is that I remain focused and not lose my way. If its fricative hiss is behind me, I know that I'm making headway and progressing in the right direction.

I was almost at the door when the light came on and I saw her silhouette sharply outlined in the window. No curtains to shield her from passers-by. She has no need out here, alone in the woods with only the owls and foxes for company. I thought at that juncture, that I had been caught, that she had seen me and was about to call the police, but then her face peering through the glass told me that she wasn't sure of what was out there. She wasn't alarmed– more curious, frightened even, her eyes wide as saucers as she scanned the area before turning away.

I almost laughed, relief disentangling itself from my taut limbs when she disappeared. I stayed hidden round the back of the house, my curiosity piqued as to why she was up at such an hour. I know her life-

style, her sleeping patterns, what time she turns off her lights and how often she leaves the house. I don't believe for one minute that she suspected I was close by, crouching in the darkness, enveloped by branches and foliage. I've been as unobtrusive as possible on my stake-outs, making absolutely certain I haven't been seen. My only travelling accessory is a small torch which I keep low to the ground, the beam stunted by a limited trajectory. I don't even carry a weapon. I don't need one. My words and my hands are all I need. Those plus the long, jagged knife that is sitting in the wooden block by the cooker in her kitchen.

Tonight isn't the night. I need to catch her off-guard, softened by sleep, her thoughts and co-ordination slow and sloppy. So I head off back to where I'm parked up and climb in, closing the door with a silent click. My car cuts through the nocturnal dimness, my headlights dipped, my cap pulled down low to shield my face from anybody who might be driving in the opposite direction. So far, I've been alone on this road. Once I'm back on the main drag, it won't matter who sees me. I haven't done anything wrong or committed any crime. Yet. Besides, this area is so isolated, the chances of ever passing anybody are slim to non-existent. She has made it easy for me. Without even realising it, I. L. Lawrence, or Lesley Harcourt as I prefer to call her, has reached out and unintention-ally given me a helping hand.

36

She could hear them moving about below her, the characteristic bellowing of her parents' voices as they padded about the house opening and closing cupboard doors, making her skin crawl with fear. A serrated knot of unease sat in her belly. She could judge their moods by their vocal intonations, the highs and lows of her mother's voice a giveaway to either her growing anger or drunken contentment, her usual sharp edges smoothed out by the alcohol leaving her a fuzzy warmer version of her normal self. Heather hoped the latter was the case but knew that even if it were so, it wouldn't last for long, her mam's mind sharpening up as the drink wore off, revealing the less buffed up corners of her nature beneath the polished haze of the booze. At least her dad was predictable, his mood wavering rarely. When he was drunk, he was loud and often on the cusp of flying into a rage. When he was sober, which of late, was becoming less and less frequent, he was also loud and nearly always on the cusp of flying into a rage. The only thing that set her parents apart was their intended target. Her dad preferred to direct his ire at the TV or stalk around the house shouting the odds about the neighbours or some bloke who had wound him up down at the pub, only occasionally lashing out at Heather whereas her mam was fond of venting her spleen on her only child at regular intervals, doling out slaps and punches on an almost daily basis, or throwing whatever came to hand – picture frames, old ornaments, anything that could hit hard and wound. She once threw a chipped teacup, catching Heather on the back of her head. She bled for the rest of the day and had to use a small towel in a bid to stem the bleeding so as not to leave filthy red stains on the pillowcase when she went to bed. Grime and general dirt were acceptable. Blood was not. Her mam saw it as a way of Heather garnering sympathy, being a martyr to the cause.

'Can't afford a new one so you'd better get it cleaned up!' she once roared after Heather fell and scuffed her knee while playing in the street, accidentally smearing a ruby red trail on the living room rug when she came inside, hoping for sympathy, yet all the while knowing that none would be given.

'It'll toughen you up,' they often said, if she ever dared to complain. 'You don't get owt in this life if yer stand there all soppy and doe-eyed. And cut out that crying. If there's one thing I can't stand, it's kids who weep at the slightest bloody thing, so stop with that trembling bottom lip and bloody well grow up.'

Heather dreaded the onset of her periods. That would be another mountain to climb. She had already thought about using old flannels and dishcloths to catch the flow when the day finally dawned. Approaching her mother for help was unthinkable. It was something she'd have to manage on her own.

A sudden screech dragged her thoughts into line, the sound of her mam's voice below her setting her nerves alight.

'Fuckin' stop it, Gary. She'll be home soon. Get yer filthy hands off me, you big drunken brute.' Then a giggle. The rustling of clothes and shuffling of feet.

Heather placed her hands over her ears, teeth gritted together.

She knew what came next, how it would progress, this type of behaviour. This lurid act.

'And? It'll only take a couple of minutes. Come on, yer big tease.' Heather's dad's voice cut through the protection of her clasped fingers that she had pressed tightly against the side of her head, his big voice and clunky slurred sentences too loud and vulgar to ignore.

'Get off, Gary. What if the bairn comes home, eh? What then?'

If she closed her eyes, Heather could see them – the slight curl of her mam's lip, her short locks that were plastered down with hairspray, thick clumps of hair bobbing about as she fought off his advances, the twinkle in her dad's eye as his hands roamed over her mam's slim hips. Her absence never stopped them in the past. She was tired, her mam, that's what it was, the drink rendering her weak-limbed and exhausted, and was using her own daughter as an excuse. Not that Heather minded. She hoped her dad would take the hint and fall sleep on the sofa, his snores rumbling around the whole house. Anything was better than what he had planned. She didn't want to have to listen to *that*. It knocked her sick, making her stomach roil with disgust, the way the bed would bounce and squeak, the way her mam and dad would grunt and moan as if they were actually fighting rather than doing what they were doing. She knew what it was. She had heard the other girls talking about it at school and wondered what would possess anybody to do such a thing. It sounded revolting, two bodies stuck together like mating dogs, all their bits jiggling about in a mad frenzy. She had already decided that she would never get married. She might consider having a boyfriend but if he ever tried any of *that,* she would tell him to piss off, to sling his hook and never come back. She would be happier on her own. People weren't to be trusted anyway. She had learned that much over the years and today down by the stream proved that she was right.

Squatting on the beam was beginning to make her legs ache but she couldn't work out how to manoeuvre herself around without falling or making a loud clatter. The wooden struts groaned under her weight if she attempted the slightest of moves. She counted the seconds, each second turning into minutes until eventually she heard him – her dad and his pig-like snores. That meant that her mam was probably asleep too although she couldn't be certain. Sometimes she would sit, feet up with the TV on, a cigarette dangling from her fingers, the small thin mountain of grey ash growing and growing until it toppled, at which point she would jump up, frantically brushing down her clothes and shouting and swearing. 'Fucking hell! Stupid fucking ciggies.' Then she would take a final drag, crush it on a nearby saucer or plate and stumble up to bed for the rest of the day. If that was the case, then Heather would just have to wait. She could do that. She was young and agile and good at playing basketball and badminton. Those sorts of pastimes kept her fit. She was good at them too, playing in matches in P. E. lessons at school. Never at home though. Who has enough money for racquets and shuttlecocks?

'Who do you think I am?' Her dad had shouted when she once broached the idea of him purchasing a small kids' badminton set complete with net for her so she could play outside and practise her shot. 'Bloody Rockefella? Get yerself outside and kick some tin cans around or do some handstands or some bloody thing but stop bothering me!'

Again, she began to count. It helped her concentrate, to not get bored and then slip because she wasn't properly focused. That would be terrible, if her legs gave way and she fell off the beam and burst through the ceiling, landing on her bed or worse still, her mam and dad's bed while they were sleeping on it. A rumble of laughter bubbled up in her throat at the thought of it, making her eyes water as she tried to stop the giggle from escaping.

A twinge took hold in her lower abdomen. She had forgotten to go to the toilet before climbing that ladder and not only that, she didn't bring a bucket with her. Or any toilet paper. She would have to wait until her dad was in a really deep sleep and then sneak down to the bathroom. Nothing woke her dad once he had had a skinful. Once Heather had stood next to him and roared in his ear as loud as she could and he didn't even stir. Her mam, unfortunately, was very different. Unpredictable. Like a wild predatory animal, angry when roused.

Fingers slippery with sweat, Heather turned on the torch, keeping the beam pointed upwards away from the hatch, and as slowly and as carefully as she could, she swung it around, looking for a bucket or anything that would serve as a makeshift toilet. In the far corner stood a medium-sized plastic container. An old toy box perhaps? She didn't recall ever seeing it before but it didn't matter because thinking about peeing had now turned her bladder into a peanut-sized thing trying to hold two gallons of liquid.

A pain shot across her pelvis when she clambered over the beams, her movements nimble and cat-like. She crouched in front of the dark blue box, her lower abdomen throbbing, nerves jangling. What if she opened it, took off that lid and a rat came scurrying out? Or two rats. There could have been a whole family of them living inside it. She leaned down and placed her ear against the container, hearing nothing but the dull *thud thud* of her own heartbeat that pounded like a big bass drum in her neck. Her bottom lip quivered when she placed her fingers around the rim of the box and lifted it off, hardly daring to peer inside, the light from the torch flooding a small area at her feet.

Only when there was no movement did she attempt to glance down. Dizzy with relief, she wanted to clap and laugh on seeing that it was empty. Instead, she pulled down her underwear, squatted over it and let the warm stream of pee land on the plastic surface, stopping every couple of seconds and listening out to make sure nobody had heard her. It was silent below. They were both asleep, brains soaked in booze, breath reeking of it as they slept, slack-jawed, hair matted, clothes askew. She still had to be careful though. Experience told her that things could change as quickly as the wind.

Heather finished and pulled up her underwear, rearranging her clothes, although why, she didn't quite know. Sitting there in the dark with only a torch for guidance through the pitch-black surroundings and an old plastic toy box as a toilet, it didn't really matter whether her clothes were straight, or on backwards or upside down. She was alone, in trouble, and nobody had any idea where she was. She could have been sitting there naked and it wouldn't have mattered.

Swinging the torch around again, she searched for somewhere where she could lie down and sleep. Her legs and back were beginning to ache. Squatting on her haunches in the darkness was draining, boredom eating away at her. Her bed suddenly held a certain amount of appeal, the thought of its stained unwashed sheets suddenly not so unpleasant after all. Just somewhere she could stretch out and rest was all she wanted. Somewhere soft with a half-decent pillow where she could lay her head and shut her eyes, and attempt to block out all the horrors of the day.

The heavy thump almost sent her reeling. Her head blazed with fear, fireworks exploding in her veins as the bang came again, this time nearly knocking her off the beam. And then the voices, the shouting she could hear that was coming from outside. All that separated her from *them* was the thin membrane that stretched across the rafters, and a row of roof tiles. And her silence. They were here. It *was* them. She knew it, could tell by the pitch and volume of their voices, the anger in their tone. Lesley had told them everything, had lied and now they were after her, baying for

220   J. A. BAKER

her blood. She would just have to wait it out, be as quiet as she
could be, and pray that they would leave and go elsewhere looking
for her.

Like a frightened baby bird, too scared to flee the nest, she
stayed there, perched on a large beam, fingers hooked around it.
All she had to do was stay there, crouched in that same position
and not make a sound, and then she could think about what she
was going to do next.

37

I sigh, disappointment and dread running through me, and run my fingers through my hair. How could I have forgotten that I was doing a talk in town today? I sit and stare at my calendar. I could cry off, call up and claim I'm too ill to attend but then the gossips would start, tongues clacking wildly about my recent collapse at the library. Everyone would put two and two together, adding fuel to an already simmering fire, and come up with five. I don't want that. Better to go, do my bit and leave. Far easier than giving people a story to feed on. I've got two hours to get myself ready, park up in town and get into the bookshop to prepare. It's one of the larger stores with a generous space at the end dedicated to author talks, so there might be a bigger audience. I need to get myself ready, quell my growing nerves and just get on with it.

Within an hour, I'm showered and dressed, have walked Whisky and am in the car, heading out onto the main road at speed. Driving the hire car doesn't faze me but I'm longing to get my own vehicle back, preferring the familiarity of it. This thing has the most bizarre radio stations set up and I spend most of the journey twiddling knobs and pressing buttons, trying unsuccessfully to tune into my favourite local radio station. I'm just pulling up into a space in the car park when I finally manage it, my ears pricking up at the topic of conversation for the usual morning phone-in.

'Well, I think they should stay in prison for longer, Andy. I mean most kids know exactly what they're doing. I taught mine the difference between right and wrong and if they did anything like that, I'd expect them to serve a lengthy sentence for it. Do the crime, do the time, that's what I say.'

'Thanks for that insight, Melissa. In case you've just tuned in, today we're discussing recent events that have hit the headlines this morning about a young girl who murdered her own younger brother and only received a sentence of eight years in a young offenders institute. With parole she could be out in five. What do you think about the way the judicial system works in this country? Are we too lenient and do you think children who carry out the most heinous crimes should be given a second chance to redeem themselves or do you think that they should be given hefty punishments and not be released until they have served their full sentence? Call us now and let us know what you think.'

I listen to another caller who is shouting down the line that children today have it too easy and that in his day, if he had stepped out of line, he would have been given a sound beating and that it never did him any harm.

'Soft, that's what we are, Andy. A nation of bloody softies.'

I take a shaky breath, unease crawling up my throat and swelling behind my eyes. A throbbing ache sets in. I rub at my face with cold fingers, my vision blurred as I continue to listen.

'Right, thank you, Ian. Let's move on to Grant who is currently studying child psychology at university. Grant, I gather you have a completely different take on this subject?'

'Hi, Andy. Yes I do. What about if the child has suffered some kind of trauma themselves? A child's brain is still being shaped and moulded and *that construction can be affected by their environment. We don't know all the facts about the case so it's difficult to pass judgement but from what I've read, the child in question was often left to care for her younger brother without any adult intervention. The defence claimed that the death occurred as a result of neglect and that it could have been accidental. He fell from a table while his older sister was present, that much we do know, and witnesses have testified to seeing the girl hitting her younger sibling on more than one occasion. That doesn't make her a murderer though, does it?'*

I'm almost panting, my temples pulsing with pain. The conversation continues but I've already tuned out, the sound of their voices no more than white noise in the background. A line of static is fizzing in my head, unsettling me. I'm on edge, my blood running hot and cold, meeting and merging in a violent clash. There's a reason for me to feel so emotionally invested in this dialogue, I know it. It has struck a chord with me. But why? I think back to those dreams, those memories that are slowly resurfacing. That article in the newspaper. Am I a child murderer? Is that who I am? There was no mention of my name in the story. So why is this radio interview resonating with me so deeply? I want to whack my head against the dashboard over and over until it all comes tumbling back, the missing years of my life. I want to scream and rant and swear. But I don't. I need to stay calm, be steady and reasonable, so I keep it all inside, all the fury and the fear. I tuck it away with a promise that once this talk is over, I will go home and dig some more into my past, and keep on digging until I get some answers.

I turn off the radio and climb out of the car, my gait slow and sluggish. A fist squeezes at my throat, limiting my breathing. I would sooner be at home than here. I usually enjoy these talks but lately they've become an infringement on my life. A life that is slipping out of my control.

My reflection in the car window is jarring. A middle-aged

dishevelled-looking woman stares back at me. In the confusion after last night, I remembered to shower but have forgotten to comb my hair and put on any make-up. Even a slick of lipstick and some blusher would have helped freshen up my appearance. I'm pale and washed out, my skin the colour of ash.

I frantically rummage and scrape the bottom of my bag for some make-up and find nothing but old tissues and receipts. Time is against me. It slips through my fingers lately, each day merging into the next.

My heels clip on the concrete flooring, echoing though the car park as I hurry into town, copies of my books tucked down into my large carrying case. I hope nobody asks me about my inspiration for *The Memory Man* again. I'm tired of coming out with the same old tropes to satisfy their curiosity and I don't think I've got the strength to tell the truth and reveal my own disability regarding the black hole in my brain. It's a weakness, a liability. In the early days, I tried various things to see if it would help shake things up a little – hypnotherapy, yoga, even aromatherapy in an act of desperation, but nothing worked. And then in recent weeks, since the appearance of Chalk White Woman, my memory has started bubbling up to the surface. That's the trigger for this. It's her.

The walk there takes only a matter of minutes. I enter the shop, make my greetings and head to the stand at the rear. It doesn't take long to set things up, and already people are coming in and taking a seat, idle chatter filling the room. I keep my eyes lowered, looking up only briefly to give the assistant a smile and a swift nod to let her know that I'm almost ready to begin. I'm deliberately averting my gaze away from the door. I don't want to see Chalk White Woman today – or any day for that matter – and I don't want to see *her* either – the other lady who spoke to me, saying those words that sent me reeling. I just want to do my bit, sign some books and leave without any drama. I don't think that's too much to ask. Being a writer is a purportedly quiet, sedate occupation and yet just lately, I end each day feeling wrung out and deflated, as if all the life has been sucked out of me. I couldn't be more on edge or tired if I was doing eight hours of manual labour or working in a lab to find a cure for some dreadful debilitating disease. I make up stories for a living. I sit at my computer and type out ideas that spring into my head. It should be easy. I should feel privileged. And yet just lately, I don't. Just lately I feel like a stranger in my own life. An imposter. Somebody who has lost their way and is mimicking another person, acting out the idea they have in their head of who and how they should be. Maybe today will be different. Maybe today will be the day that everything returns to normal and I can say goodbye to all my fears. I almost laugh, impressed at my own fortitude and positivity. I'm all those things when everything is okay and I'm in a safe environment. I'm none of those things when fear takes hold and I'm faced with the unknown.

The clock behind me ticks away, a relentless reminder that soon it will be time to begin, each second that passes a loud clatter in my head until at last, I force myself to look up at the sea of waiting faces that are sitting there expectantly, expressions eager and friendly-looking. Not hostile but warm and welcoming. I breathe a little more easily and scan the crowd and that's when I feel my heart sink. She's there, the other woman. Not Chalk White Woman but her. In many ways, she is scarier. She has approached me; she knows where I live. And the more I think about it, the more certain I am that she is the one who posted that comment on the book review site. And now she is here, sitting opposite me, a smug look on her face. She knows she has the upper hand, always one step ahead of me. She knows that what-ever she says or does, I am powerless, unable to retaliate in a public arena, the eyes of my readers upon me. I need to remain calm, unruffled even though my insides are alight, white-hot flames scorching my stomach, my lungs and throat. I stand up straight, managing a tight smile that feels more like a grimace, and begin to speak.

* * *

It goes smoothly. It almost always does. Apart from that one time. She sat throughout, smiling at me, nodding in appropriate places as if we're old friends and all the while, I was on red alert, keeping my eyes peeled for Chalk White Woman.

People line up to speak to me, copies of their books clasped in their hands. *She* doesn't line up with them. She remains in her seat, watching me through tapered eyes that glisten like coal. I shut her out, focus on the people I can trust. My real readers. My faithful little following.

'Another wonderful speech. If you can dedicate this one to Alfred, that would be brilliant, thank you.' The lady standing before me smiles and shuffles away once I've signed her copy and handed it back.

'An author! You've done well for yourself, Lesley. Your parents would be so proud.'

I freeze at the use of my real name. None of my readers know it. I always go by my pen name, I. L. Lawrence. Always.

I look up into the face of a stranger. A man I guess to be in his eighties, possibly even his nineties is smiling at me, his large slightly crooked front teeth sit on his bottom lip. He stares down at the book in his hand.

'Doreen sends her love. She doesn't get out much now but when we heard you were a writer, we both felt that one of us should come along and show our faces. We're holidaying here for a bit of a break. We're staying over at the big hotel in the market square. They've got a lift for Doreen now her legs aren't so good.

Anyway, I'm rambling. What about you, a famous author. Who'd have thought it, eh?'

My brain is working at a hundred miles an hour, synapses firing in all directions whilst I try to fathom who he is. Clearly somebody from my fragmented past. It was only a matter of time before somebody recognised me. Not that I've ever done any talks on Teesside. I've stuck to North Yorkshire which isn't so far but far enough to lose touch with my past. A past I can't remember.

'Ah okay, thank you. I'm very lucky. It's a dream job.' I hope I've said enough to appease him. Enough to send him on his way without him knowing about my accident and subsequent memory loss. I pray he doesn't ask me any probing questions about my family. The family I never see. My parents are dead, that much I do know and if I do have any siblings or cousins, they have never made any attempt to contact me. The documents I have at home point towards me being an only child.

'It was a terrible thing that happened to your parents, losing your nana that way. Such trauma for them to go through. I saw you at your dad's funeral but of course that was quite a few years back. And then for your mam to follow so soon afterwards. Such a terrible shame.' He shakes his head, eyes brimming with sorrow.

Was he a friend of my parents? A neighbour perhaps? I can't ask. He thinks I know him. And yet, this man could help open a door in my mind, a way to force that memory through, squeeze it out of the darkest corner of my brain and back into the open once more.

'Yes, it was awful about my nana.' My heart is thumping, my voice disembodied as it rattles around my head. Is this such a terrible thing I'm doing, pretending to know what he is referring to and playing along? Or do I deserve to know about my own past, my family history? I want him to elaborate and yet at the same time, I don't, frightened of what I may hear.

'I mean, I know it was years and years ago but it was such a shock for everyone. Left a lasting impact, it did. I said to Doreen at the time, it was no wonder you moved away as soon as you were old enough. Must have been hard for you.'

I nod and smile, eager for him to continue, also unsure what to say in return.

'We spoke of you over the years. It was as if you disappeared off the face of the earth, and now here you are.'

I attempt a smile, my mouth hitched up at each corner. 'Here I am,' I murmur. I really don't know what to say. Actually, I do. I have lots to say, a whole realm of questions stored up but don't know where to begin.

'Anyways, I won't keep you. Good to see you doing well for yourself, lass. After what your family went through, you deserve it.' He starts to walk away. Panic claws at me. I can't let him leave, not without knowing. I need to find out who I am. This might be my only chance.

'I'd love to see you and Doreen again, if you'd like to meet for a coffee while you're in the area?'

Everything stops, time standing still as I wait for his reply. I think that perhaps I've overstepped the mark, frightened him off. He will think me strange, overfamiliar. A little unhinged even. I'm flooded with relief when he smiles, his soft blue eyes wide with gratitude.

'That sounds grand! Doreen will be over the moon to see you after all these years.'

'How about tomorrow in Masters, the coffee shop two doors down from here? 2 p.m. sound okay for you?'

'The coffee shop it is. Doreen will be glad of a trip out. Today wasn't one of her better days but I'm sure she'll perk up at the thought of seeing you again. Two o'clock gives us time to get her ready. Things take so much longer what with her wheelchair and everything.'

I don't ask what her illness is. It's none of my business. Already my gut is somersaulting at the prospect of meeting them. This is a big thing I'm doing, taking this chance and trusting these people. I will have to tell them about my accident and memory loss. There is no way I can carry it off for an hour, covering up by smiling and nodding in all the right places. It will prove to be too big a task. Impossible. At some point I will have to explain my predicament and hope that they understand and help me fill in the gaps in my existence. As frightening as it seems, meeting them and opening up to them also feels liberating. I daren't even consider feeling excited at finding out more about my past. One step at a time.

He gives me a small wave and I watch him disappear into a crowd of people outside. Tomorrow is when I will find out everything I need to know. Tomorrow will give me the answer to who I am. I've read the article. An old lady died. Was she my nana? I think that perhaps she was. The article didn't mention me. Was I there when it happened?

Is it wrong to feel excited as well as nervous? I've lived in the dark for the past year and I need to know so many things, to work out who I was before I became me, I. L. Lawrence the enigmatic writer, the virtual recluse. The lonely old woman in the woods.

38

I let her be. For once, I just sat there, hands clasped in my lap, watching everything happen. I don't have to do anything any more, that's the thing. Me just being here is enough. It unnerves her, makes her fidgety and on edge. Besides, something happened. Somebody appeared from the past. Our past. The past she appears to have dismissed and forgotten. Trevor, the man from number 48 Mitchell Street. I saw him. I watched as he made his approach and spoke to her at length, their talk not voluble enough for me to hear. I wanted to move closer, to show my face, see if he recognised me, just to make sure I've changed as much as I think I have. But I didn't. Because if he had spotted me, what would I have done then? Turned and ran or braved it out? I think I already know the answer to that question. Of course I would have run. I would have fled for my life. I can't risk being recognised. I've come too far to lose it all now because of an impulsive move. I did the right thing staying put, sitting there and watching them. I don't think he would know who I really am. Who I was. But I'm not prepared to risk it. I have changed a lot, I know that for certain. I'm no longer that poor ragged kid, the one who was left to God and providence, bringing herself up as best she could and just about managing, until tragedy struck. I brush away that thought. I've spent far *too long dredging up my past and how bad it was, how I was mistreated and thrown to the wolves. Time to focus on the future. Time to plan, set the wheels in motion. Make sure things are properly balanced. I can't do anything tonight. I'm busy seeing my daughter and her husband, acting as the good mother and mother-in-law, which I am. It's just that they don't know about the inner machinations of my mind and what I've got planned for I. L. Lawrence aka Lesley Harcourt. That's my dirty secret, my one and only guilty pleasure.*

*I wish I could have picked up on what they talked about, Lesley and Trevor; whether it was about that day by the stream. That's how I think of it, how I approach the idea of it in my own head, labelling it as **that day.** The day when everything went so horribly wrong and my life was ripped apart. I'm willing to guess it was just friendly chatter, harmless talk about how much she's changed and how great her life is now she is famous and wealthy, the subject of that day too dark and thorny a subject to broach. She will have enjoyed that – being put up on a pedestal, a weak old man from our past, an ex-neighbour lavishing her with attention. Not that the content of their talk matters. It's irrelevant. I was there watching because I need to do something before this acid that continually swills about in me eats through my gut and begins its toxic journey into my bones. I need to be rid of it. So the night after next is when it will happen. It's set in stone now. No going back. My mind is made up and once it's over, I can go back to how things were, getting up each day as if nothing has happened. As if I haven't just made a famous author atone for her sins, ending her life as abruptly as she ended mine. Then we'll be even. Only then will the scales be readjusted and tipped back to how they should have always been.*

39

SUMMER OF 1976

The heat was suffocating, the low humidity drying her throat. Her flesh was hot and itchy and sweat coated her torso, running down her back and chest making her clothes stick to her skin. It was uncomfortable but she had to stay still. Being stuck up there was infinitely preferable to being outside facing the wrath of dozens of neighbours who would have believed Lesley without question. Lovely, fashionable, pretty, sweet Lesley with her nice house and clean clothes. Lovely Lesley with her clean hair and lip gloss and innocent sparkling eyes. Lovely sweet Lesley with her hidden bruises and fractured family. She covered it well, oozing credibility. Not like Heather who was full of sharp edges, coated with dirt and grime. Nobody sided with kids like her. Especially not with her parents being who they were. She knew that. That was why she was up there, hiding. Nobody would believe a word that came out of her mouth. They had probably been waiting for her to make a wrong move for years and years so they could point the finger and say *I told you so*. Nobody would miss her if she disappeared anyway. She would be one less thing to worry about. Another troublemaker out of the way. It didn't bother her so much. She'd got used to being discarded and ignored. If she was being honest, she preferred it that way. It meant she could do her own thing, be whoever she wanted to be without any pressure from other people who were always so keen to judge. When she grew up, she would never be like that. She would let people be whatever they wanted to be, let them do whatever they wanted to do. The world would be a better place if people were just allowed to get on with their lives without anybody else interfering and telling them what to do. That was her take on it, anyway. Too many cooks spoiling the broth or something like that. She'd heard her dad say it before now and although he was often daft and drunk, there were times when what he said made sense. That was what had happened with her and Lesley. Irena had showed up, throwing her weight around and that's when everything started to go wrong. An iron fist clutched at her stomach at the thought of Irena, the vision of her waxy skin and staring eyes beneath the water filling Heather's mind.

It wasn't my fault!

It wasn't my fault!

She wanted to scream and rage and weep until she ended up a dried-up shrunken husk but couldn't. Instead, she had to sit there and wait, sweat blinding her, muscles locked in position until everybody had left and it got dark and she had an idea of what she was going to do next.

Another series of thumps at the front door almost knocked her off the beam where she was balanced. Her damp fingers clung onto the rough surface of the wood. So many angry shouts out there – men and women hollering and swearing, threatening to kick the door in if it wasn't opened. She could imagine it, the carnage below. Everybody who lived in their street would be out there, gawping and chattering, drinking it all in, thinking that yet again the Oswalds had brought shame upon the neighbourhood with their sinful unorthodox ways. She shut her eyes and took a deep breath, mystified as to how her mam and dad slept through it. For once her mam's erratic and unpredictable sleeping pattern had served Heather well. She must have had a proper skinful to knock her out like that. The thought of drinking that much made Heather grimace. She once had a mouthful of her mam's gin when nobody was looking and couldn't understand what all the fuss was about. Her throat had burned and it had made her feel sick, hitting her stomach with an unwelcome punch. Sometimes adults did things that she just didn't understand. That's why she had to hide. None of them would ever see it from her point of view. Ever. She was alone in this thing; this horrible frightening situation. It was a good job she had learned to take care of herself over the years. She was a tough nut. A survivor. She would get through this. She had to. There wasn't anybody else around to help her. She thought of her grandparents in York, wondering where they lived and whether they would see through all the nonsense and look at it from her point of view, realising that she was a poor kid from a poor town who needed help. Not that she even knew their address. That would have been somewhere she could have gone to, but with no knowledge of where they lived and no money to get there even if she did, it was out of the question. She was alone. That was okay. At least she wouldn't let herself down. It was all other people did – let her down and abandon her when she thought they were on her side. On the odd occasion when her mam or dad showed her affection, it was quickly followed by an insult or a slap. Best to remain vigilant, be suspicious of those around her and not trust anybody. She trusted Lesley and she shouldn't have. Lesley was the person who had led those people here to her house to find her. To blame her. She had nobody on her side now. She was completely alone.

More shouting and hammering on the door followed by a long silence. Then footsteps moving away. Heather's breath rattled out of her chest like a flurry of tiny insects exiting her body. They were leaving, all those people. They had given up on trying to find her. Thank God. A tremble took hold in her jaw. She snapped her mouth shut and closed her eyes, appreciating the quiet and still-ness that followed the departure of the baying mob. She would probably have to stay up in the loft until it got dark and everyone was asleep in bed. Then she could flee to the hills, gather up some belongings and take herself off up there. She knew the route like the back of her hand. Knew it better than most of the adults in the neighbourhood. They wouldn't know where to look for her. Money would be good though. If she could get hold of some, she could take a train or a bus somewhere further south. Somewhere where nobody would know who she was. Probably London. She would wander the big city, find a bus shelter or somewhere warm where she could lay her head and sleep for the night and then in the morning, with a clear head, she would start to plan the rest of her life. It wasn't the best or the most precise strategy but it was all she had and it was better than the alternative.

A pain took hold in her belly, hunger gnawing and scratching at her, burrowing deep into her intestines. She manoeuvred her way across the beams and grabbed at the dry broken biscuits she had managed to find in their near-empty kitchen cupboards, stuffing them into her mouth, making sure no crumbs fell. There wasn't enough to allow for any wastage. Every morsel counted. She took a swig of water to counteract the dry texture that coated her gums, placed her meagre rations on a beam then settled back in position, ready to do vigil until nightfall.

* * *

It was the pain that woke her, the throbbing ache that travelled back and forth over her shoulder blades before ricocheting in a triangular fashion up and down her spine. The back of her neck hurt too, the hard wood of the beams pressing into the soft flesh of her neck. If she had owned a watch, she would have taken it with her but didn't possess anything that expensive so was stuck there with no idea if it was day or night, whether her mam and dad were still asleep or whether they had woken and gone back to the pub for their next drinking session.

The torch was lying next to her. She needed to sit up, grab at it and find her way over to that plastic container. Clambering silently over the beams was problematic with a full bladder but she managed it without making a sound, her poise and agility a surprise even to herself.

Keeping down the noise of her pee hitting the plastic container proved more difficult than clambering over beams and ducking under low rafters. The stink of it was powerful too but nothing she couldn't deal with. She was used to it, her olfactory senses already accustomed to the stale tang of her everyday clothes and dirty bedsheets. It wasn't pleasant but neither was it the end of the world. She doubted that Lesley would ever be able to do what she doing. Her moneyed upbringing had stripped her of any survival skills, cushioning her against the raw realities of life. A tic took hold in her eye as she remembered the bruises on Lesley's arms, the tell-tale signs on her pale flesh that told her that her friend's life wasn't as rosy as she painted. Heather flicked a finger over her eyelid, pressing down to alleviate the pulse that tapped away there beneath her skin. She wouldn't allow herself to start feeling sorry for her friend. Ex-friend. Things had changed. Everything was too far down the line to let pity get in the way of her need to escape from the monstrous situation in which she found herself. She had to look out for herself now, self-preservation dictating her thoughts and movements. She also needed to shut Lesley out of her mind, conserve her energy and make sure she got away from this house, from this area, and ended up on her way down to London or somewhere equally busy where nobody could find her. Nobody cared about her so she had to care for herself, that's just how it was.

She took a swig of lukewarm water, gagging as it hit the back of her throat. It was getting hotter up there, everything dank and clammy. She just wished she had an idea of what time it was, whether she was safe to gather up her things and make a run for it. The only thing to guide her was the level of noise from below and at the minute it was silent. All she needed to do was pull open the hatch ever so slightly and peer down below to get an idea of what was going on down there. The biggest problem was the metallic scrape of the ladders as they slid down. As far as she could work out, there was no way of escaping it, aside that is, from dropping down straight out of the hatch and hoping she didn't break anything when she landed. It wasn't impossible but it was risky. She wouldn't be able to flee to the hills with a fractured ankle or worse still, a broken leg. And yet she couldn't stay up in the loft indefinitely. Something had to give.

Taking another gulp of the water, Heather clenched and unclenched her fists, took a deep steadying breath and slowly lifted up the lid.

40

I can see them from where I'm standing. They're already there in the café over the road, sitting in the window seats, Doreen's wheelchair resting against the wall next to the bay window. I don't know how I'm going to approach this one, what my opening gambit will be. It's been a busy morning and my mind isn't as sharp and focused as I'd like. I had to return the hire car first thing and sign a thousand pieces of paperwork before I could collect my own vehicle. Whisky insisted on a longer walk than usual which then made me late collecting the car, and now here I am, trying to prepare for a meeting with people who clearly know all about me and my parents while I remember nothing about them. My stomach lurches as they spot me and wave enthusiastically like we're all old friends. Which in a way, we are, except they don't know about the black hole inside my head, the missing parts of me, and I don't know where to begin to explain it without appearing rude and disingenuous, as if I've tricked them into this meeting, getting them here under false pretences, especially given Doreen's obvious mobility issues. This was an effort for them, making this journey. I need to be as honest and forthright as I can be.

Butterflies flit around my chest as I cross the road and push open the door. I'm barely inside when he jumps up and pulls out a chair for me, his eagerness to see me and impeccable manners shaming me. I am going to have to be upfront and admit straight-away that I don't know who they are. To do anything else would be rude, an insult to their intelligence.

It occurs to me while I'm making my way over to where they're sitting that I don't even know his name. Suddenly it feels over-whelming, this meeting, like scaling a mountain or swimming against the tide.

'Hello there! I just said to Doreen, there's Lesley over there. She didn't recognise you, did you, Doreen? But me? I've got a good head for faces. I remember everyone.' He shakes my hand as if we didn't meet yesterday and haven't seen one another for decades. He also fails to mention my scar, his near-perfect manners steering him away from what could be a possibly sensitive subject. 'Here we are, love. Now what would you like to drink?'

'Oh, honestly, I'll get my own coffee and whatever you would both like.'

I try to catch the attention of the lady who is clearing the table next to ours but he's too fast for me, calling her over and placing an order for three cups of coffee and three slices of chocolate cake.

A lull descends as she bustles away, the noise of her heels fading into the background. It feels like somebody has their fingers clasped around my windpipe when I start to speak, my voice a strangulated squeak when I attempt to explain my quandary.

I give them the condensed version, doing what I can to leave out the most distressing parts, about how I was left for dead on the roadside, then clear my throat and lower my gaze, relieved that I found the right words to tell this kindly old man and his wife about my lack of memory and the fact that I don't know who they are, despite being the one who suggested the meeting.

'A hit and run?' Doreen's eyebrows shoot up to her hairline. 'But that's dreadful!' she says, her voice full of compassion and incredulity.

I nod and continue. 'I try to not dwell on it. I'm hoping that one day it will come back,' I murmur, taking a deep breath as if to brace myself for what I'm about to say. 'I do get flashbacks. They're disjointed though, and really unpleasant.' I think of that stream. The screams. The newspaper article. Those deaths. Darkness descends inside me.

'So you don't recognise us or remember who we are?'

'No, really sorry but I don't. I wanted to let you know as soon as possible. I didn't want you to think I was misleading you.' My face feels hot, beads of perspiration arcing around my hairline. Above us an electric heater blows out warm air. I shrug off my jacket and roll up my sleeves. I glance at the elderly man and smile affably. 'And I have to admit, I'm afraid I don't even know your name. I'm so sorry.'

'What an awful turn of events for you. I'm Trevor.' He smiles and cocks his head to one side. 'Doesn't ring any bells for you, then?'

'I wish it did.' If only it were that easy, being reminded of something or somebody from my past and for it all to come flooding back at the mention of a name. If only.

Doreen leans over and gently taps my hand, kindness in her expression. She has warm skin and smiling eyes that twinkle under the glare of the yellow strip light. They believe me. I don't know why but I was so sure they would think me a fraud or worse still, completely unhinged but it's clear that they are on my side. They're good people. I can trust them. I don't have any evidence to that fact other than my gut instinct which is telling me that it's safe to open up to them.

'So you have no memories from when you were a little kid then?' Trevor says quietly, his voice lowered as if we're discussing state secrets. 'It's so odd for us as we remember you from when you were a small child. Such a sweet thing you were. Desperate to grow up and become a teenager but always happy and polite.'

I shake my head. 'None at all. Nothing from before being knocked down. I'm a stranger in my own life, I'm afraid.' A lump is wedged in my throat. Saying it out loud feels alien and having people close by who do know me and appear to care has unknotted something inside of me that has been pulled taut for so many years now that its sudden unravelling catches me unawares. I fight back the tears and force a smile, my bottom lip trembling with thinly disguised emotion.

'Oh dear.' Trevor runs his fingers through his feather-like silvery hair and sighs. 'And I put my big foot in it with what I said yesterday about your parents and your nana.'

'No, definitely not! If anything, it has helped.' I look from him to his lovely wife then back to Trevor again. 'I'd be happy to hear anything you've got to say about my childhood.' I swallow and rub at my eyes, suddenly enveloped by a deep weariness. 'Especially my nana. I'd like to know everything. If you're willing to tell me, that is?'

For one awful moment I think that I've said too much, scared him off and made him clam up. He glances at Doreen and then at the floor before looking back at me, his skin suddenly ashen. His eyes are distant. He's trying to work out how to say it, how to tell me what I think I already know.

'Aye, well it's not easy to explain. It was an awful, awful thing. A terrible time. And that lass that did it. Well, all I can say is—'

'Careful, Trevor.' Doreen lays her hand over his and keeps it there, her eyes narrowed. 'We've always said we don't know the whole story. Doesn't do to point the finger without knowing all the facts. We always said there was more to it than meets the eye, didn't we?'

He sighs and shakes off the mood like shedding dead skin. 'Aye, sorry you're right, love.' Trevor smiles and squeezes his wife's hand, tapping at it softly before looking again at me and continuing, speaking slowly and methodically, stopping every now and then to take a trembling breath or to rub at his eyes with large fingers, his coarse skin flaky and dry like sandpaper.

I listen without moving. I don't interject, trying to absorb every word, to store every single detail in my head. Small bolts of electricity sizzle beneath my skin on hearing the story. It's as I dreamt it. The stream, the shouting and screaming. And then the deaths.

'She said you were somehow to blame, that other lassie, but the police dismissed her claim. We all did. We knew you'd never do anything like that. You were a lovely happy kid. Especially considering...' He shakes his head, his voice trailing off.

Goosebumps rise on my arms and neck. I'm suddenly cold. I have questions, lots of them, but the words won't come, my mouth and brain refusing to work as they should.

'Here you go. Sorry about the wait. We're a bit short-staffed at the minute.' A young woman appears and puts down a tray on the laminate surface. The sight of the large slab of chocolate cake that is shoved in front of me is enough to make me want to heave. I swallow and slide it to the edge of the table, my mind still trying to piece together the parts of Trevor's story, my flesh crawling with disgust. As he was speaking, I convinced myself that I didn't know any of it, and yet I'm sure deep down, that I did. My memory was never lost, just hidden, biding its time before revealing itself. Those dreams, the choice I made to live in a cottage in the woods away from the rest of the world, my writing pseudonym taken on before every thought and memory I had leaked out of my head – it all makes sense now. I was trying to escape my past. Trying to put some distance between me and that day down by the stream. That's what any rational person would do, any sane compassionate person. They wouldn't want to be associated with such a hideous turn of events.

'What was her name again?' Revulsion and disbelief are muddying my thinking, making my comprehension slow and disjointed. I need some time to put it all together.

'Heather.' Trevor passes a cup of coffee over to Doreen and picks up his own mug, sipping at it, the lava-like temperature doing nothing to put him off. 'Her name was Heather Oswald.'

I wait for pieces of the puzzle to slot into place in my brain, for a slow recognition to spark into life. Nothing happens. The name doesn't mean anything to me. She can't be Chalk White Woman. The age difference is too great. She could be the other woman though, the whispering sneering woman. That could be Heather. But why appear after all this time?

The coffee burns the roof of my mouth and my throat. I swallow it down, not minding the flash of pain, welcoming it even. It's a reminder that I'm here, feeling discomfort and all the usual range of emotions. I'm not a ghost or a stranger in my own life. I'm me.

'And the other girl?' I ask. 'The one who died in the water. What was she called again?' I need to hear her name spoken out loud, to remember her.

Trevor lowers his cup and reaches into his pocket, pulling out a large black phone. 'Irena.' He shakes his head and sighs. 'Poor Irena. That lass had her whole life ahead of her. A few stupid thoughtless seconds and it was all snatched away. And of course, your poor, poor nana...' He blinks and stares out of the window, as if his thoughts are still firmly entrenched in that moment in time, like shackles of the past he can't leave behind.

I don't know how to respond. I should feel sorrow for my grandparent but with no memory of her, no tangible connection, there is an absence of emotion. I feel for her as anybody would for a stranger who has been murdered but the deep visceral response that would usually accompany news of the death of a loved one simply isn't there. And as for the girl that died – I think that maybe I feel a flicker of recognition at her name but can't be entirely certain. What I do feel is sick and confused. Perhaps not confused. Not any more. It's all coming together. And not before time.

The crunch and whirr of the coffee machine behind me cuts into our conversation, Trevor's words drowned out by the sudden crash of crockery smashing. Next to our table, the young girl who served us bends down and starts to pick up the shattered pieces of porcelain.

'And this is the picture that our Amanda sent me.' Trevor is watching me, his hand outstretched, waiting for me to reply.

'Sorry?' I blink and rub at my eyes, suddenly weary.

'Trevor was saying that our niece Amanda found some old photos recently and sent them to us on that Facebook thingy. I don't use it but Trevor has an account and one of them has that poor girl on it. She was in the same class as our Amanda. Gave me a proper fright it did, seeing her face again after all these years.' Doreen gives me a sympathetic smile and takes a gulp of her coffee. 'It was all over the papers at the time but of course things move on after a while and people forget, don't they?'

'Maybe seeing this will jog your memory?' He hands me his phone and I take it from him and hold it up to the light to get a better view.

'Here,' he says, leaning across and placing his fingers on the screen. 'I'll zoom in for you. It's a bit grainy because it's an old picture but if you look closely, you can just about see—'

'It's okay,' I say a little too abruptly, moving the phone out of his reach and lowering it into my lap. I'm dizzy. Dizzy and bilious.

I don't need to look closely. I can see who it is, the sight of her making my skin prickle. I hang onto the edge of the table, trying to not slump onto the floor. I can't think straight. I blink and rub at my eyes. My vision is blurred, a film covering my eyeballs. I'm walking through thick fog, staggering into madness.

'Are you sure?' I say, my voice croaky. I stare at Doreen and Trevor. 'Are you sure you haven't got the photograph mixed up by mistake?' Even while I'm saying it, I know he hasn't. This is the right photograph. This is her. This is Irena, the dead girl from the stream.

Except it isn't. Not to me.

I can feel their eyes on me, their bemused expressions burning a hole in my flesh. I will remember this day whether I want to or not. It will never leave me. I'll always recall this moment as the point when I knew for sure that I was losing my mind, unspooling fast with nobody around to catch the damaged parts of me. Nobody around to try to put the broken bits of me back together.

'No, this is definitely her. Is everything all right, lovey? You look a bit pale. Would you like a glass of water?'

A tumbler of cool liquid is placed in my hand. I drink it down and stare again at the picture on the screen, the decades-old photograph of a young girl who is probably in her mid-teens but looks a lot older than her years and I know who it is. I don't need anybody to confirm her identity. Her face is so familiar to me, frighteningly familiar. Chalk White Woman stares out at me from an old school photograph, her sullen countenance turning my guts to water.

I make my excuses and dash to the toilets where I bring up the contents of my stomach until there's nothing left and then sit on the cold tiled floor, legs curled under me, wondering what I'm going to do next, wondering who is going to help me and how I'll ever move on from this point in my life. The point when everything finally came together and yet at the same time, catastrophically fell apart.

41

SUMMER OF 1976

She was met with a cool breeze. Her breath rattled in her chest as she leaned down and gulped in mouthfuls of it, desperate to alleviate the tightness in her chest and rid herself of the burning sensation that bit at her skin.

It wasn't completely murky down there just yet. If she was going to grab a few things and run, now was the time to do it. It didn't get properly dark until about 10 p.m. She could get up into the hills before that time. It wasn't as if she had many belongings to take with her. Her meagre possessions didn't amount to much. Her plan of living off the fruits of the land while sheltering under the trees and shrubbery now seemed rather flimsy but she could think of no option other than sitting up there in that hothouse until hunger and heat forced her out.

She stopped and listened for any noises from below before lowering the ladder as quietly as she could, her legs unsteady, her pulse racing.

And then she heard it, the sound of their voices turning her blood to ice, a fusion of fear and the realisation that she had made a terrible error of judgement, making her dizzy and disorientated.

There wasn't any time to take anything with her – no water, no scraps of food. She was going to have to leave with only the clothes she was wearing and nothing else.

The scrape of a chair from below sent her reeling. They were down there. They had been sitting there waiting in near silence and now they were coming for her.

She peered over the banister and down to the tiny hallway below. Her only choice to get away from this horror show was to bolt down the stairs and out of the front door taking nothing with her. With trembling legs, she made a dash for it, feet twisting beneath her, heart battering like a herd of wild animals stampeding behind her ribcage.

Her palm slipped on the door handle – the noise it made as it catapulted back and forth before finally opening sounding like a bomb detonating in her head. Voices shouted behind her. She didn't stop to look back, just kept on running, her legs heavy with terror. They wouldn't catch her and even if they had a car, the track she would take to the hills wasn't accessible by any vehicle except a bike. She knew the hidden tracks, the routes that only street kids knew. Adults didn't have a clue about such things. They thought they knew everything, had the answers to the most difficult of questions but they were wrong. They didn't know her and they couldn't see inside her head to what she was going to do and where she was going to go next.

Behind her, a police siren wailed. She didn't slow down. The sound of it forced her to pick up her pace. They were closing in on her but if she took the back streets, running down the narrow alleys between the rows of houses, it would only take her a matter of minutes to get there, for her to find some solace and sanctuary amidst the shrubbery and the dense towering trees.

Her chest was dry. Flames licked up and down her calves but somehow, she found the strength to keep going, a reserve of nervous energy pushing her on. She had nobody. None of them were on her side. All she had was her own strength, the skills she had learnt over the years to keep herself safe as she had roamed the streets from dusk till dawn while her parents drank themselves stupid. They had unwittingly done her a huge favour leaving her to fend for herself. She smiled at that thought. For the first time ever, she was able to thank them for something.

Perhaps it was the fact she had allowed her thoughts to roam untethered or perhaps it was because they were grown-ups and knew the area better than she realised but whatever it was, she knew the minute she heard it that she had made a mistake, that she had misjudged their competency and accuracy for the finer details regarding the back streets of the town. Behind her, blue lights flashed, sirens screeched, voices called out her name. She was at a dead end, quite literally. In her agitated state she had taken a wrong turn, headed up the wrong alley and was faced with a dead end. Police cars one way, a high brick wall the other. To her side was a gate. It led to a row of gardens. Without thinking, she leapt up, straddled the wooden gate, slid down the other side and ran as fast as she could. No time for meticulous planning now. Everything she did was going to have to be instinctive, her gut telling her which way to go.

Shouts behind her, the sound of feet hitting the tiles of the alleyway, echoing into the growing darkness. She still had time to get up to the hills. She still had a chance to escape before it got too dark to see properly.

Her body felt weightless, insubstantial and papery, her limbs made of gossamer as she leapt from garden to garden towards possible freedom. Thinking had knocked her off course, made her mind woolly and unfocused. She had to concentrate on simply getting there, escaping the crowds of people who thought that she was a monster when all that had happened was that she was in the wrong place at the wrong time.

'She's here! Quick, I've just seen 'er!'

A cacophony of voices filled the air; people screaming and hollering for her to stop. She didn't. She wouldn't. She was going to keep going until she had no oxygen left in her lungs. The hills beckoned, their darkness and seclusion calling to her. She would get there. She would take a sharp right once she reached the end of the row of houses. No matter what, she would swerve and dodge the police cars and the swarms of locals who wanted her arrested and locked up, and she would just keep going until she left them all behind, their screeches and hatred a dim and distant memory. And when she reached a place of safety and isolation, she would find a stream, drink from it and slake her thirst, and then she would lie down in the shrubbery where she would keep watch for hours and hours until the coast was clear. They had to give up at some point. If she hid deep enough, burying herself amongst the foliage and camouflaging herself with leaves, they would eventually stop look- ing. Was she *really* worth all that effort? She didn't think so, but then, a teenager and an old woman were dead so maybe they would be relentless, not giving up until they found her. All the more reason for her to keep going.

Two dead people.

A buzzing took hold in her head. She couldn't let herself think about that just yet. It would slow her down, filling her limbs with terror and dread. Once she was in place, hidden away in the dark- ness, she could go over the details again in her mind, think about how it all happened. Convince herself that none of it was her fault. Which it wasn't, but she wasn't stupid; she knew how these things panned out. They would want to blame somebody. Random deaths didn't go unnoticed. Somebody had to be punished. And right now, that somebody was her.

The final fence was taller than the rest; most of the others she had tackled and mounted with relative ease only three or so feet high. This one was nearly six feet up, its smooth planks making it almost impossible to scale. Her fingers slipped down over the surface, splinters sliding under her skin making her wince with pain and all the while the voices behind her grew closer. She stepped back, took a run at it, and managed to get a grip on the top of a solid strip of wood, her legs and feet madly scrambling for purchase, kicking at the solid surface as she pulled herself up and hoisted herself over it, landing in a heap on the other side.

She was up on her feet and running within seconds, no time to sit nursing her wounds. Every second wasted put those people and the police a second closer to her. Only another five minutes, maybe even less, and she would be on the track that led up to the hills. The narrower the path, the more difficult it would be for them to follow her. With their big cars and even bigger beer bellies, she would outrun them in no time at all. She wondered if her mam and dad were after her too or if they had stayed in the house, too stupid and too full of drink to even care about who was chasing their daughter. Or perhaps they were too ashamed to show their faces, knowing the neighbours would hate them for what had happened. They hated them anyway and her mam and dad hated them right back so they were equal really. Except now that everyone was sure Heather had done those bad things, the neighbours' hatred towards the Oswalds would ramp up a hundred notches.

Her breath was ragged as she ran towards the small cut that led to the track to the hills. She was close now, so very close to escaping, and that's when it happened – the fall. She didn't see the huge hole in the ground. Somebody had filled it full of grass but it wasn't enough to stop her going down, her ankle twisting as she fell. The pain took the breath right out of her, sucking every pocket of air out of her lungs. A hot line of cramp screeched up her leg, tearing at her bones. She tried to not cry but the tears came anyway, an involuntary flood of them, running down her cheeks and dripping off her chin. Snot bubbled out of her nose, running over her mouth. It didn't matter. She had to get up, get moving.

The sound of screeching tyres and sirens blaring forced her up onto her feet, the weakness of her ankle evident as she tried to set off again. She could hardly walk let alone run. It was stupid and embarrassing to be caught out by falling, like one of those pathetic weak-willed women in horror movies who fall over their own feet and then the baddie catches them and does unspeakable things to them. Heather had always thought that it served those sorts of characters right for being soft and idiotic and now she had done the very same thing.

A blistering wave of pain pinballed up and down her leg whenever she tried to put any weight on it. Her foot felt hot and swollen and she wondered if she had broken it. Not that it mattered. She had to get moving. No waiting around for the hurt and swelling to subside. Time was against her.

The cut was riddled with more holes, the parched dry ground making it even more difficult to keep her balance. It was like walking on deep craters and she ended up straddling the narrow path before limping and hobbling her way to the end where the blare of a siren and the flash of a blue light stopped her. She was trapped. She could hear their voices. They were coming for her. She spun around, flames of agony flaring up her leg and around her foot, and saw a figure standing at the end of the opening. Waiting for her. With an uninjured foot she would have been able to hurl herself over the fence but her ankle was throbbing. She wasn't sure she was capable of escaping them now. She was trapped. Doomed, everything and everyone closing in on her. And yet she still didn't want to give in.

Ignoring the screech of agony that tore at her foot, with one huge effort, Heather dragged herself over the side of the fence into the dense bushes and crawled on her hands and knees through the shrubbery until she found herself on the black path behind a row of terraced houses that sat at the foot of the hills. Positivity unfurled in her chest. She could still manage to do this. They were close but they hadn't caught her just yet. She could definitely make it up there. She could get away and escape their clutches. The clutches of people who had got it so wrong. People who knew nothing about her but were so certain they knew everything. She could wait until the swelling went down and then—

'Right, up you get, love. It's all over now. Time to stop running.'

It was the shock that caused it. The stream of warm urine that burst out of her and travelled down her legs, a dark humiliating spread of liquid that pooled beneath her.

This was it. It was all at an end. She put a hand up to her face, covered her eyes to block out the horror of what was happening, to block out her future, her present and her past. She opened her mouth and let out a long piercing scream that went on and on and on.

42

I knew. As soon as I saw that photograph, I knew. Maybe I've always known and been in denial since the first time I saw her at one of my author talks. Except I didn't see her. Not really. She was never there. It was all in my mind. What I saw was a flashback, a memory that was trying to muscle its way into the forefront of my mind. And yet as I slide into the driver's seat of my car after pulling myself together and making my goodbyes to Trevor and Doreen, promising that I'd keep in touch, the incident in the library sticks in my mind, the one where she approached me. I then think of the receipt, the lack of evidence that she had ever been there at all. And then there is Alicia's response when I questioned her about Chalk White Woman, claiming she hadn't ever seen her. Did she think I was talking to myself? Did I even say anything at all or was that conversation all in my head? And why now, after all this time, am I suddenly seeing her? Something has triggered this. I think of my medication and possible side effects. Could that have contributed to this episode? Or am I truly slipping into an abyss of madness?

I turn on the engine, mulling it over. I know that memories don't appear in a sudden rush, hurtling back into the brain at lightning speed. They slowly edge their way in, dipping their toe every now and again to test the temperature before being slowly and carefully immersed, twitching and shifting every so often to make sure nothing gets burned and damaged. I read up on it after the crash, sifting through as many medical and psychological articles as I could find. Maybe that's what is happening with me. Maybe, bit by bit, it will all come back. The problem is, will I know it's a memory, an image from the past? Or will I, like I did with Chalk White Woman, mistake it for something else? The lines between past images and the present tangible things have become blurred and I'm clearly unable to distinguish between the two. Or maybe stress and exhaustion have played their part, making my thinking disjointed and skewing my judgement.

The drive home feels surreal as if I'm operating on autopilot, my lower order skills taking over, every turn of the steering wheel, every change of gear I make, a reflexive action.

I pull up outside my cottage and sit for a short while, gathering my thoughts until I hear Whisky whining inside, the sound of crunching gravel alerting him to my presence.

He's sitting at the door waiting for me when I head inside, his large paws spread out on the doormat. The sight of him never fails to pull me up short, reminding me of what's important in this life, how brief and sweet our time is on this planet. How we need to make the most of it. I think of my grandmother, that poor lady and her grisly demise and then the girl – Irena – how little she lived and how lucky I am to have survived that accident, the one that ripped every thought out of my head. I could have died and I didn't.

Eena.

Alicia's words come rushing back to me. My semi-conscious ramblings. Irena has always been there in my head, hidden. My memories haven't disappeared completely. They're in there somewhere, lying in wait. Biding their time before creeping out and showing their face.

I drop my bags and bend down to ruffle Whisky's face, his wet nose rubbing against my cold cheeks, his rough tongue lolling in appreciation of being hugged and fussed. Holding him feels good, a tangible reminder of how life isn't always sad and harrowing. There is good in this world. It's just that sometimes, you have to search that bit harder to find it.

'C'mon, lovely boy, let's get out there and get filthy, shall we?' He waits by the door while I pull on my wellies and old anorak. 'Okay, all ready. Let's get out there.'

We step outside, the breeze rustling through the trees, the sound of it music to my ears. After the meeting with Trevor and Doreen, I need to touch base with my surroundings, to feel the wind on my face and hear the distant cooing of the wood pigeons, I need it to remind myself that I'm here and I'm alive.

That woman. She's on my mind as we stride through the thickets. The words she whispered in my ear. The note on my car. That push. And the caustic barbed phrases that she wrote on the book review site. She alluded to it, the part I played in those deaths and yet according to Trevor, I was innocent. I pray that he's telling the truth because if he isn't, I'm not sure how I will ever be able to wake up each day, look at my reflection in the mirror and convince myself that I'm a half decent person. Is she the trigger for all of this? Her presence at the talks, did it bring back visions of Irena? It's a possibility. If life has taught me anything, it's that no matter how outlandish and far-fetched something can seem, anything is possible.

I briefly shut my eyes, enjoying the sensation of the cool breeze that passes over my skin. Whatever it is, this episode of my life, whatever it brings, I'll remain stoic. That's my promise to myself. I will be stoic and resilient and I will live through it. I've survived worse. This is something I can definitely do.

* * *

I'm warm after the walk. Whisky is tired too. Outside, it's starting to get dark. Another day gone and yet today feels like a turning point, as if I've achieved something momentous. Maybe today will mark a point when my life starts to make sense. I hope so.

By the time I've fed Whisky and prepared my own meal, I've managed to convince myself that everything is going to be okay. Perhaps not okay, but slightly better than it was. I no longer have to be frightened of Chalk White Woman. I am, however, still wary of *her*, the other lady. The one who is possibly linked in some way. The one who is possibly Heather Oswald. Should I contact the police; tell them of my suspicions? And then what? Is an over-stretched police force really going to take action against somebody because I have a hunch she may be an ex-convict? It's unlikely. It would also be one step closer to confirming my suspicions about my own mental state. So for now, I'll be vigilant, make sure my security is as tight as it can be and wait to see what tomorrow brings.

43

Sitting waiting in a layby for hours at a time paid off. I had planned on walking down to the house, when I saw her drive past in her vehicle. This time, luck really did play a part. I waited until she was a safe enough distance away and started up the engine and followed her into town, driving just far enough behind to remain unseen.

What a cosy get-together it was, the three of them sitting there chatting like they didn't have a care in the world – Lesley, Doreen and Trevor. They didn't see me. None of them have ever really seen me. I fell through the cracks; teachers and neighbours all too busy and distracted to notice the skinny bruised child, the feral streetwise child. I was written off as wayward and feckless. The naughtiest kid in the street. Nobody cared about me back then when my life was falling apart so I doubt they spared the time to think about me now, all these years later when the scars still run deep, the wounds inflicted by my healthy serving of injustice still raw and bloody. The fact I'm not on their radar gives me hope, makes me think they've forgotten about me and I can move amongst them ghost-like, a spirit in their midst. I can be the stone in their shoe and they won't be able to guess where their problems stem from. I don't care about Doreen or Trevor. I didn't care much for them back then and care even less for them now. They were the sort of neighbours who would turn a blind eye to the child who was obviously neglected and hungry. All they saw was dirt and surliness, not taking the time to look closer; not caring enough to see beyond the grime, to look just that little bit harder for the hurt and the trauma and the signs of neglect. They could have done so much. It takes so little to do such a lot, to make those all-important changes for people who are in need. I wish people would realise that. The tiniest of efforts can make the biggest of changes. But nobody did that for me. They thought I was tough. A street kid. Somebody who could take care of herself. I thought that too, but I was wrong and so were they. Children don't have all the answers. They might act as if they do and by God, I certainly acted like the toughest child on earth but it was just that – an act. Children need care and guidance and love. I needed those things as much as the next youngster and yet they were lacking in my life. Even the most hardened of kids need to feel cherished and wanted. My main memories from back then before I was locked away for killing two people are of a cold loveless house where food was scarce but arguments and violence were aplenty.

Not that any of that matters any more. It's all in the past, over and done with. No amount of raking over it will change what happened. It's about what comes next, how I redress the balance, make sure Lesley understands that no crime goes unpunished. Four decades it's taken for me to do this. It's long overdue.

So tonight is when it will take place. I'm both eager and nervous in equal measure but make no mistake, it will happen. No backing out now.

I trace my fingers over the outline of the key in my pocket, the key to Lesley's cottage. I'm ready to do this thing, to take the next step and do what needs to be done before going back to my mundane little life with my small business and wonderful daughter who has inherited all of her father's gentle characteristics and none of my bitterness and bile.

Tomorrow the sun will shine a little brighter, the sky will be that little bit bluer, the grass that little bit greener and the world will be a better place without Lesley Harcourt in it.

44

SUMMER OF 1976

They gave her something to eat and drink at the police station – a glass of orange juice and a cheese and ham sandwich followed by a shortbread finger. It was the most delicious thing she had eaten in weeks. Aside that is, from the food that Lesley had bought her, those lovely plates of chips lathered in ketchup and big bowls of ice cream with sprinkles on top that they bought in town. And of course, there were those big bags of stolen sweeties. They tasted like heaven, the fact they were stolen and forbidden adding to their appeal. She wondered if the police would ask her about those as well while she was there or whether she should just own up straightaway. If she did that it might mean that they would go easy on her. She had seen it happen on TV and read about how if criminals pleaded guilty, they would get a lighter sentence.

There was a woman at the station who was sitting beside her with a weird look on her face, as if she felt sorry for Heather whilst also knowing there wasn't really anything she could do to help her. It was the way her mouth trembled whenever she looked her way, how her eyes twinkled whenever Heather spoke, before a veil of darkness descended. It didn't matter. She'd learned how to cope on her own a long time ago. She didn't need any useless limp-looking adults telling her what to say or how to behave. She would manage just fine.

'Your parents are here at the station, Heather. They're waiting in another room. This is Norah. She's here to help you. We're going to ask you some questions about what happened down by the stream.'

And so they asked their questions and she told them everything. How it had all been an accident and that Lesley was a big fat liar for saying it was all Heather's fault and that it was Irena who had poked the stick in the old woman's face and it was Lesley who squashed Irena down under the water and that everything had happened so fast that she couldn't have stopped any of it even if she had wanted to and that she was tired and wanted to go to bed because she had run for miles and miles and hurt her ankle and maybe even broken her foot and how long were they going to keep her here for because she was really, really fed up and tired and wanted to go home even though home was rubbish and stinky and she was always hungry when she was there but she had nowhere else to go to and sometimes her mam and dad slapped and hit her but it was mainly her mam who did it but it was still her home and how long were they going to keep her here for because she also needed the toilet and had tummy ache, and with her bad stomach and aching foot she just wanted to lie down somewhere where people weren't going to shout at her and hate her for saying she had done things that she hadn't really done.

Tears streamed down her face; her breath was hot and ragged, pockets of stale fetid air floated around her as she spoke. It was as though something had died in her stomach and was rotting down in there. Maybe that's what it was. Maybe she was a bad person after all and even her own body was repulsed by what she had done and was doing its best to turn her into a stinking foul pile of rotten meat like a dead person. Like Irena and Lesley's nana. She swallowed and wiped at her eyes with her threadbare sleeve, tears and snot smearing over her face.

Norah, the woman sitting next to her, handed her a tissue and patted her hand. It felt quite nice, the feel of Norah's soft skin against hers. The warmth and closeness of it. She cried even harder knowing deep down that they wouldn't believe her and that something bad was going to happen. Something she couldn't control. A longing to see her mam and dad suddenly tugged at her, like a sharp-clawed animal scratching beneath her skin. It didn't even matter if they shouted at her or lashed out with their big hands; she just wanted some familiarity, to see their faces, to be able to know that they were close by.

The hand covering hers stayed put. She didn't dare move for fear of it being snatched away so instead sat as still as stone, a breath held in her chest, time slowing down around her until at last she had to let it out, that long juddering rush of warm sour air that wouldn't stay put. She knew then that that was the moment when it would all change, when everything around her began to speed up, people rushing around, watching her closely, waiting for her to crack, waiting for her to admit that she was a murderer and then tell her that she was about to go to prison for the rest of her life.

She couldn't stop the tears. Maybe they had been there all the time, years and years of them stored up, ready to come pouring out. Maybe she should have cried more often in the past and then she wouldn't have been sitting there hiccupping and sobbing, hardly able to speak, hardly able to breathe properly while her chest heaved and her chin trembled, her mouth quivering and flapping uncontrollably.

They thought she was guilty. She could see it in their faces.

They were sure of it and she was sure of one thing and one thing only – there was no way out of this mess and she was about to go to jail for something she didn't really do.

45

Whisky's long walk earlier means he will only need a short one before I turn in for the night. I'm relieved. As much as I love being out and about and roaming through the woods with him trotting along beside me, I'm tired. After eating my evening meal, I plucked up the courage to check the book review site and noticed that her toxic words have been removed, the whole thread no longer visible. I felt dizzy and liberated as if I'd been freed from being held hostage by her hatred. Perhaps she has given up her campaign and I can go back to living my low-key life, to writing and loving my old dog. I've thought about that too, today, my unglamourous subdued existence, and decided that maybe it's now time to start living a little, especially since I know the truth about my past. Getting out and about a bit more might help to free up my thinking. I can shake off all thoughts of Chalk White Woman and be on the lookout for new plots rather than shrinking away from everyone. Low-key has been nice but being sedentary and isolated has been, if I'm going to be perfectly truthful, a lonely experience. Meeting up with Trevor and Doreen made me realise just how secluded I have been, living apart from the rest of the world. It's time to spread my wings, be the person I should have always been. There's no harm in mingling and being more gregarious. I have no secrets in my life, nothing to hide. I'm an ordinary woman with a rather sad but distant past. She is still out there, and she is an unknown quantity, but am I about to let her ruin what's left of my life? The thing that scared me the most wasn't her capacity to physically harm me, it was the fact she hinted that I was involved in that crime. I wasn't. It was being exposed that terrified me. I know now that I've got nothing to hide. I'm clean and blameless. And if she comes at me again with any more physical threats, I *will* contact the police. My past is nothing to be ashamed of. I don't know why I ran from it all those years ago. Maybe it was a clean break I was after, a need to put some distance between me and what happened. And unless my memory comes back fully, I will never really know.

The snap of my laptop as I close it breaks the silence. Even Whisky's heavy breathing and usual glass-shattering snores are absent. I glance outside into the gloom, and shiver. As beautiful as it is living here in the woods, once the sun dips, this area turns into something quite sinister, the impermeable darkness and hoots of the owls reminiscent of a cheap horror movie. I keep reminding myself that Chalk White Woman doesn't exist. She isn't outside, waiting in the shadows to do me harm. As for the other woman – well, I'm just going to have to be on my mettle. My problems haven't gone, not completely, but there is a certain lightness in my step, as if a load has been lifted. For all I know she could be out there waiting for me, or with the removal of that review, she may have given up. I guess, I'll have to wait it out, see if she reappears in my life. And if she does, I will have to think about what I'm going to do next.

I lock all the doors and head up to bed, Whisky rising from the rug where he is lying and following me, his pace slow and cumbersome, his poor old body ponderous with exhaustion.

In the bathroom, I take one of my pills to help me sleep. I don't think I will need it, not the way I'm feeling, but swallow it down anyway, just to be sure.

The sheets are wonderfully cool when I clamber into bed. I try to read but my eyes are heavy and after just two pages, I put down my book, switch off the bedside lamp and slide down under the duvet with a sigh.

46

I'll always be on the bottom rung of the ladder of life. I know that. I'm not stupid. Doing what I'm about to do won't elevate me in any way, shape or form. I'll still continually worry about being recognised. I'll still live a double life, my daughter in ignorance of who I really am, but for once, I will allow myself to feel happy and at ease. It's as if doing this comes naturally to me. Maybe our upbringings will always define who we truly are and those deaths weren't an accident. Maybe everyone was right and I really am a savage and a psychopath. A natural-born killer.

I knew that even though I had the spare key to Lesley's house, there was that small chance that she would leave her own key in the lock on the other side. I could have somehow managed to dislodge it which would have proven to be a noisy messy affair, one that risked waking her and the dog. But that didn't happen. The lock was clear. That was my one and only piece of good fortune. I felt like I'd earned it, that a leg-up in life was well overdue as I slipped in my key and it turned with ease, no extra manoeuvres required. I thanked a god I haven't ever believed in and stepped inside effortlessly as if I actually lived there.

Now that I'm here, inside her private space, her chaotic haphazardly equipped cottage with its oversized antique furniture and low beams, I'm aware of the things that can go wrong. I think of her dog and the possibility of him alerting her to my presence. I pause to listen. He doesn't appear to have woken. Another stroke of good fortune. Her big lolloping old canine friend stays asleep, but I've got my treats ready in case he does. This is my only chance to get inside her house and confront her, and I've got to get it right, to be prepared for every eventuality. I even deleted the thread on the book review site and all the comments that followed it. Every single word has gone, as if it were never there at all. Once this is over, I don't want anybody to discover any links I may have had to I. L. Lawrence. I want to flee this place leaving no trace behind.

I place my shoes by the front door, the wooden floors not lending themselves to unannounced callers, then make my way into the kitchen, the small torch I've brought along providing just enough light to guide me but not enough to wake Lesley or her dog.

It's exactly where I spotted it last time, the long silver knife. I lift it out of the block and run my finger along the sharp serrated edge, impressed at its sheer heft and solidity. At the damage it could inflict, the pain it could cause. Being violent doesn't scare me. Not really. I've seen plenty over the years, in prison and as a child. I'll cope.

I tiptoe upstairs to the dog basket where the old German Shepherd lifts his head and snuffles up the treats that I give him, licking at my palm with his large warm tongue leaving a layer of sticky residue on my hand. Satisfied and unbothered by my arrival, he lays his head down and closes his eyes. I put my gloves back on and count to ten, giving myself enough time to steady my breathing and to allow my pulse to slow down, because it is definitely racing. I'm angry, fucking hell am I angry, but I'm not a psychopath, not really. Nor am I a cold-blooded killer without empathy or feeling. Just filled with hatred and the nerve to do something about it.

A few seconds pass. I count them in my head.

1, 2, 3, 4, 5...

Then, clutching the knife between my fingers in one hand, I reach out with the other and turn the handle that leads to her bedroom.

47

My head is pounding. I can't recall the dream but something has woken me with a start. I lie still, my throat dry, the top of my spine and shoulders knotted with tension. Sleep eludes me despite lying here, heavy-eyed and yawning. I try counting down from one hundred but soon lose track, infuriated at myself for being unable to stay focused, my mind still fogged up with sleep.

I shuffle up in the bed, rub at my face with hot fingers and lean over to turn on the light, my hands fumbling with the switch. I stop, disturbed by an alien noise. My skin prickles with anticipation. Whisky? It doesn't sound like him but there's no other explanation. Apart from the hoots of the owls that filter in from the woods outside, even the wildlife has to sleep at some point. It's not a sound I'm familiar with. My movements are sluggish and lacking in dexterity. I flick on the light and let out a shriek.

She is sitting there in my bedroom chair, hands clutching the arms, her knuckles prominent, the flesh stretched across them waxy and bone white. Her face is carved out of stone. Eyes staring straight ahead at me. I can't breathe. The bed seesaws beneath me. The room spins.

I try to speak, my mouth opening and closing, lips trembling like jelly, but nothing comes out, just a dry whining sound like the peep of a distant whistle. And then I see something else, as if her presence isn't disturbing enough. A knife. My large kitchen knife, the one I use to slice meat and gut fish – it's laid across her lap, its glint catching my eye. I swallow hard, a pain shooting across my skull.

'What?' I manage to say after a few seconds, my voice a mere squeak. I hoped for power but it failed me. 'What are you doing here?'

I already know the answer. I want to hear it from her. She isn't some deranged stranger, a reader of my books. A random stalker. It's her. I know that it's her.

She laughs but says nothing. She's trying to scare me.

'I know who you are and I know why you're here.' While I'm speaking, I think about how far the phone is from where I'm propped up, wondering if I can slide my hands along underneath the quilt to grab it without being seen. Why did I put it on the other side of the bed? My broken mobile suddenly now seems important. I should have had it fixed but it's too late now.

'Really?' she says, her voice soft and child-like.

She's trying to lull me into a false sense of security with her soft inoffensive voice. It won't work.

'You're the girl from the stream when I was a child.'

'The girl? The fucking girl? Is that all you've got to say about it? Do I really mean so little to you? And you weren't a fucking young child so stop saying that!' Her dark eyes spark into life, her mouth twisting in anger. 'You were eleven years old, almost twelve and acted like a grown woman, and you fucking well abandoned me and left me to rot in prison after telling a pack of lies to everyone, so don't start playing the victim here, Lesley. You walked away from it all unscathed while I lost everything! Every fucking thing I had, which let's be honest, didn't amount to much, was taken from me. I lost my freedom, my identity. All of it, gone!'

I fight back tears, curled fists pawing at my face, angry at myself for being so weak. 'I don't remember any of it. I only know what I've been told. I know you won't believe that but it's the truth.'

'What the hell are you talking about, you don't remember any of it? You were there for God's sake! You were there when Irena died. It was you who was lying on top of her in the water! It was you who stopped her from getting up and escaping. Don't tell me you don't remember because that is a big fat fucking lie!'

'I was in a car accident.' I bite at my lip, angry at myself for playing down what really happened. 'Actually, it wasn't an accident. It was a hit and run. Somebody knocked me over on the back lane and left me for dead. I suffered head injuries and lost my memory. I've got amnesia. I can't remember anything from before the accident. Not a thing. It's all gone. Just a big fat nothing. So it's not a lie. It's the truth.' Not the whole truth. There are fragments there. Ill-shaped pieces searching for their rightful place.

I can't swear to it but I think that I see her smile before she looks away, her expression dark and unfathomable. She's angry, not just at me but at the world in general. And if what she is saying is true, then she has every right to be, but how do I know what she's saying *is* true? She could be a fantasist for all I know, a manipulator of the truth. Nobody wants to be branded a murderer – even murderers. They plead innocence, convincing themselves they did nothing wrong. We all want to be thought of as decent people, even the very worst of us.

The knife is still laid on her lap. I can't stop looking at it. At her. She moves one of her hands and places it over the blade, running her thumb up and down the sharp edge with practised ease, then glances my way.

'You don't remember anything? Or is that a story you made up to avoid having to talk about the past?'

'Talk about it to who?' My voice is raised, frustration edging its way into my thoughts. I stare around, my movements exaggerated for emphasis, and then look back at her face. 'I live here on my own. Why would I make up such an outlandishly stupid tale?'

'Because of me. You're hoping I'll somehow forgive and forget if you claim you can't remember.'

I almost laugh. It's absurd, her reasoning. Absurd and not even worthy of discussion. 'If you're going to do something to me,' I say, courage finally finding me, giving me a voice, 'you'll do it regardless. Am I right?'

She stares hard, her expression murky, her posture rigid. 'I saw you with them today – Trevor and Doreen – all three of you cosied up in the café. Have a nice time, did you? Had a good laugh at my expense, eh?'

I shake my head. I should pity her, the fact she lost her childhood years, but feel nothing but contempt. She has broken into my home and has done her level best to try and ruin my life.

'Why would we talk about you? Your name wasn't even mentioned.'

'You're a liar, although I do believe you about one thing.' Her pupils are dark pinpricks, a smirk teasing at the corners of her mouth. 'The car that ran you down. I believe that part of your story.'

Cymbals clash in my head, a line of white noise ricocheting across the inside of my skull. I know it then. It was her. She was the one who drove her car at me. I want to slide down under the covers and hide until this is over but know now what she is capable of, the lengths she will go to, to hurt me. That was her attempt to kill me and she failed. She's back for a second chance. I think of the knife, knowing its capabilities. Its robustness and heft.

'Get up.'

I stay put, my fingers gripping the duvet as I try to work out how quickly I can reach the phone and dial 999. Quicker than it would take her to run at me with that knife and push it deep into my abdomen? Probably not, but I'm not about to give in to her demands so easily. I can reason with her; I feel sure of it. There is something there, something in the timbre of her voice and a look in her eyes that tells me she is being driven by something other than pure psychopathy.

'No. I'm not getting up until you put down that knife. Do you really want to go back to prison, Heather?'

'I'm not Heather. Heather died many years ago. I'm a different person now. I have a daughter but no husband. That's your fault as well. He left me when he found out who I really was. Everything bad that's happened to me since that day is all your fault. You've broken me, taken away anything that ever mattered to me. Can you even begin to imagine how that feels?'

I shake my head, trying to look sympathetic; compassionate and empathetic even though I cannot envisage what she has been through. 'No. No I can't imagine that and I'm sorry you feel you've been treated badly but I'm not sure how any of that is my fault?'

She snatches up the knife and is on her feet, waving it about in front of her as if it is a harmless object, not a weapon designed to maim and kill. 'I've already told you! I got the blame when it was all a horrible accident. I had to go to prison because you lied and said I killed them.'

Many times, I've longed to be able to know about my past but no more so than now. 'I wish I could help you, I really do but I have no idea what I said or did. All I can say is that I'm sorry and if I could go back and change things, then I would.' My voice shakes. I bite down hard, my jaws locking together. She can't see that I'm scared. I won't allow it.

And I have every reason to be afraid. There is a rage in her expression, a look of detachment in her eyes. I need to talk her round, to soften her up. If that's possible. This is the woman who hates me so much, she tried to kill me, driving her car at me on a dark lane then heading off leaving me injured or possibly dead. Why would she change her mind now? What words of wisdom can I possibly come up with to make her think differently?

'You said you had a daughter. You must be very proud of her. What would she want you to do if she were here now?'

'My daughter?' She tilts her had to one side, gives me a sympathetic side-eyed look. 'Aw, you still haven't put it all together in your tiny little head, have you? Why don't you ask her yourself what she would want me to do?'

Thoughts pop and fizz in my brain until it hits me. I've been side-blinded. Stupid. So stupid of me. I should have seen it. Should have worked it out before now.

'You mean...?'

She cuts in, practically spitting the name at me. 'Yes, that's right. Alicia is my girl. And what a gem she is, isn't she?'

As she speaks, I think about it; Alicia's visit here, her evasive manner when I quizzed her about knowing my address, everything suddenly slots into place. I feel like such a fool. A prize idiot.

'I followed you here after one of your talks at the library. You really need to be more cautious you know; start being more vigilant and taking notice of your surroundings. For a crime writer you're pretty piss poor at observing those around you.' She laughs and sighs softly. 'I even knew some of the dates of your talks before you did. And I may have let it slip about knowing where you live, saying I'd read it somewhere in a crime magazine. Funny old world, isn't it? Smaller than you realise. And before you ask, no she doesn't know my real connection to you. My daughter is completely innocent in all of this. She knows nothing of my past and just thinks I'm a reader of your novels, letting me know when she's going to book you in for a talk because she thinks I want to meet you and get my paperback signed. That's how sweet she is, how kind and completely unaware, so don't you dare try to bring her into it.' A veil of anger drops behind her eyes. She starts to shout, the knife wobbling in her hand. 'Don't even mention her name. You're not a good enough person to let it pass your lips. She's worth a hundred of you. A fucking thousand actually!'

I shake my head, careful to not make any rogue movements that might send her into a rage. The mention of Alicia has unlocked something in her mind. This could go either way. Time is slipping away from me; every second I wait bringing both me and Whisky a second closer to possible death. If I can somehow get past her to the door and...

'Get up! I said fucking well get up!'

She moves across the floor and is so close, I can feel the heat from her body and smell her stale breath, the sour tang of hatred and vitriol poisoning the air around us.

'It doesn't matter if you kill me. I'm dying anyway.'

She stares at me, eyes tapered into suspicious slits.

'I've got cancer. So go ahead and do your worst.'

I think of Whisky and what would happen if I die before he does. Without treatment, according to the doctors, I've got a year or so left. Whisky is fourteen. Ancient for his breed. His back legs are already failing him. The vet has said he will be lucky to make it to the end of this year. Six months at best. What will happen to him if this woman gets her way and ends my life here and now? Who would take care of him then?

I brace myself, my fists clenched beneath the bedsheets, my body tensed for what happens next, and then slowly and carefully get out of bed.

48

Cancer? She's lying. She has lied her entire life. Why should I believe her now? She's saying it to slow me down, to make me feel sorry for her. I'm not going to fall for it. Once a liar always a liar. Some things never change. It's sad how low she will stoop to evoke my pity. I would rather she just begged me to not do it. I'd have more respect for her, but to use a serious illness to stop me from doing what I'm about to do is beyond the pale.

I need her out from under that quilt. I don't want to risk missing, the thick padding providing a barrier between the knife and her flesh. I want to see her squirm and bleed. She is standing there before me, her pyjamas concertinaed up the back of her legs like a small child, a barely visible tremble causing her hands to shake. It's a small thing and I can see she's trying to hide it, clenching her fists together until her knuckles are white, but it's there all the same – her terror. For all her talk and apparent confidence, she is scared. Really scared. This fills me with hope that I can do this thing without too much of a struggle. If she's ill, she will be weak. And if she really is weakened, I can catch her unawares, make the most of her nervous disposition, which is another chink in her armour. She won't be ready for me, all her senses attuned to her survival and how to escape, not focused on my attack.

*One lunge. That's all it will take. One hard lunge and I can turn and head out of here, leaving no suggestion that I've ever been here at all. And yet, now that she's standing here so close to me, it doesn't feel so easy. I'm angry at her, my God am I angry. Raging actually. I have enough bile and hatred in me to last this lifetime and two more besides, but am I really a killer? I thought I was but now that I am here, faced with the prospect of sticking a knife into another person, I suddenly feel out of my depth, as if I've come here under false pretences. But I **am** here and if I leave now, she will call the police and I'll be arrested. And then there's Alicia to think of. I can't let her go through it; seeing me in court, my past being dredged up, my real identity exposed in the press. Her wonderful flawless name dragged through the mud by the gutter gossips. Having a hunk of metal between me and Lesley felt less invasive, my car a large barrier between us, but as it is now, I've got nothing and it's making me feel vulnerable. Perhaps not vulnerable. That's too strong a word. Less inclined to be mind-numbingly violent and brutal.*

I take a long shuddering breath and run at her, my fingers curled around the handle of the knife. My voice echoes around the room as I let out an involuntary roar.

She moves quickly, stepping sideways out of the way. I catch her across her stomach with the jagged blade, dots of blood springing through the fabric of her pyjamas. She doesn't fall to the floor. She doesn't collapse as I'd hoped. Instead, she dodges past me and runs for the door, arms outstretched, fingers ready to grab at the handle. I can't let her leave this room. It's not going to happen. I'm not going back to prison. I'd rather stick this blade in my own chest than let that happen.

The handle of the knife is slippery in my palm, my own reticence creeping in and undermining me, making me sweat. I'm being knocked off balance by my own cowardice. I have to stop this, to dig deep and just do what needs to be done.

I jab at her, the blade connecting with her side. She lets out a scream and at the same time, turns the door handle and then sucks in her breath and lets out a loud whistle, its tonal pitch setting my teeth on edge. Before I have a chance to do anything, I feel him, the bristles of his fur rubbing against my leg. And then I feel something else – a searing pain that takes my breath away, rendering me helpless, even with a large knife clasped in my hand. My initial reaction is to drop it and fall to my knees to stop the waves of pain that are shooting up and down my leg, but I can't. I need it now more than ever to protect myself, to stop this animal from sinking his teeth any further into my leg, this dog that I thought I had won over. He snarls and flings his head from side to side, tugging at my flesh with his long, pointed teeth.

My vision is marred, bubbling tears throwing a thick mesh over my eyes. I wave my arm about, the metal blade making a swishing sound as it cuts through the air. If I can reach down, I can stick it in this dog and unlock his teeth from my lower leg. It feels like a flamethrower is scorching my calf, a hot wave of agony throbbing and pulsating deep into the bone. I thought he was a gentle old soul, this lumpen mass of fur. Not this. I didn't expect this.

'Get him off me or I'll stick this in him!' Through the tears, I can see her, standing watching me. She thinks she's safe now that her fucking dog is trying to rip off a chunk of my flesh. She's wrong. All she has done is added fuel to an already simmering fire. I had my doubts as to whether I could do this. Those doubts have fled. I'm ready now. I'm more than ready to shove this knife deep into her ribs and leave her here on the floor to die.

I lean down, trying to jab the animal with the knife, doing my damnedest to get through his fur and get him to open his jaws. Snot and tears mist my eyes as I blindly thrash about. The hold on my leg grows tighter, a vice clamped onto my calf.

My feet twist as I try to pull away from him. I slip about, the floor wet and slimy. I blink and look down. I'm standing in a pool of blood, its stickiness and stench repulsing me. Beside me, she waits motionless, her hand clutched to her abdomen. A smear of crimson is seeping out through her fingers and running down her arms. I don't know if the blood on the floor is hers or mine but hope that I've seriously injured her. Nobody would visit this place. She could die here, her body mummified before anybody noticed she was missing.

I continue jabbing at the animal, who still has his teeth set deep into my lower leg, and hear a whine. I have no idea if I connected with him. I don't want to hurt him. This isn't how I planned it. She turned everything on its head. It's all her fault.

I let out a roar as the pressure on my leg eases and I'm able to move again. The pain is immense, debilitating even, but at least I can move. I'm able to get out of this place. Away from her and away from this fucking dog. She can die here on her own. Just her and her vicious mutt.

One glance over my shoulder and I can see that she is on her knees, the dog whining at her side. She rests her hand on his back and he nuzzles his face into hers. For one second, I'm touched by the picture before me. But only for a second. No time for being soft, for regrets or capitulation. I need to get out of here. She's obviously seriously injured and will probably die anyway. I can leave while her hound is otherwise engaged. He'll stay and protect her. Too busy worrying about his owner to think about me. He isn't injured. He'll be just fine.

I drag myself to the top of the stairs, blood trailing behind me. I pull off my sweater and try to mop up the sticky mess, aware I can be traced to this crime scene. I thought I was being faultless, operating with logic and precision and look what has happened. My DNA is all over the place. The best I can hope for is that she dies and isn't found for weeks and weeks, if at all. She's a loner, a recluse. I'll leave food out for the dog, open cupboard doors so he can get to more if he needs it. Right now, it's the best I can do. I'm not a complete monster. All I wanted was justice. To let her know how badly I suffered because of her lies. Like all half decent people, I never wanted the dog to die.

I'm about to head down when I feel it, the push. I yelp and suck in my breath, knowing she has caught me unawares. And so much power behind it too, that push. Too much strength for a purportedly dying woman. I fall forwards, my hands clutching at thin air, the knife spiralling out of my grasp and landing with a clatter somewhere behind me. My teeth are gritted as I prepare to hit the first step. I feel the crack against the side of my head, the wooden boards slamming against my skull so hard that I bite my tongue, blood spurting out of my mouth and spraying over the wall. It's the last thing I see, those miniature ruby droplets peppered over the cream wallpaper before my eyes grow heavy and everything goes black.

49

THREE MONTHS LATER

It feels as if it all happened in another time, another existence. I think perhaps my mind has done its utmost to protect me, blocking it out and allowing me to move on with my life in so many positive and pleasurable ways. It was a catalyst, that evening, the night she entered my cottage and tried to kill me. A catalyst for change. A rejuvenation of the old me, like the splitting of a chrysalis and a new life emerging.

After her tumble down the stairs, I sat by her side, praying she wasn't dead. Her first words to me when she opened her eyes were, 'I'm sorry,' and then, 'Why?'

'Because I had to save myself,' I replied.

'No,' she whispered, her breathing low and ragged. 'Why didn't you kill me while you had the chance?'

'Why would I want to kill you?'

She sat up and rubbed at her face, an egg-sized lump visible on the side of her head where she had hit the first step.

'I wanted to kill you,' she murmured.

'Wanted to? And now?' I replied, confident she was now no

threat to me. She looked weak and helpless. No fight left in her. 'Do you still want to kill me now?'

She hesitated before shaking her head, a listlessness about her that indicated it was over. She was weary of her plight, of her anger and the direction it had taken. How it had brought her to this point in her life.

Despite the severity of the situation, the knife, and her tumble down those stairs, our injuries appeared to be survivable. Just. I wasn't a medical expert, far from it, but we were both still here, breathing and talking. Her leg was a bloody mess and the lump on her head was clearly visible but she wasn't dead. She had caught me twice across my abdomen but neither wound seemed deep or serious enough to warrant a visit to the hospital. At least that's what I hoped. I wasn't sure how I would explain it to whoever tended to my wounds if I did have to receive any treatment. I did wonder if she had put in little effort with that blade, that subconsciously she had been unable to go through with it. I suppose I'll never know. And her fall didn't result in any broken bones although it could so easily have ended up as a very different story and how I would have explained it and dealt with the aftermath, I will never know. The thought of it still makes me go cold.

It was quarter of an hour or so before she felt well enough to stagger up the lane to her car. I wasn't about to offer her a lift but did walk beside her, just to make sure she didn't hang around. I wanted her gone, out of my life, never to return. The fifteen minutes we spent together slumped at the bottom of the stairs while we tended to our wounds and gathered our strength, didn't turn us into the old friends that we supposedly once were but at least we were no longer arch enemies. Lethargy had set in and neither of us had any anger or resistance left in our injured weary bodies.

Or at least that's what I thought. But that wasn't quite the case.

In my wearied state, I hadn't thought about that knife. I didn't scout around for it to make sure it was out of her reach. I should have. Stupid really. In my defence I was tired and wounded but I still should have looked. Had I done that, what came next would never have happened.

She was ahead of me, limping along. I had her in my sights until she stumbled and fell. I carried on walking, thinking she would pick herself up and follow me. She did just that. But the sound of her quickened pace on the loose tarmac alerted me. I turned and that's when I saw the flash of the knife, the glint of the metal catching my eye before she could plunge it into my chest. I was tired and bleeding and she was sluggish and bruised but we still became engaged in a tussle. More than a tussle. I'm being less than truthful. I tried to grab the knife out of her hand, both of us falling to the floor, our limbs entangled, locked together in a fight for survival. I don't know how it happened, what came next. All I remember is the feel of the metal beneath my fingers, the tug of war between us. And then the blood.

I sat for a few seconds, watching her chest rise and fall, wondering what to do. Whether to drag her body into the under-growth and bury her or not. All it took was a few seconds for me to think it through. I wasn't a killer, a psychotic individual. Maybe I did make a mistake as a child. Maybe some of it was my fault, those people dying, but if I was the same person back then as I am now, I know that it was an accident.

My legs were like rubber as I ran back to the cottage and grabbed my car keys. This wasn't an ideal answer but it was the only one I had. I would deal with the consequences afterwards, if there were any.

I parked up, opened up the back door of my car and lifted Heather inside, laying her down across the back seat. She was still breathing, the knife still lodged just below her right shoulder.

There wasn't any time to do anything else. I drove to East Cleveland hospital, taking as many country routes as I could, to avoid being seen. To avoid being caught on any CCTV cameras. I didn't know for certain if there were any. I prayed there weren't but it was a chance I had to take. It was dark out, in the early hours of the morning, hardly anybody about. It wasn't the closest hospital, but it was more isolated than any of the others. It was all about damage limitation at that point.

I drove onto the A174 and before the turnoff that led to the hospital, I stopped and pulled over. It was pitch black. Nobody around. No other cars. Before I could change my mind, I clambered over to the back seat and checked Heather's pulse. Still there. I kept my eyes away from the knife that protruded out of her body, knowing I did that. Then I took her arms, opened the back door, and pulled her out onto the grassy bank next to the hospital. It was a mild night, no rain, no howling cold winds. She wouldn't develop hypothermia but she could still bleed to death. I prayed that she wouldn't because I'm not a monster. Then I jumped back in my car and drove away, hoping somebody would find her. I didn't want her to die. I made my way back home, stricken.

* * *

I look around the graveyard, at the rows and rows of headstones. So many dead people. I could have been one of them had she had her way. Perhaps not the last time she tried but the first time, when she aimed her vehicle at me and drove at speed, leaving me for dead. I'm not sure I have any lives left. I've used up my share of chances which is why I've opted to have the treatment for my cancer. It may save me or it may just prolong my life for a while, but after my recent encounter, I've decided that life is definitely worth living. Whisky needs me. He needs a healthy positive me and after my most recent visit to see the specialist at the hospital, things seem brighter. I have a chance, and I'm going to grab it with both hands.

It was easy enough to find the graves of Irena and my nana. The staff at the council were enormously helpful, giving me a detailed plan of how to locate them. It was the least I could do, to bring some flowers and pay my respects. Unless a miracle happens and my memory returns fully, I suppose I'll never really know what happened that day by the stream. I only have Trevor and Heather's accounts to go on. I hope I didn't lie to save my own skin and I hope that I wasn't involved in their deaths in any way. It's been a trying, grisly episode, this encounter with Heather. Or should I say Mary. I hope she finds peace in her life and can move on and enjoy some time with her daughter. She is right about one thing though – Alicia is a delightful charming young lady and I will miss her. She contacted me to tell me about a traumatic incident involving her mother and that she would be taking some compassionate leave to help look after her. She didn't go into detail and I didn't ask. I simply wished her well and bid my goodbyes.

The car is still warm when I clamber back inside. Only a few more things to pack and I'm ready to go. I have loved living in my little cottage but the time has come to move on. Does the thought of living there after what happened scare me? If I'm being honest, yes it does. For all her claims that she no longer wishes me any ill intent, if I'm still living in that place, there will always be a small part of me that is anxious, waiting for that time when I hear her creeping about my house, her mind angled towards doing me harm. Her mind angled towards retribution for what I did to her. I can't live like that. Although I no longer crave solitude the way I used to, I do need security and peace of mind. Only my agent, my bank, the hospital and doctor's surgery and a few other necessary utility providers know my new address. Perhaps once I'm settled and feeling less jittery, I will loosen a little, become less security conscious and more welcoming towards near strangers. But not just yet.

Funny thing is, I could have sworn I saw Chalk White Woman yesterday. She was walking across the road as I pulled up at a pedestrian crossing. I blinked and when I looked again, she was gone. Maybe my lost memory is in there, flexing its muscles, waiting to show its face. I'm not sure how I will feel if that happens, if I wake one morning and remember everything. Maybe it's best I forget the whole sordid affair.

I've met Trevor and Doreen a couple of times since the night Heather entered my cottage and there were some things they told me about my childhood and my parents that have made me think I'd be better off as I am – ignorant of my past and what went on. As loyal and considerate as they are, Trevor let slip a few things about my parents and their propensity for being short-tempered. Doreen refused to let him continue as he tried to tell me about a time when my mother banged on their door after my father took a swing at her during an argument. So for the most part, I'd rather my memories of that torrid time remained in the shadows, just out of reach.

The engine purrs as I put my foot on the accelerator and weave my way along the narrow path and out of the cemetery, out into the welcoming sunshine of a bright new day.

50

It's busy in here today. An author is up there on the lectern giving a talk. Not her though. She's gone. My hand trails up to my breastbone as I think about that night and how lucky I was to survive. She must have driven me to the hospital. At least she had the good grace to try and save me. Has that softened my feelings towards her? It's too early to tell. The doctors who tended to my wounds asked me what happened, how the knife came to be lodged in my shoulder, how my leg was damaged. I didn't have an answer. That's because there isn't one. Not an answer that anybody would understand, that is. What took place that night was between me and Lesley and will stay that way. Once they had administered painkillers and stitched me up, I discharged myself, somehow managing to limp to the nearest bus stop where I sat slumped until first light.

Alicia thinks I fell onto shards of glass. She doesn't know about the knife or the dog bite and hopefully never will. I'm not sure she fully believes my version of events but hasn't pushed it. I sometimes catch her looking at me. Trying to work out what's going on in my head. What I'm hiding. I'll never tell her and pray that after I'm gone, she doesn't find out by other means.

I'm back to being on red alert, waiting for that call from the police or the probation services. It hasn't happened yet and I hope it never will, but you just don't know. There are eyes and ears everywhere – dashcams, CCTV cameras, private security cameras on residential properties and businesses. I'll never be able to rest.

I watch Alicia as she dashes about the place, smiling at people, organising everything whilst remaining cool, level-headed and calm and wonder where she gets her efficiency from. Her hair and make-up remain immaculate, a smile always on her face. And such delicacy and patience when dealing with people. She's a gentle soul and makes me proud every day. I'm in awe of how understanding and thoughtful she is, a world away from how I was at her age. I like to think a half decent and balanced upbringing helped shape her or perhaps people are what they are from birth, their personalities already embedded deep in their DNA, their path in life pre-ordained. Things could have been so very different for me, so much brighter and better, but they weren't and I guess I have to accept that and move on, try to see the positives in each new day.

I hold my phone on my lap, keeping an ear out for anybody approaching. For my daughter approaching. She doesn't need to know what I'm doing. What I'm searching for. Who I'm searching for. She's been through enough. We both have, but something is still rumbling about inside of me, a boulder rolling and crashing and it won't stop until I do what needs to be done.

I scroll through my Google searches for I. L. Lawrence and find plenty of sites about her books but nothing about the woman herself. No changes from the last time I looked. I type in her real name, Lesley Harcourt, and am disappointed again, to be presented with nothing that leads to her. She has moved from her cottage and opted out of the open electoral register long ago so it will prove difficult to find her new address. Difficult but not impossible. I'll keep going, will keep on digging and searching. Because after all, I'm tenacious. I've suffered plenty and am a patient woman who has nothing to lose...

ACKNOWLEDGMENTS

Where to start. I have so many people to thank, so many names running through my head as I write these acknowledgements so forgive me if I miss anybody out.

First and foremost, I would like to thank my publishers, Boldwood Books, for taking me on and allowing me free rein with my ideas. Emily Ruston, you are an amazing editor and always know the right path for my stories and you were on point with this one! I hope I did your comments and guidance justice with the end product. This book would, without doubt, be a rambling mess were it not for your interventions and careful and considered counsel.

Jenna Houston and Nia Beynon, thank you for your ongoing support and for getting my books out there and noticed in what is a tough and competitive industry, especially the psychological thriller genre which is packed to the rafters with brilliant gifted writers.

Anita Waller and Valerie Keogh, you once again warrant a mention because the pair of you are superstars, propping me up through the difficult times and laughing with me through the better moments.

To my husband and family – you mean the world to me so thank you for just being there. To my friends, especially Dawn, you are the best.

Finally, a huge thank you to the people who read my books and to those who take the time to review them, including book bloggers. You help to get my books noticed and give them an arena where they are allowed to shine. I'm always so very grateful to you.

If anybody would like to follow me on social media or fancies a chat or feels kind enough to give me a break from writing and stop me from falling into a word-induced coma, I can be found at:

www.facebook.com/thewriterjude
www.twitter.com/thewriterjude
www.instagram.com/jabakerauthor
jabaker.substack.com

Thank you!

ABOUT THE AUTHOR

J. A. Baker is a successful writer of numerous psychological thrillers. Born and brought up in Middlesbrough, she still lives in the North East, which inspires the settings for her books.

Sign up to J. A. Baker's mailing list here for news, competitions and updates on future books.

Follow J. A. Baker on social media:

facebook.com/thewriterjude
twitter.com/thewriterjude
instagram.com/jabakerauthor
tiktok.com/@jabaker41

ALSO BY J. A. BAKER

THE
Murder
LIST

**THE MURDER LIST IS A NEWSLETTER
DEDICATED TO ALL THINGS CRIME AND
THRILLER FICTION!**

**SIGN UP TO MAKE SURE YOU'RE ON OUR
HIT LIST FOR GRIPPING PAGE-TURNERS
AND HEARTSTOPPING READS.**

SIGN UP TO OUR
NEWSLETTER

BIT.LY/THEMURDERLISTNEWS

Boldwood

Boldwood Books is an award-winning fiction publishing company seeking out the best stories from around the world.

Find out more at
www.boldwoodbooks.com

Join our reader community for brilliant books, competitions and offers!

Follow us
#BoldBookClub

Sign up to our weekly deals newsletter

https://bit.ly/BoldwoodBNewsletter

Milton Keynes UK
Ingram Content Group UK Ltd.
UKHW040337220923
429080UK00004B/126